Praise for Betty Hechtman's National Bestselling Crochet Mysteries

"Will warm the reader like a favorite afghan."
—*National bestselling author Earlene Fowler*

"Get hooked on this new author . . . Who can resist a sleuth named Pink, a slew of interesting minor characters and a fun fringe- of- Hollywood setting?"
—*Crochet Today!*

"Fans . . . will enjoy unraveling the knots leading to the killer."
—*Publishers Weekly*

"Classic cozy fare . . . Crocheting pattern and recipe are just icing on the cake."
—*Cozy Library*

Praise for the Yarn Retreat Mysteries

"If you haven't read this series yet, I highly recommend giving it a go. The mystery will delight you, and afterward you'll be itching to start a knitting or crochet project of your own."
—*Cozy Mystery Book Reviews*

"A cozy mystery that you won't want to put down. It combines cooking, knitting and murder in one great book!"
—*Fresh Fiction*

"The California seaside is the backdrop to this captivating cozy that will have readers heading for the yarn store in droves."
—*Debbie's Book Bag*

More Books by Betty Hechtman

Yarn Retreat Mysteries

Yarn to Go
Silence of the Lamb's Wool
Wound up in Murder
Gone with the Wool
A Tangled Yarn
Inherit the Wool
Knot on Your Life
But Knot for Me
Knot a Game

Writer for Hire Mysteries

Murder Ink
Writing a Wrong
Making It Write
Sentenced to Death

Killer Hooks

BETTY HECHTMAN

BEYOND THE PAGE
PUBLISHING

Killer Hooks
Betty Hechtman
Copyright © 2023 by Betty Hechtman

Beyond the Page Books
are published by
Beyond the Page Publishing
www.beyondthepagepub.com

ISBN: 978-1-960511-30-0

Killer
Hooks

BETTY HECHTMAN

BEYOND THE PAGE
PUBLISHING

Killer Hooks
Betty Hechtman
Copyright © 2023 by Betty Hechtman

Beyond the Page Books
are published by
Beyond the Page Publishing
www.beyondthepagepub.com

ISBN: 978-1-960511-30-0

Acknowledgments

Thank you to Bill Harris for the great editing and everything else. Jessica Faust continues to help me negotiate the roller-coaster ride through the publishing world.

Thank you to my loyal blog commenters Linda Osborn, Patty, Sally Morrison, Miss Merry and Chkntza. And top fans Valley Weaver, Melissa Phillips Cook and Catherine Guerin. Thanks to Margaret Stanislawski, a loyal reader and super-generous crocheter who turns 100 this year. Mirium Lubet for posting pictures of my books on Facebook. And all the other fans of the Crochet Mysteries who let me know that you wanted more Molly books. I really missed writing about Molly and the Hookers and the rest of the crew, too.

Jan Gonder is my reminder of our writers' group. I am forever grateful for her help with commas. Lee and Denene Lofland put on another fabulous Writers Police Academy. I always learn something and am grateful to have the chance to talk to first responders and find out about their lives. Hank Phillipi Ryan gave an inspiring keynote speech about celebrating the possibilities rather than just the achievements. Thank you to Tami Hoag for gifting the registration that I won.

Jakey has taken me back to kid-land and it's even better this time around. I have become a connoisseur of playgrounds. Thanks to Max for being the driver through Malibu Canyon and around the rocky area in Chatsworth, so I could observe the scenery without becoming part of it. Over the years Burl got me the opportunity to be a featured extra, and to be backstage and on film sets, along with being a guest at interesting parties. Madonna let me go ahead of her in a buffet line.

Thanks to Buttercup for making her debut in the book. Sorry Kitten, maybe in the next one.

Chapter One

"No, no, no," I said, hoping that repeating it three times made it more forceful, but Gabby just ignored my words and set the sleeping baby in her car seat down on my front porch. A man in a dark suit was behind her and deposited a suitcase, a stroller and a big quilted bag next to the baby.

"I have to go," she said, waving to the driver to return to his car. "I can't miss my plane. Tell Peter it's on him. He's her father. I can't possibly take her with me without the nanny." She blew a kiss at the baby and rushed down the two steps and sprinted back to the waiting limo.

I stood in shock watching the black car drive away.

Just then Marlowe opened her eyes and began to wail. "I know how you feel," I said, pulling myself together and grabbing the handle of the car seat and going inside. I was greeted by my menagerie of dogs and cats, who had been hanging around the front door since the doorbell rang. Cosmo and Felix began to bark at the crying baby. Princess began to go in circles. Blondie took off for the bedroom to get away from the sound. The two cats swirled around my feet to make sure I knew they were there. Not sure of what else to do, I hung on to the car seat while I made repeated trips to bring the rest of the stuff inside.

This was not how I expected to start off my Monday morning. There had been no phone call or text to warn me about their arrival. Marlowe's mother—and my son's ex-not-quite-wife—had just shown up in a panic saying the nanny had quit just when she was supposed to leave for the airport. Gabby had made it sound like it was all about the nanny being irresponsible and unreasonable, but I knew Gabby well enough to figure they had more likely gotten into an argument caused by some demands Gabby made and the woman decided life was too short and walked.

And where was Gabby going that was so important? She had a position as an associate producer on a TV movie that was shooting in

1

Vancouver. I got it. There was no way she could take Marlowe with her unless there was someone to actually take care of the eight-month-old.

All that seemed beside the point now. It was more about dealing with her crying and figuring out how I was going to handle my workday.

"You probably don't know who I am," I said, trying to determine what was bothering the baby. How could she know who I was since Gabby had kept her away from all of us. "I'm your grandmother, but you don't have to call me that. How about something like LaLa? That sounds like someone fun, doesn't it." I had Marlowe's attention and her crying had turned to more of a whimper. "I'm sorry we haven't spent much time together. Not my choice. But it looks like we're about to make up for lost time." I noticed she was wearing a dress that seemed all about looks and zero for comfort and appeared to have irritated the skin on her arms. "Maybe that's the problem. Let's find you something more comfortable." It took some fidgeting with the straps but I managed to undo them and got her out of the car seat. She regarded me with interest as I carried her and the quilted whatnot bag to one of the leather couches in my living room. I had a whole entourage of dogs and cats following me, curious about the small visitor. I checked the quilted whatnot bag and found a yellow stretchy one-piece number.

"I used to call these baby suits when your daddy and his brother were little like you. I think the real name is onesies." I felt around in the bag and found a diaper. "You probably need a fresh one of these too." It had been awhile since I'd been dealing with diapers and baby clothes and I was a little nervous at handling it all.

It turned out to be like riding a bicycle. As soon as I started undoing the itchy dress it all came back to me and I had her all done up in a new diaper and the yellow stretchy suit in no time. The dogs viewed the proceedings from the adjacent couch, but the two cats had lost interest and gone off somewhere.

"I bet you're hungry. Babies are always hungry." There was a tin of formula and some new-style bottles in the bag. "You can have that later. I was just going to have breakfast and I'd be happy to share." I put her back in the car seat since I didn't have anything else to use and it seemed like it was meant to be used as a general-purpose seat, and took her into the kitchen. "Lucky for you I haven't downsized as your father has suggested. And I tend to hang on to things." I set the car seat on the built-in table and arranged it so she could look out through the big window and see the backyard and the orange trees that were covered in fruit. I rummaged through a cupboard and found the old baby food grinder I'd kept from the time when my sons were small. It wasn't completely about nostalgia; it actually was great for making egg salad. I took some of the scrambled eggs that were waiting on my plate and put them through the grinder. I did the same with some strawberries. The three dogs had followed us into the kitchen and were keeping their eyes on the food. Marlowe obliged and dropped some of the eggs on the floor, which were hoovered up in no time. The three of them looked up at her hoping for more accidents as she ate her fill. She was drifting off to sleep as I finished my coffee.

Now that I'd managed to deal with the short term, there was the long term to consider, like I had to go to work. I grabbed my phone and called Peter to let him know that his daughter had been abandoned on my doorstep. That was a little more dramatic than what really happened. Gabby did tell me she was leaving Marlowe instead of just dropping her on the porch, ringing the bell and taking off. But I wanted to make a point to my son. Of course, I got his voice mail. There was no immediate answer to my texts either. I checked my watch and was running out of time. I made some more phone calls and sent more texts without success. I looked at the peaceful baby, wondering how long that would last. "I guess it's going to be 'go to work with Grandma day.'" I'm not sure what was more jarring, the thought of dealing with a baby while I tried to work or calling myself Grandma.

I knew that Gabby dismissed my work as not being on the same level of importance as going off to Vancouver and dealing with a movie set. I would be the first to admit that it wasn't brain surgery, but it was still important to me. Working at Shedd & Royal Books and More had changed my life and started a whole new chapter when my husband died. And it had kept me going recently when the bottom fell out of my life again. I pushed away even thinking about the details. It was still too fresh

I had been hired as the event coordinator, which included arranging for the Tarzana Hookers to have a place to gather—that's hookers as in crochet hooks. The Tarzana part referred to our community in the San Fernando Valley. It wasn't long before I became one of the Hookers after teaching myself how to crochet with a kids' kit. We had all become friends and partners in crime when I'd gotten involved in some murders. Solving murders, not committing them. It had embarrassed my older son Peter no end that I had been referred to as Tarzana's super amateur sleuth and interviewed by a local news person a few times.

The point was that it had all started with my job at the bookstore. Recently, I had been promoted to assistant manager when Pamela Shedd and Joshua Royal got married. They were still involved in the bookstore, but spending more and more time taking long lunches and doing fun things like taking mambo lessons. So, it wasn't as if I could just call in and say I was taking the day off at the last minute.

It took me forever to figure out how to put the car seat in my vintage Mercedes, but Marlowe amused herself with the toy thing strung across the front of it and didn't seem to care that it was taking so long. The fact that I talked the whole time, telling her what I was doing, might have helped too. Once I finally got it installed, it took only five minutes to drive to the bookstore in what was considered the heart of Tarzana. It turned out to be a lot easier to unhook the car seat from the foundation. The parking lot was behind the bookstore and even with the bucket-like handle it was a hassle hauling the seat, the quilted whatnot bag hung cross-body, my purse, and the tote bag with my crochet project around to Ventura Boulevard and the entrance to the bookstore.

Normally, I would have checked over the display window before I walked in, but with all that I was lugging, I just wanted to get inside and make it to the information booth, which served as my office. It was an enclosed cubicle in the middle of the store and I figured it would work to contain Marlowe if I let her loose from the car seat. I had just made it past the cashier area and the entrance to the café when Adele Abrams Humphries came up next to me.

"What's going on, Pink?" she said, looking down at the baby girl and then at all I was carrying. Before I could say anything, her expression darkened. "Don't even think about trying to leave her in my area."

Where do I begin to explain Adele? Maybe I should start with why she insisted on calling me by my last name instead of Molly. Even though I think she has forgotten by now, it was her little way to annoy me. Adele had already been working at the bookstore and expected to be promoted to the event coordinator position. She was more than a little resentful when I got hired instead. She refused to even consider that I was more qualified. I had spent years helping out with Charlie's PR firm so arranging author events and community gatherings was easy for me.

To pacify Adele, Mrs. Shedd had given her the children's department, which was where she was afraid I was going to drop Marlowe off. Adele didn't have any children of her own and frankly didn't really like them, but they loved her. She was tall and amply built and towered over them, but it didn't seem to matter. Adele lived for drama and costumes whether it was a cape and crown for story-time or outfits that were overly embellished with crocheted flowers and motifs. Adele could have been the national spokesperson for the yarn craft. She dismissed knitting and knitters as unimportant in the yarn world. Crochet ruled as far as she was concerned. Needless to say, she was one of the Tarzana Hookers and had been with the group since they first started meeting at the bookstore.

First, I assured her that I had no intention of leaving the baby in the children's area, then I explained who Marlowe was and why she was with me. Adele eyed me with disapproval. "Pink, I never would have let that happen. Your family is always dropping something on you. How many dogs and cats have they left with you? And now a baby."

Marlowe seemed totally enthralled with Adele and had reached out to touch the crocheted sunflower on the sleeve of Adele's sweater. My coworker started to scowl and then she reached in her pocket and pulled out a loose crocheted sunflower with two pieces of golden yellow yarn hanging off of it. She went to tie it to the string of amusements across the front of the car seat. I was surprised by the gesture until it became obvious that it wasn't totally altruistic. "I might need your help on something," Adele said. "Now that you're dealing with a kid, you'll be perfect." She gave me the mysterious look she gave the kids when she came to a cliff-hanger during story-time. "I'll tell you the rest later." She reminded me that story-time was beginning shortly and she had to prepare.

My cell phone was ringing as I squeezed into the information booth. I was sure that it had to be a return call from the SOS I'd put out earlier and rushed to set Marlowe down so I could grab it.

I answered, expecting it to be Peter, but it was my younger son, Samuel. He let out a disbelieving chuckle when I explained the situation. "She just dropped the baby and ran," he said. "That's something since she wouldn't even let us see the baby." He asked about his brother and I said I'd left voice mails and texts with no response.

"Looks like it falls on Uncle Samuel to be the hero," he said with a sound of pleasure in his voice. Peter was like Charlie, all about work and ambition, while Samuel was a little more laid-back. He had moved back home a while ago and was responsible for bringing the two cats and one of the dogs into my household. Samuel was a musician. He had moved up from open-mike night to actual gigs at some small bars.

He was also the musical director when my mother's singing group the She La Las went on the road. He had a day job managing a local coffee place. Peter had always excelled at everything and I knew that Samuel felt lesser for it. "Let me make some phone calls and I'll pick up Marlowe when I finish my shift." He gave me an idea of when it would be and was about to hang up. "With the way things turned out for you," he said, "I'm glad I can be there to help out."

I knew he was being deliberately vague because he knew I didn't want to talk about the train wreck of my personal life. I appreciated his support without judgment.

• • •

Samuel was still wearing his green apron and name tag when he came to pick up Marlowe. His sandy hair was in one of the current styles that I didn't understand, long on top and shaved on the sides. It was as if somebody said we've run out of ideas for styles so let's just go for crazy. He had a little swagger in his walk and a confident smile, as though he was pleased with himself. "Don't worry, I took care of everything. I called some friends who have kids and scored sort of a combo sleeping and play thing." He held up a bag. "It turns out we have some great baby snacks at the coffee place. I brought a lot, so she won't starve. I also found out why you haven't been able to connect with Peter. He's out of town on his way back. Bunny and Irv are coming over later," he said, referring to my parents. "And don't worry about me being able to take care of her in the meantime. Remember, I was the guitar guy at that day camp." He looked over the counter of the information booth and started singing. Marlowe stopped rolling on the floor and stared up at him with a delighted giggle.

He put Marlowe back in the car seat with ease. I gave him a grateful hug and put the whatnot bag on his shoulder. He still had the swagger as they went to the door.

"At last," I said with a huge sigh of relief when Marlowe and all her stuff were gone. It was time to change gears and prepare for what I had to do. I headed to the café to revive myself with a red-eye before I had to deal with a situation regarding an upcoming author event. Mrs. Shedd and Mr. Royal might have been spending a lot of time away from the bookstore, but that did not mean they didn't keep their eyes on the bottom line. They'd come up with a change in an author event we had planned, sure that it would make it more profitable, and now it was up to me to convince the author to go along with the change.

Daisy Cochran had been a reporter and columnist covering the entertainment business for forty years. She was supposedly retired, though I wasn't sure if it was her idea or had been forced on her by the way things had changed. She had put together a book with behind-the-scenes stories about old Hollywood, which went along nicely with the March theme of movies because of the Academy Awards. But March was also National Crochet Month, and since the bookstore hosted a crochet group and CeeCee Collins was one of the main members of the group—and because she happened to have been nominated for an Academy Award for her role as Ophelia in a movie about Anthony, a vampire who crocheted to control his bloodlust—the bookstore owners' idea was to have Daisy interview CeeCee about being nominated for an Academy Award as part of her presentation. It was actually more than an *idea*, they were insisting on it. They had already put together a table display featuring copies of Daisy's book, DVDs of the Anthony movie, and copies of the whole series of books the movie was based on, along with crochet kits to make a vampire scarf. There was a photo of CeeCee from the movie with a banner touting her being nominated, copies of a biography of her, and even a book about the *CeeCee Collins Show*, which had started her career.

I had no idea how Daisy was going to react to the suggestion that was really a command from the owners. She was more than the author of the self-published book she was pushing. She had been kind of a celebrity in her own right, and probably still saw herself that way even now that she had slipped from the public eye.

She thought she was coming in just to go over the setup for her appearance and getting copies of her book delivered. I felt my heart rate take an uptick as she came into the bookstore. She gave off an air of importance and was dressed in her trademark outfit of slacks and a sweater. The pale blue shirt she was wearing under the sweater had the collar popped and she wore a colorful silk scarf like an ascot. Her mink-colored hair didn't have a thread of gray and she still had the same blunt cut she'd had in the photo that had appeared with her column. She wasn't alone. The woman with her had short brown hair with a bright green overlay and was wearing comfortable jeans and a leather jacket. She seemed to be taking in the bookstore. She nudged Daisy and said something.

I went to greet them and Daisy gave me an automatic greeting of a hug and an air-kiss. She saw my gaze go to her companion. "This is Leslie Bittner," she said, and the other woman held out her hand. "She's my assistant and is working with me on my new venture." Daisy did the same survey around the bookstore Leslie had done. "I thought there were signs up about my appearance," she said, seeming perturbed. I didn't want to tell her that my bosses had taken them away, planning to replace them with new signs touting what was now being called an evening with Daisy Cochran and CeeCee Collins. The new signs were waiting in the storage room to be put out as soon as I talked to Daisy.

"About that," I said. "The owners of the bookstore had a revelation about how to make the evening even more exciting and a bigger draw, which I'm sure you'd appreciate. More people means more sales for you."

She gave me a wary look. "What exactly are you talking about?"

I explained about March being National Crochet Month and the theme of the Academy Awards and how CeeCee Collins had a connection to both. "Wouldn't it be more exciting to have an actual actor here who could talk about what it was like to go to the Academy Awards as a nominee?"

I had hoped to get her to agree to the new plan before CeeCee arrived, but the actress- crocheter was early and was on her way across the bookstore before Daisy had a chance to make a comment.

"So good to see you again, dear," CeeCee said as she joined us. CeeCee had blondish hair she'd worn in the same simple style her whole career, which made it seem like she'd never aged. Instead of her usual jewel-colored velour tracksuit, she was wearing slacks and an untucked white shirt with a cowl in shades of pink and rose.

Until her role in the vampire movie, CeeCee was generally referred to as a veteran actress, which meant old, been around a long time, or past your prime. She had taken it all in stride, going from starring in the *CeeCee Collins Show*, to guest slots on other sitcoms, to cameos in whatever came along, to where she was now. The Ophelia role and the Academy Award nomination, even without a win, had put her back in the public eye. She had been around long enough not to get too caught up in it. Other than being a little self-absorbed, she was warm and good-hearted.

Daisy and CeeCee embraced each other and fumbled as there were air-kisses all around. Leslie introduced herself to CeeCee and called herself the producer of the new venture.

CeeCee dove right in as if the new plan was a fait accompli. "Dear, it'll be fun being part of your event." CeeCee seemed very enthusiastic. "I know it's supposed to be me talking about my Academy Award experience, but I'd like to get in that I'm up for a role in that streaming series *Wyoming*."

Daisy blanched. "I am still trying to process this change in the program." She looked at me. "That isn't how I saw my appearance going," she said. "I don't know if you realize it but there are people who think I'm like a national treasure of Hollywood information." She pointed to her head. "It's all up here. I'll tell some of the celebrity stories as a tease for the book, but really what I want to talk about is the podcast I'm putting together. It's going to be called *Were They Murders*. I'm going to shed new light on some deaths. Heads may roll," she said with a laugh. Then she grew serious. "Who knows," she said with a shrug, "it could end up with charges being brought against people who think they're home free. The book is about the past. The stories are all upbeat and amusing. All my years of doing the reporting and columns I focused on positive stories. I knew a lot about the underside of things, but it was an unwritten rule that I didn't disclose anything that somebody wanted to keep under wraps. My philosophy was if I couldn't say something nice, I said nothing. So no drawing lines between the dots.

"But it's a different world now. Everything has become like tabloid journalism with headlines meant to grab your attention but misrepresent the story. My podcast is going to bring up forgotten stories, and reexamine some old situations with new information. I have to move with the times and I'm not afraid to connect the dots now." Daisy smiled at us. "Sorry if I got a little carried away. I'm just planning to give a tease at the bookstore event about the first couple of situations, which are about deaths from mysterious falls, and ask the question were they really accidents. Were the victims really alone?"

CeeCee's smile faded. "Are you sure you want to go to the dark side?"

"The public has a right to know," Daisy said. "And it will bring me listeners and then advertisers."

"It's more like what the public wants to know," Leslie added. "There are a million podcasts out there. You have to do something sensational to get an audience."

"Dear, it's such a change from what you're known for," CeeCee said. Daisy scowled at the words *known for.*

"You have to move with the times if you want to have a career," Daisy said decisively. She turned to me. "As long as I get to push my book and talk about the podcast, I'll interview CeeCee, though it would be more exciting if she was the other kind of hooker," she said with a smile.

With the change accepted, there were just a few details to talk about regarding the setup for the event. Daisy let Leslie tell me what the columnist-author required. I was surprised at her list of demands. She had to have an area like a green room where she could stay until I introduced her. She needed her own wireless mic so she could move around while she spoke and she had requirements for refreshments. There needed to be a certain brand of bottled water and a particular strawberry smoothie, freshly made from the juice place down the street. She wanted me to stand beside her during the book signing to make sure the line kept moving. I was to step in if anyone started a long conversation.

Since she had not been a problem about changing the program and I knew how to create a backstage area using bookcases to make an enclosure and could deal with the rest of it, I agreed. The two women left and CeeCee hung behind.

"She's certainly a prima donna," CeeCee said. "It sounds like she may be upsetting a hornets' nest with that podcast idea. But I guess she feels she has to do something like that to get back in the public eye."

"It's not my problem, thank heavens," I said, thinking of what awaited me at home.

Chapter Two

All the lights were on at my house and I could see people moving around in my living room through the front window before I pulled into my driveway. It looked like the whole clan had gathered at my house and that was never peaceful. I expected that Peter was among them. I'd finally gotten a text from him that confirmed what Samuel had said. Peter had been out of the country and was traveling home.

Cosmo, the small black mutt, and Felix, the gray terrier mix, were waiting by the kitchen door and gave me an enthusiastic greeting. Not seeing Princess in the group, I assumed she was on the couch glued to someone. Her previous owner had died and I'd been the one to rescue the small white poodle mix. She had been an *only dog* and was always looking for a person to cuddle with.

With all the commotion, I was sure Blondie was ensconced in her chair in my room. The strawberry blond dog hardly seemed like a terrier mix. Instead of being feisty like Felix, she was like the Greta Garbo of dogs and preferred to be alone. The cats probably had run off to a quiet spot, too.

At least they had brought food. The counter had a platter of corned beef and an assortment of cheeses with a selection of bread and rolls. A pile of paper plates sat next to containers of coleslaw, potato salad and fruit salad. Even though I was really hungry and it smelled great, I bypassed it and went into the living room.

My parents were on one of the leather couches with Princess settled in between them. Samuel was on the other couch. Marlowe was rolling around in the portable bed/play thing that Samuel had told me about. A box of diapers was next to a shopping bag from Carter's. Another bag overflowed with stuffed toys. There was more paraphernalia for Marlowe to sit and bounce in. Peter was lounging in a corner talking on his cell phone.

My father mentioned there was food as if I could have missed it. He was a food specialist and always brought a copious amount.

Despite enjoying what he brought, he had a wiry build. He was a retired dermatologist and these days spent his time being supportive of my mother's renewed singing career. She was the lead singer of the She La Las and despite having only one big hit back in the day, they were back performing. It was sweet the way he treated her like a star.

Bunny was petite and feisty. She had kept her hair natural and there were some patches of silver in the dark brown. The turquoise linen top was typical of her clothing choice and I always felt drab next to her in my neutral-colored wardrobe. The silver bangles that jangled when she gestured were her trademark. She used them as an instrument when she performed.

My mother shook her head with disapproval as she said hello. Was she ever going to get over it? I'd be the first to admit that I'd made a mess of things and yes, I knew that everything would be different if I hadn't made such a bad choice. But giving me dirty looks was not going to change anything. And I had to stop being so bothered by the dirty looks. I was over fifty, for heaven sakes.

Marlowe started to whimper and I waited to see who would step up to take care of her. Peter was oblivious since he was still on the phone. Samuel was taking his plate to the kitchen and announced that he had to get to a gig. My mother picked up the baby but then handed her to me.

"We've been here since four and believe me, we held her plenty. We'll be back tomorrow. The She La Las are going to rehearse here in the morning," she said. "We're learning a new dance routine and I need a good night's sleep." She glanced at Peter, who was facing the wall and gesturing with his hand as he continued on his phone. "Peter's getting everything worked out. Not my way of doing things. I guess I'm old-fashioned, but I think you should get married before you get divorced." She rolled her eyes at the situation.

They followed Samuel to the door and Cosmo and Felix let me know they wanted some outside time. I balanced Marlowe on my hip as I rounded up Blondie and Princess and took the four dogs to the kitchen door and let them out.

It was dark now and the floodlights illuminated the patio and orange trees. I gave Marlowe a running commentary, telling her that the blossoms would be opening on the orange trees soon and how much she was going to like the sweet fragrance. "And we'll make orange juice for you in the meantime."

Peter had finally gotten off the phone when we went back into the living room. I really wanted to make myself a plate of food, but I realized it was better to deal with him first.

"I'm sorry," he said, putting his hands up. Even after a long flight home, Peter looked put together in dressy jeans and a sport coat over a collarless shirt. "I had no idea Gabby would do what she did. But then we barely talk. She decided she was keeping Marlowe all to herself. I'm doing my best to work things out. It's great how Samuel and Bunny and Irv came through today." His expression changed to disgruntled. "I just talked to Gabby and she's not coming back to get Marlowe. Said it was on me now. She went on about how I could just go off and not have to worry about Marlowe and could focus on my career. She's still so angry at me for what happened." I knew he was referring to the collapse of what had seemed like a sure thing.

After being a successful talent agent, Peter had formed a production company and put together a sitcom. Gabby was working with him. They had gotten a commitment for two seasons' worth of shows and were living in a Beverly Hills condo. Everything looked rosy. Gabby had gotten pregnant and they planned to get married. Out of nowhere it came out that the man who was creator, chief writer and star had had an inappropriate relationship, which was a nice way of saying he liked to hang out with very young teenage girls. And just like that everything fell apart. They lost the condo and had to move in with me. And then things blew up between them and Gabby left. I never knew the exact details, but I gathered that she got her own place and started trying to get on with her career. Peter was at the hospital when Marlowe was born, but then other than a few short visits, she kept all of us away from the baby.

"She's all caught up in this fairness thing." He put up his hands in a frustrated gesture. "Even though it was her idea, she's complaining that she's done everything for eight months and now it's on me." He sounded bewildered by it all. "I'm trying to line up childcare, but I can't see how I can keep Marlowe at my place. You know how unpredictable my schedule is and I'm so worried about this production I'm putting together." He gave me a hopeful look. "I was hoping that she could stay here with you." He rushed and added that he'd get whatever she needed and that Samuel had a friend who would be able to take care of her when I was working.

What was I going to say? It was like there was a big welcome sign on my door for anyone in need. Samuel had moved back home with pets. My mother and the "girls" used my living room as their rehearsal spot. I'd let Peter and Gabby move in and even let them pass off my house as theirs as Peter tried to get a fresh start. Surely, my grandchild would be as welcome or more.

"Of course, she can stay here," I said. "But I have my job, the Hookers and a life."

He assured me that I would be able to keep on with what I was doing, but I could tell there was something else on his mind. He seemed hesitant to talk about it and I finally just told him to get to it whatever it was.

"I can't believe that I'm going to ask you to do this," he said, half to himself. "I know I haven't been very supportive of your investigative activities." I choked back a laugh. Not supportive was hardly correct. More like he'd been horribly embarrassed that I'd gotten involved in some murder investigations and actually found the killers. He had hated it when I got interviewed on the news. It was very clear to me that when Charlie died, Peter expected me to fade into the background.

"Why don't you just get to the point."

He let out a heavy sigh. "I can't afford to have any surprise disclosures about the people I'm working with. I'm still in the process of putting everything together. Miles Langford wants to invest in the project I'm working on. I really want to take his money, but after what happened, well, I need to be sure there aren't going to be any skeletons popping out of his closet. I've done what I can to check into his background, but with all the nondisclosure agreements and quiet settlements, there's a lot that gets kept under the radar. I was thinking that you could use your skills to nose around. I can't afford to be bushwhacked again." He sounded genuinely worried and didn't have his usual confident demeanor.

I was surprised by his request since he had given me such a problem about my investigating in the past. "How am I supposed to nose around? I would need some sort of an entry."

"That's no problem," he said. "For once Gabby is a help. She hooked herself up in an exclusive mommy group and Miles's wife is in it. Gabby sent me the schedule and I'll forward it to you. You can explain you're taking Gabby's place. But they can't know who you are."

"You mean you want me to go undercover," I said, chuckling at his discomfort.

"You can't give them your last name," he said. "Go by your maiden name."

"No problem. I'll introduce myself as Molly Aronson and I won't mention you. But are you sure that they don't know who Marlowe's father is?"

He let out a mirthless laugh. "Believe me, Gabby had erased me from the picture up until now. They know the baby as Marlowe Alter. She blames me for that last production deal falling apart and wants to distance herself from me as much as possible. The only reason she brought Marlowe here was she had no choice. Apparently, her mother is out of town. Gabby said there's a dad in the group, so I'm sure a grandmother would be perfectly acceptable. They probably gossip about each other or you could make friends with his wife. You're good at being nosy." He shrugged as if it would be nothing for me to delve into people's lives and find out their secrets.

"I'd have to work it around my schedule, but I'm sure I could manage it." Suddenly taking care of Marlowe had become more interesting.

With it settled, Peter deflated and looked all in, explaining that he had flown in from London. I expected him to leave, but he hung around for a while, watching me bathe his daughter and put her into her sleepwear. He moved the portable crib thing into my bedroom and then I handed her to him while I cleared out the toys. I was still amazed at the differences in my sons. Samuel seemed at ease taking care of Marlowe even though he was inexperienced. Marlowe was Peter's daughter, but he seemed so stiff and uncomfortable holding her and clearly could not wait to hand her off.

He tried to hide it, but it was obvious that he was relieved to go home, where he could forget about everything and just deal with himself.

Chapter Three

Marlowe had fallen asleep right after I put her in the moveable bed. Finally, I was going to get a taste of that deli food. My stomach rumbled in anticipation as I walked across the house, but then my cell phone rang. As soon as I saw it was my best friend Dinah Lyons, I clicked it on.

"Tell me you'll come over," she said. She didn't have to go into detail for me to understand the urgent sound in her voice. She had recently married Commander Blaine, and while they definitely cared about each other, they were totally different. He owned the local Mail It store and led a very orderly life with an early bedtime.

Dinah taught freshman English at the local community college and made sure she never had a class before eleven. Before that she wasn't ready to deal with students who tried to write papers in text talk and made-up words. At home, she had created what she called her she-cave to deal with their different schedules. That way when he went to sleep and required that the house be quiet, she could go into her space and entertain, or at least make noise.

Normally, I would have been on my way out the door at the offer, but I couldn't now that Marlowe was a resident. I talked Dinah into coming to me, promising deli food and a surprise she would never guess in a million years. It hardly took much convincing. Just being able to make noise was a draw.

I was just finishing making up plates for both of us when she came to the kitchen door. She was still bristling with energy and swirled her trademark long scarf out of the way as she went to give me a hug, and then she went right to finding out the surprise.

"It's actually two," I said, taking her across the house to my room and showing her the sleeping baby. We tiptoed out and into the den.

"Wow, you're right. I would never have guessed that. Who is she?" I gave her a quick rundown on Marlowe's arrival.

"Gabby really did that? It sounds like she dropped her and ran."

"Almost. She certainly gave me no choice."

"What about Gabby's mother? What does she call her, Mumsy?"

"Yes, and Mumsy is out of town. I was the only one she could find at the last minute and was her last resort." I explained that my whole family was helping out and Peter was trying to arrange for childcare so I could work.

She gave me a look. "You're still the one who has to keep it all together." We kept moving back across the house.

"You're right," I said, letting out a sigh. "And the plot thickens. There's something else." I told her the assignment Peter had given me.

"Really?" Dinah said with a laugh. "After all of his fussing at you, claiming it was embarrassing that you kept getting involved in murder investigations." We'd arrived in the kitchen and picked up the plates of food and I suggested we go to the dining room.

"There's still more. I have to be incognito so the wife of the man he's considering as an investor won't see my connection to Peter. So, I'll be Molly Aronson to them. Peter is confident that Gabby hasn't talked about him to the group." I shook my head, thinking of how sad it was the way things had turned out with them.

Dinah brightened. "I love the idea of going undercover and sneaking around. Let me know if you need a sidekick or you want to play our Sherlock Holmes game." I promised I would do both. We'd created the Sherlock Holmes game trying to see what we could infer from information we had. It was fun and we actually had figured things out that way. "Do you think Peter has an inkling about what they could be hiding."

I shook my head. "He thinks there's nothing there. He just wants to be sure." We had been talking so much we'd neglected the food and finally dug in. I offered Dinah seconds but she refused, but not to the chocolate cake I'd noticed in the refrigerator. I put on a pot of coffee, which brewed while I served up the cake.

"Yum," my friend said when I returned with the cake and coffee.

"And that isn't even all of it," I said as I sat back down. "I had to tell an author we were changing her event and Adele played a mystery game with me, saying she needed my help on something and left me hanging about the details." I decided the cake needed whipped cream and went to the kitchen to get it.

"I'm sure we will hear all about it at the Hooker gathering," Dinah said. I gave both pieces of cake a squirt and then added some to our cups of coffee.

"I'm kind of glad to have all this on my plate," I said. "It's been kind of dull and quiet at my place. No surprise—my mother didn't miss the opportunity to remind me how I had ruined things."

"Have you ever thought about calling him?" my friend said.

"Him, who?" I said.

"Mason," Dinah said and looked at me to read my expression.

I probably appeared panicked at the thought. "Are you kidding. What would I say? I'm sorry I called it off with you the night before we were to fly off to a new life together so I could stay with Barry Greenberg, who I'd had an on and mostly off relationship with, because he claimed I was the love of his life."

"When you put it like that," Dinah said. "But does he even know how things turned out?"

"Mason would probably think I'd gotten my just rewards. And I probably did." An image of him flitted through my mind. I saw his smile and the warmth in his eyes. He was wearing his favorite Hawaiian shirt and jeans and holding his toy fox terrier, Spike. He was a successful attorney, was charming and fun. He had attempted to redeem himself after all the years of getting off celebrity clients who probably had done the misdeeds, by spending time working pro bono getting new trials for the wrongfully convicted. He was divorced and at first had only been interested in a casual relationship, but eventually he realized that wasn't enough and wanted us to get married.

"It doesn't matter. I'm sure he has moved on and probably found a whole line of women who want what he has to offer. Peter developed a sort of business friendship with him and I think they still speak.

Dinah was the only one I'd told exactly what had happened with Barry. All my mother seemed concerned about was that I had messed things up with Mason. He fit in with my family and she had always liked him and disliked Barry. I was never sure if it was because Barry was a homicide detective or if it was personal. Now I wondered if her disapproval had been a reason I had gone with Barry. Could I really have been that immature?

I thought over what had happened for the umpteenth time. How Barry and I had run off to Hawaii. We'd stayed at a resort on the Big Island and it had just been the two of us for the first time. He didn't get called away on a homicide or disappear to follow up on some evidence. We had breakfast on the balcony of our room, lounged on the beach and did tourist things like going to a coffee plantation in the cloud forest. It was two weeks of pure fantasy.

But as soon as we got home the bubble burst and it was back to real life. Barry got a homicide the first night and disappeared for days. The only difference was that he remembered to text me a few times. When he was off on a case, he forgot about everything and everyone else. When he finally resurfaced, we had a long talk. Despite the feelings we had for each other, it wasn't going to work out. He couldn't change and I couldn't live with the way he was.

"I have my job, you, my other friends," I said, smiling at Dinah. "The Hookers and even Adele with all her craziness. Now I have Marlowe and a mystery to solve, too. I wouldn't have time for anyone anyway."

"There you go then," Dinah said, even though I doubted she really agreed.

22

Chapter Four

When I left for the bookstore the next morning, the She La Las were making space in the living room to practice their new dance routine. Peter had gotten a playpen delivered and it was in the corner of the living room, where Marlowe could watch the dance moves. Samuel's coworker from the coffee place, Beth, was there to audition as a babysitter. My father had brought fresh bagels along with an assortment of cream cheeses and some treats for Marlowe. There were more boxes of diapers, formula and baby bottles. Samuel had gone off to his shift at the coffee place but said he would come back in the late afternoon. Peter couldn't promise a time, but he agreed to stop over and see his daughter sometime during the day. I went off to work feeling comfortable that Marlowe would be fine.

I made up for the time I'd lost the previous day. The signs were out for Daisy's author event, and now it was described as Daisy Cochran in conversation with Academy Award–nominated actress and crocheter CeeCee Collins. There was a description of Daisy's book and that she was going to be talking about her new project of podcasts that delved into some old Hollywood deaths.

I'd sent out an email blast about the event and made sure the display tables were all in order. The Tarzana Hookers were having a happy hour gathering. We all agreed that spending the late afternoon with yarn and conversation had the same mellowing effect that wine did without any of the downside. I was so looking forward to it. I was overflowing with things to talk about. That was what I loved about the group. It was about so much more than what we could create with our hooks. We had become friends, confidantes. We listened to each other and most of all cared. It was a little iffy about how much Adele cared about anything other than her own woes, but I knew she did value the companionship.

Most of the Hookers were already at the table in the yarn department when I went back there for the gathering. It had been Mrs.

Shedd's idea to add the section at the back of the store. She was always looking for ways to attract more customers by making the store a destination. It was an inviting area filled with color from the cubbies filled with yarn. There were several easy chairs for anyone who wanted to stop and knit or crochet. But the main fixture was the wood table surrounded by straight-back chairs.

CeeCee Collins had taken her seat at one end of the table and was already working on something. Her hook moved through the rosy pink yarn with only an occasional look from her. I had come a long way from when I started but still couldn't imagine being able to crochet without paying attention.

The actress seemed to be in the midst of a disagreement with Elise Belmont. Elise's looks were at odds with her personality. She had a bird-like voice and had what I could best describe as a vague expression. She was slender and it seemed like a gust of wind could blow her over. But she had an iron core and was aggressive and maybe a little obsessive about whatever she did. For now, it was mostly real estate. "I don't see why I'm not part of the evening with Daisy," Elise said with an edge to her voice. "After all, I am the one who created the kits for vampire scarves." Elise had been fixated on the Anthony character and all things vampire. She used half double crochet stitches in the kits because she thought they looked like fangs.

"I could come up with another kit. Maybe something your character would wear," Elise said, looking at CeeCee. "What about a little black shawl for Ophelia?"

"Dear, you really need to check with Molly about that. I'm just part of the evening, not arranging it." She had caught sight of me in her peripheral vision and held out her arm as she turned to face me. "You must have heard what Elise said. She thinks she should be part of the evening and offered to make a kit with something for my character."

Before I could answer, Adele chimed in. "If anyone should be part of the evening representing crochet, it should be me." She stood up and turned model-style to show off the shawl she had wound around her shoulders. It was made in free form stitches, which meant it was like jazz crochet. Totally improvised, it went from a bunch of double crochet stitches in the back loop to treble stitches with spaces in between. The yarn changed from a bright red worsted to a thick silvery textured yarn with sequins and then to a royal blue and finally a variegated yarn that went from pale to dark green.

"The sign said Daisy is going to talk about some podcasts she's doing," Rhoda Klein said. She had a thick New York accent and a blunt personality. She dressed for comfort, which meant all her pants had elastic in the waistband and her footwear was mostly Crocs. "I think people are going to want to hear about that more than vampire movie crochet kits. I know I'd be more interested in what Daisy has to say. I wonder who the subjects of the podcast are."

"She's trying to move with the times," CeeCee said. "When she was a columnist, it was all about interesting stories about celebrities. She never ruffled any feathers. But times have changed and they're reporting terrible things like that some handsome actor was a cannibal." CeeCee shuddered at the thought. She was dressed in a garnet-colored velour tracksuit with her blondish hair in the same simple chin-length style she'd always worn. "Without her column, Daisy has gotten kind of pushed to the wayside and I'm sure she misses being in the middle of things and she's trying to be contemporary. She probably knows a lot of dirt. I heard her talking and it seems like she is planning to go over some old deaths with new information," CeeCee said.

"I wonder if she's worried about stirring up trouble for herself. It sounds like some people might have gotten away with murder, and they might not be so happy to have it brought up again," Sheila Altman said in her soft voice. She was the youngest in the group and suffered from bouts of anxiety. She'd found that doing the most basic of crochet stitches helped relieve it and she always carried her emergency kit, as she called it. It was really just a small hank of cotton string and a J-sized hook. When she started to feel everything tightening up, she'd take out her kit, do a line of chain stitches and then single crochets back over the chains. The rhythm and repetition of movements always calmed her. She was capable of much more complex crochet and was an accomplished knitter as well. She had developed her own style of mixing blues, greens and lavender yarns and creating pieces that had the look of an impressionist painting. She sold them at the lifestyle store located down the street where she worked. This time her nerves seemed in check and she was actually working on one of the hazy-colored throws. It was crocheted, of course. There was no knitting allowed by Adele's decree.

"I should talk to Daisy about something I'm working on," Adele said. "She'd be perfect to hook me up with the right people."

Just then Dinah came in with Eduardo Linnares. To say he stood out from the rest of us was an understatement. It wasn't just that he was a man, but was also very tall with the kind of good looks you'd expect a former cover model to have. He'd cut his flowing dark hair and wore it short, but all it did was show off more of his angular face. He seemed to have an interesting relationship with his hero-like handsomeness. It was as if he recognized it, but then forgot about it and got on with his life.

His days as a pirate or a duke on the cover of hot romance novels were over. He'd dropped the model work when it had been suggested he be in the background as the pirate's father. He had become a personality after that doing some commercials and comedy bits playing himself on late-night talk shows. He had enough of a name that he was able to add a celebrity touch to the high-end drugstore called the Apothecary that he'd created. He was in the process of expanding his business and opening a restaurant.

His connection to crochet came from his Irish grandmother, who taught him to crochet lace when she had no granddaughters to teach. It always amazed me how he managed the delicate work with such large hands.

"What are you guys talking about?" Dinah said. "Was Molly telling you about having her granddaughter left on her doorstep? The baby was in her car seat with a bag of things on the front porch."

"It wasn't quite that bad," I said. "Gabby talked to me before she rushed off. Though more like talked at me announcing she was leaving the baby. She was flying to Vancouver for a production job and couldn't take care of Marlowe without help and the nanny had quit just as they were leaving for the airport."

Rhoda looked at the space around me. "Where is she?" She glanced around the area for the baby.

"You should have been here yesterday. It was 'bring your grand-daughter to work day' for Pink."

"Are you still calling her by her last name?" Rhoda said, giving Adele a look.

Adele started defending herself, saying that calling me Pink was a compliment, likening me to the singer. They all rolled their eyes at her attempt at a save. "But that reminds me. I wanted to tell you about my new venture." She surveyed the group at the table. "Actually, all of you."

Adele began to circle the table, making eye contact with everyone as she did. "It has become unmanageable living with Mother Humphries. I know it upsets Eric that his mother is so bad to me, his wife, but I don't think he knows what to do. Lucky for him, I do. We have to get our own place. I'm sure you all know of my super success with the children's department. Everybody loves Queen Adele. We have a waiting list to join story-time. So I asked myself why can't I use my talent to make a profit. The answer was so obvious. I'm going to put on kids' parties." She looked directly at me. "I just need to connect with the right people. Then Queen Adele will be trendy and everyone will want to pay a ridiculous amount of money to have me host their kids' party."

"You do realize it takes more than you in a costume to put on a party," CeeCee said.

Adele shrugged it off. "That's why I need Pink, she can fill in the rest of it."

Rhoda gave Adele a scolding shake of her head. "You know it might help your situation if you stopped calling her Mother Humphries."

Adele flashed her eyes and made it clear that was not going to happen.

Dinah grabbed the floor. "Molly has more than a baby visitor going on." She turned to me. "Tell them what Peter wants you to do."

They all knew how my son had reacted to my sleuthing and I was sure it was okay if I didn't mention any names. They all chuckled at the irony. Except Adele.

"Here goes Sherlock Pink again," Adele said in a scoffing tone.

"We're really here for crochet," CeeCee said, holding up her work and giving Adele a pointed look. "We haven't done a charity project in a while and I think it's time."

"That's what I was going to say after I talked about the party business," Adele said, interrupting. The rest of the group got the *here we go again* look. CeeCee was the leader of the group, but Adele somehow thought she was.

CeeCee ignored the comment and said she'd bring in some ideas.

"After you run them past me," Adele said, trying to stake out her position. There was a collective rolling of eyes.

Chapter Five

"Here are the directions. It's in Malibu at a playground," Peter said, handing me a printout. "I can put them in your phone since your antique car doesn't have GPS." It was the night before the first meeting of the mommy group and Peter said he was there to prepare me. He had waited until the rest of the family had left and seemed more uptight than usual.

Just because he asked me to investigate his possible partner did not mean he completely trusted me to do the job. He went on and on about what I shouldn't say, like the obvious that I was trying to check the background of Miles Langford. He told me over and over that I should act casual and not ask any direct questions, like *Is there anything scandalous in your family's past that is likely to come up?* Like duh, I thought, shaking my head in disbelief at my son.

"Remember, don't give your last name or mention me. I can't have Miles Langford find out that I sent my mother to investigate him."

"You're sure they don't know who Marlowe's father is?" I said, and Peter shook his head.

"Gabby made sure to distance herself from me, and Marlowe goes by her last name." I asked what he knew about the people in the group and Peter seemed impatient. "All that matters is that you keep a low profile and find out what you can about Miles Langford. I really don't expect anything to show up. He seems to be a pretty mild guy. The money comes from his family and he wants to get into show business."

I thought that was going to be the end of it, but then he said he had talked to Gabby. I asked him what her plans were. Was she going to get a new nanny and come back to pick up Marlowe? Peter looked uncomfortable.

"No and no," he said. "Nothing has changed. She's leaving things as they are and put it all on me." He looked at the array of his daughter's stuff in my living room. "Okay, it's on you more than me."

I had explained the situation with Marlowe and the mommy group to Mrs. Shedd and Mr. Royal and they were very accommodating about letting me switch around my hours. Of course, they knew nothing about the other reason I was going to the meetup.

I had been able to get a little more information out of Peter. The different members of the group took turns hosting. It was an exclusive group and Gabby had used a connection in the group to get the production job. This one was being hosted by Taylor Palmer in Malibu.

• • •

Marlowe was snuggled in her car seat the next morning and had fallen asleep before I even got on the 101. She didn't stir when I got off the freeway at Las Virgenes and headed toward the ocean. The first part of the trip was all straight road surrounded by meadows and mountains in the distance. It was all very green from the winter rains. The scenery changed as we passed through Malibu Creek Park. There were trees and bushes and somewhere in it all was the creek.

From there the road became twisty as it hugged the mountainside. The name had changed to Malibu Canyon Road. Craggy mountains loomed on the other side of the road and it seemed hard to believe we were so close to the people and congestion of the Valley. I thought of other times I had gone on this drive with Mason. He was an expert at romantic gestures, like taking me off to an exotic spot for lunch or going to the beach to toast the sunset with cappuccinos. It had been about us being together and sharing the experience. Wasn't that the way a relationship should be? I felt horrible all over again for the way things had turned out. Particularly since the whole thing with Barry had imploded so quickly. How could I have not seen that it would never work out? Well, I'd made my bed and now I had to lay in it— alone.

It was always a thrill when the blue of the water was suddenly visible and then the road began to descend, giving a bigger view of the ocean. Peter had given me very specific directions, like turn left at the second stoplight and then listed landmarks I would pass before I had to turn left again. He could have just said the street names and the name of the elite shopping center.

There was a haze making the sky seem iridescent as I pulled into the small shopping center in a flat area at the foot of the mountains. The stores and restaurants were all high-end. There were more exact directions from Peter about where to park and where to walk around the line of shops to get to the playground. Marlowe awoke as I put her in the umbrella stroller Peter had gotten her and she looked around with interest while I wheeled her to our destination.

The playground was nothing like the places I had taken Peter and Samuel when they were small. The moms had sat on green wood benches in leggings topped with sweats that had chocolate fingerprints smudged on the shoulders, while the kids played on dull-colored swings and slides.

The equipment here was more colorful and varied. There were bridges and slides with a structure resembling a fire engine. A swing set was set up for different age kids and an area set aside for babies Marlowe's size. Kids were on the move, running and climbing. The play area was fenced in and a strip along it had brightly colored chairs and benches. A group was huddled at one end and I assumed they were who I was looking for.

I sized them up as I approached. There were two woman and a man. They were all in their thirties and seemed wrapped up in a sense of their own importance, reminding me of Gabby. I already felt like the odd man out and realized it wasn't going to be so easy to do what Peter requested.

I put on my friendliest smile and wheeled Marlowe to the group. They all looked up when I approached and reacted as if I was an intruder until they recognized the baby.

"I'm Molly, Marlowe's grandmother," I said. The easiest thing to do was give no last name. "I'm standing in for Gabby."

"She sent me a text that Marlowe was staying with you while she was on the film shoot," one of the women said. "I'm Taylor, the host of this meetup." She was slender with a determined demeanor, as if she was the kind of person who set her sights on a goal and got it. She turned to the other two people.

"I'm Kath," the other woman said. She had long dark hair that the breeze was doing a number on. She peeled it off her face and twisted it into a topknot. With the hair off her face, I noticed that her features seemed a little too perfect and I tried not to stare at her pillowy lips.

The man nodded a greeting. "Garth, working-from-home husband," he said with a grin. He seemed the least concerned with his appearance and was wearing jeans and well-worn ankle boots.

Two other women sat a little off from the rest and Taylor gestured toward them in a dismissive manner. "They're stand-ins." She lowered her voice. "Nannies because their mothers couldn't make it."

"You mean like me?" I said, wondering if I was going to be banished to the fringe.

"No. You're family, so it's okay." She looked down at Marlowe. "You can take her into the play area. My housekeeper, Elena, is there to watch the kids." A woman about my age dressed in comfortable jeans and a hoodie was catching a little boy who looked about two on a slide. Another child about Marlowe's age was crawling on the ground. Once I'd left Marlowe, I glanced back at the adults.

It seemed like the first bit of detective work I was going to have to do was to figure out who Miles's wife was. I knew that Taylor's last name was Palmer, so she was out. Peter had said *wife*, so Garth was out. I didn't want to be overt and simply ask Kath her last name. Even if Peter hadn't given me the ridiculous warning not to be obvious, I knew that on my own. Asking a question like that would likely prompt them to ask me why I was asking. It would be even more complicated dealing with the nannies and finding out who they worked for. They were both older and plain-looking. I wondered if their age and appearance had made them choice candidates after so many stories of husbands running off with younger caregivers. It seemed doubtful any husbands would want to take off with them unless the guy had a mommy complex.

They all had coffee drinks and Taylor pointed to the coffee place just around the corner. When I returned with my drink, they had a chair in the middle for me. I took a sip of the coffee as I considered what to say. It was delicious with a chocolatey aftertaste. I made a mental note to mention it to Bob for the bookstore café.

A good icebreaker seemed to be asking how they'd started the group. It turned out they'd met at a celebrity-owned Malibu children's boutique. Along with a play area that had snacks for the kids, there was a wine and espresso bar for the adults where they hung out as a clothing consultant showed them merchandise. I found out that Taylor had a five-year-old son named Andrew who was in school. The boy she had with her was a toddler named Oliver. Garth had three-year-old fraternal twins named Edgar and Lucy. Kath had a daughter named Plum who was Marlowe's age and was a surprise addition. Her two older kids were in high school. As I glanced at her face again, I realized she was older than I'd thought.

"What about them?" I said, pointing at the two nannies.

Taylor seemed annoyed. "We should really consider whether we want to keep their mothers in the group. I don't remember the last time Lindy and Vanessa came with their kids. And they always have an excuse why they can't host when it's their turn. We had to ask Benita to leave when she refused to do her part."

I was hoping that neither of the no-shows or Benita was who I was looking for, which left Kath. I thought if I could get her talking about herself there might be a clue.

I had barely put together a question to ask her when she solved the problem and also dashed my hopes that she was who I was looking for. She began talking about her professional life. She turned to me to explain. "My husband is a plastic surgeon and we have a number of clinics. I deal with the marketing and advertising. We're in the process of putting together a new infomercial." She looked at me to see if I understood what she meant and then explained anyway that it was a half-hour show about their services that was really an advertisement for them. "We call the clinics Beau Visage, which means beautiful face even though the clinics do everything. We were going to call them Beautiful Body, but in French it comes out as Beau Corps." She laughed. "Corps and corpse sound the same. Not the image we wanted."

She turned to Garth. "When do you think you'll have something to show me?" Trying to keep me in the loop, she explained that Garth was writing the script for the half-hour ad.

"It's different than what I usually do," he said, telling me that he was between gigs writing sitcoms. "But I'll have it for you in a couple of days," he said, answering Kath.

"As long as we're giving our credits," Taylor said, "I wear a number of hats. Mother, wife, and I was the director of *Dust and Sagebrush*." I nodded with a smile as if I was impressed. I vaguely remember the movie from one of the streaming channels.

Just then another woman joined the group with a boy about four. She sent the boy to join the other kids in the play area and turned model-style in front of us. "What do you think?" she said, seeming to show off the wrap she was wearing. It seemed somewhere between a shawl and a jacket and was white with a blue stripe. The back spread down from her shoulders but was stitched together so there were arms holes. "This is the sport model and it's made out of linen." She slipped it off and held it out for someone to try on.

Garth took it, smiling as he slipped it over his hoodie and mimicked a model on a runway, and they all laughed. "What do you call these things again?" he asked.

"The style is called a cocoon, but I call mine the Cuddle."

Garth handed it back to her and she started to sit, but then Elena came up to the seating area with the kids in tow. She handed off Plum to Kath, and Marlowe to me.

"Now we move to my place for lunch," Taylor said.

"My favorite part," Garth said, coming up next to me as we trooped to the parking lot and our cars. He seemed to pick up that I was an outsider like him. "Be sure to stick with the convoy. We can't take the shortcut since it means driving through the creek, which is too high at this time of year.

"You probably noticed that Taylor is the leader of the group. If you want to get on her good side, compliment her on the house. It was the Beltron family's summer house. Lots of history with the place. If you have any aspirations to work in the 'business,' Taylor is the one with the connections. Gabby got her job as producer from hanging out with this group."

Garth seemed friendly and gossipy and I was going to ask him about the last arrival, but his phone rang. He answered the call and gave me a wave, talking as he and his twins went to their car.

Chapter Six

I packed Marlowe up in her seat and rushed to keep up behind Garth's black SUV. I was glad I had somebody to follow instead of instructions. It started with us going past a gatekeeper and then eucalyptus-lined twisty back roads past estates until everyone turned into a driveway. The cars in front of me pulled into a motor court. My ancient blue-green Mercedes seemed lost in all the SUVs, which all seemed to be big and black.

The house was massive and had a classic old California look with the creamy-colored stucco and terra-cotta roof. Tall arched mullioned windows were on either side of the covered entranceway. I got Marlowe out and gathered with the others around Elena. We followed the housekeeper around the side of the house past a tennis court, pool and yard to a guesthouse, where we left the kids with the housekeeper. The woman in the cocoon wrap took a small box out of an insulated bag. "In case he gets a nose bleed." Elena pushed it back on her and assured her the refrigerator had popsicles that worked even better. The two nannies stayed with the kids and I followed the others to a French door that led into the main house.

We walked into a large room with a tiled floor that seemed like a den. A woman in a gray uniform came in pushing a cart and began to set out platters on an antique wooden sideboard. "I kept it simple," Taylor said, urging us to help ourselves. Simple, ha! There was a platter of fruit with wedges of pineapple, slices of melon, huge whole strawberries surrounded by blueberries and blackberries. A bowl of chopped salad had a stack of small dishes next to it. And finally, there was a platter of triangular half sandwiches. Another smaller one had more sandwiches, which Taylor said were all vegan. There were bottles of wine and glasses and a pitcher of lemonade with slices of lemon floating on the top, and finally an airpot with coffee. At the very end of the table was a tray of brownies. As we all gathered around the food, I noticed they all stared at the chocolate treats, but only Garth took one.

I remembered what Garth had said about the house and was curious about a wall of photos. I tried to detour to have a look but Taylor came along and sent me toward the two long beige couches that faced each other and had a coffee table between them.

There were only five of us now that the nannies had stayed with the kids. I'd been concerned about finding my way and then getting Marlowe situated. Now I was ready to go back into detective mode.

Unless one of the two mothers connected with the nannies or Benita was Miles's wife, the woman with the cocoon wrap had to be her. But I still needed to confirm it. I wished Dinah had been there so we could play off each other, but I was on my own. Maybe if I brought up the name. I considered talking about jazz, then I could say I was a fan of Miles Davis and see if it got a reaction. Or what about talking about poetry. The Robert Frost poem had the line "miles to go before I sleep." Would it be too weird if I brought up how miles was both a name and a measure of distance? None of it seemed very good. The two couches were extra-long and could have easily accommodated three people each, but the new woman had taken a chair instead. I felt her gaze rest on me.

"Are you another nanny?" she said. She said it in a condescending tone and I expected her to follow up by suggesting I join the other two in the guesthouse if I said I was.

"No, no," Taylor said. "She's Marlowe's grandmother."

"Molly Aronson," I said, not wanting to be known by that title. I was still getting used to the term and fighting the image I had of a woman in a shapeless dress standing over a stove making chicken soup.

After that, the new woman seemed only a little less dismissive as she introduced herself. "I'm Lily," she said. "Alexander is mine."

Lily who? I wanted to scream. I didn't know what else to do and launched into a discussion of how they all had introduced themselves with first names only.

"It's not a problem for me," Garth said. "Mine is Ross." He looked to the women.

"I'm sticking to my maiden name. It's what I've always used professionally," Kath said. "I'm glad I didn't take my first husband's name. Imagine how confusing it would be now that I'm married to Michael."

"It all depends on whether your husband's name means something," Taylor said. "I make sure everybody knows I'm Mrs. Palmer. It opens a lot of doors."

"It makes you a package deal," Kath said. "Fine, as long as it's positive like it is for you. But if he ends up being disgraced or in jail, not so good." She looked at Garth. "What about your wife? She's in business affairs at Winkleman Brothers Studio. What does she go by?"

Garth shrugged. "I guess I don't offer enough power like Andrew Palmer, and I'm her second husband. After the divorce, she went back to her maiden name and she said she's keeping it that way."

So far Lily had stayed out of the conversation. "My solution was just to go by my first name." Lily picked up the cocoon she'd hung on the back of the chair and showed me the label. It said: The Cuddle by Lily.

I had started the conversation as a tool to get information, but now that they'd spoken, I was thinking about what they'd said as it related to me. It had never occurred to me not to take Charlie's last name, Pink. But now that I was a widow, what if I got married again? Would I keep adding on last names? If I'd married Mason would I have called myself Molly Pink-Fields? What if everything hadn't blown up with Barry and we'd gotten married? I'd be Molly Pink-Greenberg.

"My credit for directing *Dust and Sagebrush* is listed as Taylor Owens. In that case, I wanted my own identity. I'll do the same with my future projects." Taylor turned to me. "I suppose you can't relate to what we're talking about. I think it's really people our age who are making choices about what name they want to go by."

She had done a good job of making me feel like an outsider and older than time. I really wanted to tell them that I was actually there on a case, acting as a detective, and not just there to accompany Marlowe. But it would have blown my cover.

"I think you know what we all do," Taylor said, talking to me. "But what about you? What is it that you do?" Taylor caught herself. "That is, if you do something. So many woman your age were still stay-at-home moms." I wasn't sure if she was just being friendly or trying to see how I measured up to the rest of them.

Peter hadn't said I had to hide where I worked. And, well, I wanted them to see that I wasn't just Marlowe's grandmother. "I work at Shedd & Royal Books and More," I said, sitting a little straighter.

"So then it's your bookstore?" Kath asked.

"You mean like own it?" I said, since her expression implied that was what she meant. "No, I just work there. I'm the assistant manager and I handle the special events," I said, feeling like I had to keep up with the Joneses. "We have a wonderful children's department."

"Events?" Taylor said.

"Author signings and things like arranging for groups that meet at the bookstore." I felt like I had to say more to build it up, something that they could relate to, and brought up the theme we had going. "It's because it's award season and the Oscars are coming up," I said. "We're doing an event with Daisy Cochran, who has a book out with stories from her days of writing the entertainment column, and CeeCee Collins talking about her Oscar nomination."

"We all know who she is," Taylor said. They didn't seem too impressed.

"Daisy Cochran is old-school," Garth said. "She adhered to that saying about if you can't say something good, don't say anything. In the old days when I was trying to get my break, I worked as a production assistant on a movie. Daisy came on the set and I know she witnessed the two stars having a shouting match, but she never put a word of it in her column," he said with a shrug. "I'm sure whatever stories she tells will all be upbeat."

"Maybe not," I said, trying to generate some interest. "She's trying to reinvent herself and go with the way things are now. She's doing a podcast and is going to investigate some of those things she didn't say. She didn't go into detail with me, but she said it involves some deaths that might not be what they seemed."

"CeeCee Collins is going to be there?" Taylor said. "I suppose it was a big deal to be nominated for an Academy Award after being sidelined for so long." Something in her tone irritated me. CeeCee was so much more than an actor. Even though Adele fought the idea, CeeCee was the leader of the Hookers and the one behind all the things we made for charity.

"Actually, she's going to be there in a dual role," I said. "It's also National Crochet Month and we're combining the theme of the Academy Awards with crochet. CeeCee is the heart of the Tarzana Hookers." They all started laughing at the name and I didn't bother trying to say more.

They were all on second glasses of wine, while I nursed my coffee. No way was I going to try to negotiate Malibu Canyon with a fuzzy head. Everyone had switched seats and the spot next to me on the couch was open. Garth came back with a plate with fruit and more brownies and took the empty spot.

He seemed interested in the bookstore. "I'm a writer," he said with a sheepish smile. "I love anyplace that specializes in words." He was interested in the event that I'd talked about.

"I bet Daisy made demands. She always seemed to view herself as one of the celebrities." He talked about working as a production assistant on a telethon. "I would do anything to make connections. Including working for free," he said. "All those celebrity guests volunteered their services, but their people submitted a list of demands of things they had to have in their dressing rooms. It was crazy stuff," he said with a laugh. "Very specific, like wanting a bowl of M&Ms, but with no yellow ones. Someone even gave the temperature they wanted their diet soda cans kept at."

"I can relate," I said with a chuckle. "It's ironic. CeeCee is the real celebrity and she asked for nothing, but Daisy had a list. Nothing as bad as having to pick out yellow M&Ms, but she insisted on having a green room." I described how I could create a backstage area by making an enclosure with the bookcases. "She was very specific about her water and a juice smoothie. A strawberry concoction that had to be made just as she was about to begin."

Garth looked up with a sigh as Elena and the two nannies came in with all the kids. "Party's over," he said as his twins rushed over to him. "It was nice talking to you. We both deal in words," he joked.

Marlowe was in her stroller and seemed ready for a nap. Taylor took charge and led the way through the house to the entrance. I tried to take in the details of the house, but there was too much commotion. The entrance hall was impressively large with a curved staircase coming from the second floor.

Garth glanced up at it and held on tight to Edgar and Lucy's hands. "Those are not stairs to play on. With no landing, once you start to fall it's going to be all the way down to the bottom." He made a thud sound.

There was a din of conversation as everyone prepared to leave and was saying their goodbyes. Taylor came through the crowd and stopped at me. She wanted to know how long I'd be subbing for Gabby, and when I said it was indeterminate, took my contact information, and then she dropped a bombshell.

"Then you'll be taking Gabby's place and hosting the group when it's her turn," she said. "You can give us all details when we meet next time."

She didn't give me a chance to respond but moved to the double front doors just as one of them opened and a tall man with white hair came in. He greeted her, but most of his interest was on the little boy at her side. He picked him up and gave him a hug. "Everyone, Andrew," she said, and he gave a nod as a greeting to the group. Lily pushed through the crowd and stopped in front of him. Through the din of conversation, I caught a few words. She had said something about Miles. Hallelujah, I was right! I felt like day one of my detective work was a success. I had at least figured out who I was supposed to be interested in.

Chapter Seven

Dinah was sitting in the café with Samuel when I got to the bookstore. I saw the mug of coffee in front of my son along with the cookie bar of the day. "Checking out the competition?" I said with a smile. His green apron from the coffee place where he worked was rolled up on the table.

He drained the cup. "We'd win, hands down." He picked up the cookie bar and finished it off. "Okay, Bob has an edge on what the café offers to go with the drinks." He touched the coffee mug. "I needed an extra blast of caffeine before . . ." He patted Marlowe's head. His point was lost for the moment because she was slumped to one side, having fallen asleep again after I got her out of the car seat. "That won't last. Then it's Uncle Samuel the entertainer." He got up and took over the stroller. Peter had set up a car seat in his brother's car so there was no problem with the handoff.

"So, tell me everything," Dinah said when he was gone. It was a relief to talk to somebody where I didn't have to worry about what I said. "What a snooty group," she said when I'd finished describing them.

"Garth seems okay," I said. "He was at least friendly and didn't treat me like I was a million years old. I get that from Peter, too. It's as if they think they'll be thirty-something forever. They all have a profession with being parents as sort of a sideline." I went through the list. Taylor was a director, Kath was an infomercial producer, Garth was a writer, and Lily had a clothing business. "She's the one I'm most interested in," I said. "She made a point that she is CEO of the Cuddle by Lily Designs."

Dinah already had her phone out and had typed something in. "Here's her website." Dinah handed me the phone and I read the details. Her whole business was the one style of cocoon wraps in different fabrics and colors. She had a "flagship" store in Malibu. There was a list of other retailers who carried the cocoons and they were available online. I went right to the About Us page and there was a glowing story about how the idea for the cocoons had come to her in a dream. There were a lot of words like *artistic energy* that really said nothing. There was mention that her creations were a favorite among celebrities with no names given. It was noted that she was married to Miles Langford and had one son named Alexander. I shrugged it off. "There's nothing there to cause a problem," I said.

"Kath is a walking advertisement for her husband's clinics, though she seemed a little too perfect-looking. And the lips—" My eyes went skyward. "They looked like they were swollen from someone busting her in the mouth."

Dinah seemed as perplexed as I was as to why someone would want to look like that. "Here's something to play our Sherlock Holmes game with," I said. "Taylor is in her early thirties and has two boys." I gave their names and ages. "Her husband Andrew has white hair and is a big deal in the entertainment business."

Dinah thought a moment. "I'd say that it's a second family for him, or maybe even third family, and since the older son shares his name, I'd guess that he's Andrew Junior or maybe even Andrew III."

"And I deduce that he only had daughters in his other families," I chimed in. "Let's see how accurate we are." I gave her Andrew's last name and she typed it into her phone.

"We're good," Dinah said with pride. She'd found a biography of Andrew on an entertainment database that listed wives and kids. He had two daughters with the first wife and the two boys with Taylor. She read over his credits. He had a production company and had produced a number of blockbuster movies.

Dinah drank the last of her café au lait. "I have a class," she said, collecting herself to leave. "It sounds as if it went well."

"Except that Taylor, who seems to be in charge, dropped the news that I have to host one of these meetups."

Dinah temporarily leaned back in her chair. "Easy. Do it here. The café can offer the treats and Adele can do a special story-time."

"Easy?" I said with a laugh. "Nothing is ever easy with Adele."

When Dinah left, I went into the bookstore to see what was waiting for me.

I saw several people sitting at the table in the yarn department and went to investigate. As I got closer, I saw that it was CeeCee and Elise and it appeared they were fussing about something. I went to hopefully make peace.

"Mrs. Shedd agreed that I should be part of the evening since I created the kits," Elise said in her chirpy voice. "I think we should go over what we're going to talk about."

"The evening really has a Hollywood/Academy Awards theme. I fit in because I have a connection to the Academy Awards," CeeCee said.

"But you didn't win," Elise said with defiance.

"It doesn't matter. I went to all the festivities before the award show and had my picture taken with all the other nominees. I can give some behind-the-scenes color. I thought I might even wear the dress I wore to the show."

"But how are we going to segue into talking about March being National Crochet Month?" Elise asked.

"The obvious thing is that I talk about the movie vampire, Anthony, and his love of crochet," CeeCee said.

"Which could lead into the kits that Elise created," I said, approaching the table. If Mrs. Shedd had given the go-ahead to Elise, I had to make sure she was part of the event. "The scarf pattern she created is like the one Anthony wore in the movie." I directed the comment to CeeCee, who didn't seem happy with what I was saying. Then she capitulated.

"I suppose if Mrs. Shedd wants Elise included, I have to go along," the actress said.

I mouthed a thank-you to the actress and turned to Elise. "It would be good if you brought one of the finished scarves."

"Bring one," she said with a twittery laugh, "I'll wear one. And bring a display with several." Now that they were on the same team,

Elise started trying to direct things. "We should work out now what we're going to talk about since I'm sure Daisy Cochran will want to spend all the time going on about her book and that podcast thing."

"I know it would make Mrs. Shedd happy if you mentioned our yarn department, and that we have knitting supplies, too."

They were both crocheting as they talked and I took out the simple project that I kept in the yarn department for times like this. It was a basic scarf that didn't take much attention. Even so, I could only combine talking and crocheting so much, which meant the scarf was taking forever to finish. "You could also mention the Hookers and that we do projects to donate to different charities."

"Good point," CeeCee said and pulled out a file. "I had a few ideas for a blanket that could be made in different sizes." She slipped the file back in her bag. "I'll explain it when everybody is here."

Elise went off to look at the kits we had on the display table. CeeCee continued with her hook and I stayed to visit. She asked about Marlowe and I told her about my morning and the mommy group and the fabulous house where it had been held. "As a stand-in for Marlowe's mother, they're expecting me to put on one of the get-togethers. The kids go off somewhere to be entertained and the parents hang out and network, as Taylor Owens—I mean Palmer—did," I said with a laugh. "There was such a fuss about names. The women all seemed to want to be known by their maiden names either because it had to do with their identity or because they might get a divorce." I added Dinah had suggested I do the meetup at the bookstore, using story-time as the entertainment.

CeeCee smiled. "Good luck dealing with Adele, though since she wants your help with her parties, you might use that as bargaining power." She looked down at her work and noticed a loose loop and used her hook to straighten it out. "I know who Taylor is," CeeCee said. "She's the second Mrs. Palmer. He financed that movie she directed." CeeCee gave me a knowing look. "Supposedly, they were involved while he was married to his first wife, but then Taylor got pregnant and when he found out it was a boy after having nothing but daughters, he pushed through a divorce and married Taylor. That house is something, isn't it?" CeeCee said. Then she lowered her voice. "There was a fuss about that house after the divorce. Margo wouldn't leave despite whatever was in their prenuptial agreement and the newlyweds couldn't move in. I heard that Andrew wouldn't take legal action to force Margo to move either. It might have been that he felt guilty about the divorce or he was concerned it would get him negative publicity."

"You've been there?" I said, surprised.

"Dear, Margo loved giving parties and having celebrity guests. The *CeeCee Collins Show* was a Wednesday night fixture. Nobody called me a veteran actress then." She had a dreamy look, remembering another time. Elise had returned and heard some of our conversation.

"You mean when your career was hot," Elise said.

"You could say I'm hot again," CeeCee countered. "Being nominated for an Oscar is a big deal. My agent sent me a script I'm considering."

"Really?" Elise said. "For what?"

CeeCee looked Elise in the eye. "I know you think it's for a part in a horror movie. But actually it's for a western and the part is for the matriarch of the family. I'll have to ride a horse—well, learn how to ride a horse." She let out a sigh. "We'll have to see if that's negotiable."

CeeCee turned the subject back to the mommy group and wondered about who else was there. She didn't know who Kath was but was familiar with the Beau Visage commercials. Now that I thought about it, I was too. "They are all over the TV with before and after photos. And the doctor must be Kath's husband. What's his name?" Then it came to me. "Dr. Michael Zander. He was always smiling and saying how proud he was of his work."

"I wonder if he's proud of the complaints," Elise said. "I was thinking about upgrading this—" She gestured to indicate her face. "Shave off a few years and maybe add a little to my lips. But when I asked around, I heard that not everybody was happy with the results. Things didn't turn out as they expected. Though it seemed a lot of it was about Brazilian butt lifts."

Elise put her work away. "Now that we're settled on who is going to be there with Daisy, I need to check the stock of kits I have at home. If I'm going to be here signing them, we'll need a lot."

CeeCee had put her work away as well. She was meeting someone for lunch. The two women left the store and I was on my way back to my cubicle.

I glanced at the front of the store and was shocked to see Taylor come in with Elena and her two sons. When I'd mentioned where I worked, I didn't consider that any of them might come in— particularly all the way from Malibu. So weird, too, after we had just been talking about her and the house.

"It sounded like a special place. And I wanted to get Andrew some new books. He's tired of all the old ones. You said there was a special children's department." She glanced at the sign advertising Daisy's appearance. "This is the event you talked about, isn't it?" She read over the copy and I mentioned there was a display of Daisy's book. As I took them further into the bookstore, I saw Adele looking over the bookcases that separated the children's department. Her eyes rested on the little boys and then flashed when she glared at me. I knew what she was thinking—that I was impinging on her domain as head of the children's department. She came out in a rush, swirling the cape she was wearing over a fairy costume. She headed right toward us and a sudden horror crossed my mind as I saw her opening her mouth and knew she was going to call my name. I couldn't let Taylor hear her call me Pink and blow my cover.

Chapter Eight

"What happened?" Dinah said as I told her about Taylor's visit to the bookstore and having to deal with the wrath of Adele when she thought I was encroaching on her department. Dinah and I were sitting in my car outside Pet World. The menagerie was getting low on supplies and I had needed a reason to get out.

I'd come home to a circus. Peter was waiting to grill me. The She La Las were practicing their new dance number while Marlowe watched from her playpen. Samuel's friend Beth was sitting on the couch watching the baby and the dancing as she continued to audition for the babysitter job. Samuel and my father were in the kitchen unloading white containers of Thai food to feed everybody. They had brought far more than was needed. It was a family trait to be generous with food.

Peter was disappointed in how little I had found out and was practically hysterical when he heard I had to host one of the mommy group meetups and was thinking of doing it at the bookstore and involving Adele.

It was all too much and I had called Dinah about going with me on an errand. She was glad to get out as well. Commander was already in going-to-sleep mode and she was still ready to do something—even if it was only a trip to the pet store to replenish the food supply for my animals.

"So . . ." Dinah said, gesturing for me to tell her the outcome of the confrontation with Adele.

"I couldn't stop her from calling me Pink," I said, remembering the moment. "I had to do something to cover it up." I laughed, thinking of the absurd thing I had come up with. "I looked at Adele and quickly added *Ballet Slippers* in an excited voice. And then added that *The Pink Ballet Slippers* was the book I'd been referring to, implying it was from some past conversation. Adele looked confused by it all and as if she was about to say something, and I got ready to do damage control, but I was saved by the bell. Well, not really a bell, more like the arrival of Eric Humphries and Mother Humphries. Adele got all unhinged about them and forgot all about me. She muttered something about they wanted to talk to her about something."

"Nothing is going to get better until she stops calling her Mother Humphries," Dinah said. I nodded in agreement. Everyone who knew about the situation had tried to tell her the same, but she never listened. But then Adele never listened to anybody.

"But that wasn't the end of things. Leslie Bittner came in." I explained that she was Daisy Cochran's assistant and podcast producer. Dinah knew about the hassle I was having putting the event together with Mrs. Shedd's demand that I mix in National Crochet Month with all the Hollywood stuff and Daisy's demands. "She dropped off another box of books so we'd be sure to have enough for Daisy to sign. She went over Daisy's demands and went over that the juice place where I'm to get the smoothie has two kinds of strawberry smoothies and I had to be sure to get the right one. She insisted it had to be the strawberry splash."

"What a prima donna," Dinah said. "Sorry I'm going to miss the event, but I'm helping Commander with a happy hour thing he's hosting at the Mail It store. Since so many of his customers work out of their homes, he likes to give them a chance to socialize." She smiled at the thought. "He is such a sweetheart in so many ways it makes up for what's hard to deal with." She looked ahead at the pet superstore and chuckled. "We better go in before they close."

We got out of the car and went into Pet World. Since we were making an outing out of the errand, we took time to look at the small animals they had for sale in the front of the store. We bypassed the snakes and salamanders and glanced at the hamsters before stopping when we got to the guinea pigs. They had bright eyes and I made eye contact with them. I had started talking to them when Dinah knocked against my arm to get my attention and pointed to the automatic door that had slid open. I froze as Mason Fields came in holding his toy fox terrier Spike.

I ducked down and waddled toward the end of the row of enclosures, thinking I could escape into the aisle of cat trees and carriers. But Mason had moved into the store and was standing in the aisle I'd have to cross, blocking my way. I stayed put and bent down as if I was looking for something, hoping he'd keep going without noticing me. All I could see were his shoes, soft brown leather slip-ons, and they weren't moving. I heard him greet Dinah and knew my cover was blown, and I stood up feeling foolish.

He was wearing jeans and a Hawaiian shirt, which I thought of as his casual, fun look, but there was no affable smile or light in his dark eyes. His expression was stone-faced. He looked so cold, I expected icy fog to come out of his mouth. Spike had no idea of what had happened between Mason and me. All he knew was that I was the person who'd played fetch with him. He wiggled with joy at seeing me. Mason set him on the ground and the little short-haired dog rushed up and put his paws on my leg.

"You won't get any peace until you pick him up," Mason said, keeping an even tone. He was a high-powered attorney who spent a lot of time in court defending his naughty and entitled celebrity clients and obviously knew how to modulate his voice to hide what he was feeling, which I assumed was anger and more. And I deserved it all. I cringed, reliving the phone call I'd made to him canceling our plans. I was sure Mason was having a good laugh knowing how badly things had turned out—that is, if he knew.

I wanted to ask him if he was still doing the pro bono work, helping innocent people get new trials. But I couldn't even look at his face after the first glance. I gave all my attention to Spike. As soon as I picked him up, he wiggled with excitement and covered my face with doggie kisses. I gave him a few cuddles before setting him back on the floor. He ran back to Mason and danced in circles, yipping.

Mason scooped the dog up. "Well, I'll leave you to it." His tone was flat. "We're shopping for his favorite chicken treats."

Just before he walked away, I muttered "I'm sorry." It was under my breath and I didn't know if he'd even heard me.

"Now you understand why I didn't consider calling him," I said to Dinah, feeling all the starch go out of me. I knew I was bound to see him somewhere eventually, but it was even worse than I had imagined.

We got the pet supplies I needed, and Dinah talked me into going to her place. I accepted, thinking there was no way I was ready to go back to the commotion going on at my house.

Her house was in the heart of Tarzana and a short walk from Shedd & Royal. Commander had gone to bed and turned off all the lights in the house, and it was like walking into a tomb. She walked through, flicking them all back on as she led the way to the added-on den, which she had made into her she-cave. The sliding glass doors that separated her space from the rest of the house had been the end of the house originally and were quite soundproof. She turned on all the lights in the large room and invited me to flop on the chartreuse couch that had been in her living room prior to the marriage. It was a little too much for Commander and had been replaced with one covered in a neutral sort of tweed.

"After that you need the heavy-duty stuff," Dinah said. She pulled off her long golden yellow scarf and dropped it on the couch, then went to the counter and filled the electric kettle from the bar sink. A few minutes later the fragrance of Earl Grey crème tea filled the air.

What would I do without my best friend.

Chapter Nine

I had a day off before our Hollywood Crochets Event. I used the time to make the arrangements for Marlowe's care since I was going to go in early and stay late. We'd all agreed that Samuel's friend Beth had passed muster. I gave her the news she was hired and set up the time for her to start the following day.

I was still getting used to having a baby in the house. More and more baby stuff kept arriving. Marlowe had a bouncy chair to sit in and another that let her push herself around the room with her feet. I'd packed away all the dresses and accessories Gabby had provided and bought a bunch of the stretchy little suits with the snap-up front. It was all comfort all the time for Marlowe now and she seemed to appreciate it.

• • •

When Beth arrived the next morning, I made sure to show her the array of baby bottles and canister of formula even though Marlowe was more into eating food. She had her own plates and little spoons. There was a selection of food I had put through the grinder in the refrigerator and a selection of commercial baby food, just in case.

It was going to be a long day and I was glad I didn't have to worry about who was taking care of Marlowe or what she had to eat.

Mrs. Shedd stopped me as soon as I walked into the bookstore. I was always struck by how ageless her hair was. I knew she was well into her sixties and still her honey blond hair had a silky texture without a single strand of gray. There was never a question that it was natural.

"We've been getting a lot of calls about the event tonight. I knew mixing National Crochet Month with Daisy's Hollywood stories would get a lot of interest," Mrs. Shedd said with a look of self-satisfaction. "Times may have changed, but I've still got my sales savvy." She had told me I could call her Pamela and Mr. Royal had said I could call him Joshua, but somehow it felt too strange to me to call them by their first names. She went on to tell me that Mr. Royal had brought in extra chairs and already rolled back the bookcases, making an open space for the crowd, and used them to create the backstage area I had asked for.

I went to look it all over and make some adjustments. I saw Adele peeking over the top of the bookcases that divided off the children's area and a moment later she joined me. Before she said a word, I knew what it was about. She was going to try to make a last effort to get herself in the middle of the evening's event.

"Somebody should be there to explain how superior crochet is to knitting," Adele said. She naturally had a voice that carried and I noticed several customers turning when she spoke. Adele saw herself as the champion of the yarn craft. Without her saying a word, I knew she had dressed hoping to position herself on the panel. Her boxy jacket was made of granny squares. Her long black skirt was done in basic double crochet stitches and her white cloche hat was covered in crocheted violet and pink flowers. She was like a walking display of the craft.

Simply telling her no one really cared except her would only cause more problems. The only way to deal with her when she got like this was to get her mind on something else, preferably to something that she would have a strong response to. I had a thought in mind and even how to handle it when she made a fuss.

I brought up the mommy group and before I could get to the point, she objected.

"Didn't you say there's a dad in it, and then there's you. How can you call it a mommy group?" Technically, she was right, but it was a lot easier than being one hundred percent accurate and calling it something like the children of assorted ages and an important family member group.

"Whatever you want to call it," I said, glossing over her comment, "they take turns hosting, which means I'm going to have to do it.

There needs to be an entertainment for the kids." Adele saw where I was going and her eyes began to flash.

"Pink, there is no way I'm putting on a story-time for them. The answer is double no." Her tone was petulant and I didn't want to ask her what double no meant. I was expecting her reaction and moved into phase two of my plan.

"You might want to reconsider," I said. "You didn't give me a chance to tell you who the other adults are."

Adele turned back to look at me. I'd gotten her interest. "You saw one of them the other day. The woman with the little boys. Her name is Taylor." I struggled with what last name to give her and figured neither one would mean much to Adele, so just left it with her first name. "She was the director on *Dust and Sagebrush*. Her husband is a big-time movie producer. Imagine if you did a party for them."

Adele's eyes began to light up with understanding as I continued. "Putting on a special story-time would be like an audition and a chance to pitch them on the parties. Imagine what it would do for your business if you could say you'd put on a kids' party for them."

Adele had forgotten all about being upset about not being included in the evening's program. Her eyes were darting back and forth, indicating that she was thinking about what I said. "Okay, I'll do it. You're right. They'll see me and want Queen Adele to put on a party."

I nodded in agreement and Adele said she was going back to the kids' department to start brainstorming on how to make the story-time extra impressive. I smiled to myself on how I had managed Adele. I was so caught up in patting myself on the back that I was startled to see that Daisy Cochran was standing next to me holding a box of books.

"I brought them for tonight," she said, setting them on one of the chairs. "If there are any left, you can keep them here—on consignment." Because her book was self-published, we didn't get them through the usual channels.

She glanced in the direction that Adele had gone. "You gave her good advice. If she puts on a party for Andrew Palmer, plenty of others will follow." She looked at me with an admiring nod. "I didn't know you traveled in such a contemporary Hollywood circle."

I explained suddenly having my granddaughter and having to step into the mommy group. She asked who else was in the group and nodded with interest as I went through the list. "I know them all, or of them," she said with a mysterious smile.

I brought up Miles Langford and she nodded. "He's trying to buy his way into the entertainment business. He invests in projects and gets a screen credit."

"I guess there's nothing wrong with that," I said, leaving her an opening to say more.

"No, I guess there isn't since he's all about the image rather than doing the work." She immediately went back to what she really wanted to talk about, which was her event and some tweaks for her backstage area.

• • •

The afternoon was fading and the bookstore was filled with shadows as I changed gears, thinking ahead to the event. I had rearranged the setup of the green room according to Daisy's specifications. The fancy bottled water she had demanded was chilling. The chairs were all set out and I took a quick dinner break in the café. It was more like breakfast for dinner as Bob gave me some leftovers of a new addition to the menu. They were called Eggy Squares and meant as a morning treat. He added a mini croissant and a red-eye to make it a complete meal.

It was dark when I came back into the bookstore. CeeCee had just arrived and was wearing a long black dress with a sequined jacket. She'd gone heavy on her makeup to resemble the character in the movie. Elise followed her in and had one of the finished scarves from the kits wound around her neck. She had brought along a stack of business cards for her real estate endeavor. Daisy was dressed in her trademark slacks, a sweater, shirt with a popped collar and a colorful scarf. Despite her insistence on having the backstage area, I'd seen her mixing with some of the early arrivals.

Mrs. Shedd was definitely right for getting extra chairs. Her idea of mixing up the Hollywood stories with Crochet Month was drawing a crowd and the seats were filling up. I had arranged and rearranged the front with a table of samples of merchandise adjacent to where the speakers would be sitting. Mr. Royal had come up with the idea of CeeCee signing the DVDs of the crocheting vampire movie and the set of DVDs from her old TV show. Elise had decided on her own to sign the kits for the crochet projects connected to the movie. There were signing tables for each of them set up for after the program.

I was sorry that Dinah was not going to be there, but I understood she wanted to help Commander with his happy hour party. I was glad that Adele had left, though with great drama, going on that she was not staying because she wasn't part of the event.

"You better get Daisy's drink," Leslie Bittner said, coming up behind me. I swallowed my annoyance at Daisy's assistant telling me what to do and went to the juice place a few doors down to get the drink. I looked at the menu on an overhanging board and noted the two strawberry drinks and ordered the one that Leslie had told me to get.

When I came back with it, Daisy was standing outside the enclosed area looking over the crowd. I went to hand her the drink, and she saw the label stuck to the cup.

"Are you trying to kill me!" she shrieked. "You were supposed to get the strawberry fiesta. Go and get me the right drink," she demanded.

I chalked up her behavior to nerves before she had to face a crowd and apologized without mentioning that it was her assistant who had told me to get the strawberry splash. When I returned with the right drink, the seats were all taken and there were people standing in the back. Daisy had retreated to the green room setup. Not wanting another confrontation with her, I set the tall covered cup next to

Daisy's name placard and then moved away. I had a sudden worry that if CeeCee or Elise saw that I'd gotten a drink for Daisy, they'd feel left out. I found two bottles of water and set them out for them.

I always felt a tingle of nerves just before an event. I went to check on the three of them and tell them I was going to warm up the crowd before I introduced them. Elise begged me to wait to start until she made a bathroom stop. When she returned, I went to the center microphone and got everyone to quiet before doing my welcome followed by the introductions. Daisy had written hers for me. She was determined to generate interest in her upcoming podcast and had gotten it into the introduction with the promise that she was going to disclose a tidbit of inside information. I had created the intros for the other two. It was easy with CeeCee, particularly since Adele wasn't there to object when I referred to the actress as being the leader of the Tarzana Hookers. I'd had to be more creative with Elise and made her out to be a yarn craft designer along with being a real estate super agent. When I did the Tarzana Hooker line I looked over the crowd for their reaction, since it always got a laugh. I was surprised to see Taylor standing in the back. I got to the end of the introductions and there was a nice round of applause as the three of them came out and took their spots. There were mics on the table for CeeCee and Elise, but one of Daisy's requirements had been to have a mic she could move around with and I'd gotten her a headset.

She slipped it on and glanced out at the crowd with a smile. "I like to move when I talk." Since the event had started out only being her, she was going to speak first. She seemed comfortable addressing the crowd and began to zigzag in front of the table. She grabbed the smoothie. "I need to get juiced," she said as a joke before she sipped from the big cup.

"Why did she get a fancy drink and we didn't?" Elise wailed in her birdlike voice, not realizing the mic was in front of her. CeeCee stepped in, intending to speak just to Elise, but it was picked up on her mic and everyone heard the actress say that they should have been as demanding as Daisy. Daisy gave them both a look telling them to shush and tried to continue.

"I got my start writing for my high school student newspaper. We had a very strict advisor who sanitized my 'News Around the School' column and took out anything even faintly negative. All the years I wrote the entertainment column, it focused on movies being made, parties given and things like my dinner with Elvis. There was never anything about dark stuff. But I still know what I know." She stopped to take another sip. "And I'm ready to tell all in the podcast I'm putting together. There will be stories, like was . . ." Her voice trailed off as an odd look came over her face and she grimaced. She began to stagger. She went to put the cup down, but it fell from her hand just as she collapsed on the ground. It was an understatement to say that something was wrong.

For a moment everyone froze and then a commotion broke out as people seemed to be going everywhere, and I pulled out my phone and called nine-one-one.

Chapter Ten

The paramedics had come and left quickly with Daisy packed up on a gurney. A couple of cops had come as well to check out what happened. I heard Mrs. Shedd tell one of the officers that it appeared Daisy had a seizure. CeeCee and Elise were still at the table, not sure what to do.

"Molly, this is a disaster," Mrs. Shedd said, stopping next to me. She looked around the area we had set up for the event. Most of the seats were empty and there were a lot of books, DVDs, and such that had been abandoned.

Muttering to herself, my boss went off and started to retrieve the unsold merchandise. She seemed to be operating on nerve and was in shock like everyone else.

But then everything changed when one of the cops got a call that she had been DOA when she reached the ER. They started rolling yellow tape across the front of the bookstore and told the small crowd that was left that they would need statements.

It wasn't the first time I'd been through something like this and I knew I was going to be there for a long time. I realized I better call home and alert them I was not coming home to take over Marlowe's care and I couldn't say when I would be back.

Peter answered and he wanted to know all the details of why I was delayed, somehow thinking I had gone out on a date. When he heard about Daisy, I heard him let out a groan. "Don't even think about it. You can't get involved with playing detective to find out what happened to her. You're supposed to be working for me. I need you to stay focused on Miles Langford. I want to have yea or nay soon—hopefully yea, so I can take his money and start putting all the pieces together."

I hung up, shaking my head in disbelief at my son's reaction. Someone had just died and still his mind was all on his business. Just like his father had been.

CeeCee and Elise both still seemed stunned and I went to talk to them. They were both upset and wanted to leave.

The two cops had been joined by four more and they circulated among the people still there and began separating everyone, ordering us not to talk among ourselves.

"Too late for that," Elise said, looking at the other people who had been clumped together and clearly were talking.

She had barely gotten the words out when the cops came to separate us.

"She works for the bookstore," one of the cops said and I was singled out. They didn't say it, but I knew it was for more advanced questioning.

I skipped to the head of the line as the cop took down my basic information and then led me to the enclosed area I had called the green room, explaining that the bookstore owner had given them permission to use it.

The three chairs I had set out were still there. Two were empty and the third was filled with Detective Barry Greenberg. "I didn't see you come in," I said while I tried to collect myself. It was the first time I'd seen him since our breakup and I had a flood of confused feelings.

"We have our stealthy ways," he said. If he felt as uncomfortable as I did, it didn't show. He was dressed in a suit that was impervious to wrinkles. The white shirt and tie appeared fresh, too. There was just a hint of a five o'clock shadow on his chin to hint that it had probably been a long day.

"Maybe you should have someone else question me," I said.

He shook his head. "I can handle it," he said. "But if it's too uncomfortable for you, I can get somebody else."

"I'm okay," I said.

"Good," he said with a nod. "We're adults. We realized we'd made a mistake and moved on," he said in his benign cop tone. He looked around the enclosure for a long time, which seemed like a way to stall before he continued. "I'm back with Carol." He was quiet for a moment. "It's not like it was with you, but it works." Our eyes met and a spark of heat passed between us and I knew he was thinking back to those nights in Hawaii, as I was. He looked down at his clipboard, trying to get back in professional mode. "She's okay with my lifestyle and the hours I keep. And Jeffrey is good at watching her kids when both of us are working." Carol was an ER nurse who probably worked all kinds of crazy shifts herself. Jeffrey was his son and was nothing like Barry. He was into theater and had always seemed mature for his age. I had a soft spot for the kid and wondered how he felt about the situation. But I didn't feel comfortable about asking.

"About Cosmo," Barry said, referring to the black mutt who was technically his and Jeffrey's dog but was residing at my house. I crossed my fingers that he wasn't going to ask to take the dog now that he was back with Carol. "He's better off staying with you." He glanced at me and then away. "No guarantee he'd be taken care of with us." I felt a twinge at the way he said "us." Could he really move on so easily after saying that I was "the one"?

"What about you?" he said. "Are you doing okay?"

The feeling of discomfort was going away and I'd even forgotten that I was there to be questioned about a death. I told him about Marlowe being dropped off, but didn't mention what Peter had asked me to do. It was none of his business and I knew he would not approve. Not that it really mattered what he thought, I was going to do what I was going to do regardless.

Then he got to what he really meant and asked if I was back with Mason.

I choked on a laugh. "Are you kidding? I'm sure he hates me." I gave Barry a hard look. "What was I thinking? I should have known it wouldn't work with us. That nothing had changed."

A cloud passed over his face before he turned away. When he turned back to face me, he was back to Barry the detective. "So then, why don't you tell me what happened," he said in his cop voice.

I straightened and began to describe the evening. "This is probably a waste of your time. It looked like she had a seizure. So no crime, no murder, no suspects."

"That's for me to determine," he said. He was trying to stay in cop mode, but he finally shook his head with a hopeless smile. "Some things don't change—like you trying to tell me my business."

• • •

When I finally left the bookstore, the Channel 3 news van was parked out front. The doors opened and the reporter and camera person hopped out and managed to turn everything on in the time it took me to walk to the corner. They rushed up behind me and Kimberly Diaz Wang stuck a microphone in front of my face.

"Hello, Molly. Can you tell us what happened?" she asked. I'd made the mistake of talking to her in the past and she'd given me the moniker of *murder groupie* because somehow I had been at a number of crime scenes. Not going to happen to me this time.

I looked at her with a smile. "No."

Chapter Eleven

There was still yellow tape across the door to the bookstore when I arrived the next morning. There were people in white suits and booties moving around the chairs and tables that had been set up for the event. While I was standing outside watching, Mr. Royal and Mrs. Shedd stopped next to me, holding cups of coffee.

"The CSI people should be done soon. We're going to sit in the car and listen to music," Mr. Royal said. He looked back at the bookstore. "The café isn't part of their investigation and the outside door is open if you want someplace to wait until they finish."

I watched the two of them walk to their electric car. They were about the same age, but Joshua Royal wore it better. He had a wiry build and shaggy salt-and-pepper hair. When I'd first started working at the bookstore, he'd been off on adventures. I'd wondered if he really even existed until one day he showed up and started coming into the bookstore as if he'd never been away.

I didn't know the whole history of his romance with Mrs. Shedd, but one day they'd announced that they'd gotten married, assuring us nothing would change—not even their names. The only change was that they were absent from the bookstore quite often. It was mostly his doing. Mrs. Shedd was still very concerned about keeping the bookstore going, though she did seem to be enjoying their fun adventures.

Sitting with a red-eye did seem more appealing than standing around the front. Bob, our main barista, looked up and smiled when I came in. He didn't even ask, but poured a shot of espresso in a cup of the brew of the day and set the cup on the counter. "It's been pretty slow this morning," he said, indicating the yellow tape blocking the inside door to the bookstore. "How about some more of the Eggy Squares?" Bob was known for making cookie bars of all types, but this was his first attempt at a treat that wasn't sweet.

I hadn't gotten home until after midnight and for obvious reasons hadn't slept well. I'd rushed out without breakfast and was glad to accept his offer.

He put two squares combining eggs, spinach and cheese on a small plate with a fork. He added a generous dollop of sour cream and a sprinkling of scallion slices.

I had thought the place was empty, but when I went to sit at a table I saw Barry sitting with a bland-looking man with sandy hair dressed in an outfit similar to Barry's. They waved me over and invited me to join them. It didn't seem social and it became clear that I was right after Barry introduced his associate as Detective Rick Carlson. "He's going to be the lead on this case," Barry said and gave him the floor.

Rick acknowledged me with a nod and then started to ask about the previous night. He had his notebook and pen out. It started with the basics, asking what I knew about Daisy before getting more specific about the setup for the event.

"Did she request anything special?" he asked. His tone made it seem that he was just gathering information.

I explained the green room setup, the mic so she could walk around and the drinks.

"What exactly were the drinks?" he asked, not looking up from his notes.

"There was bottled water and a strawberry smoothie," I said. He glanced up from his notes and looked at me directly.

"Tell me about the smoothie?" His tone had not changed, but his demeanor had. It was as if he wasn't just listening to what I said, but also checking my body language.

His question seemed a little vague to me. "What do you want to know?" Out of the corner of my eye I saw Barry's eyes close for a second, and there was the slightest disapproving shake of his head because I had just answered the question with a question.

"Who got the drink?" he asked.

There was nothing vague about that and I said it was me.

"And what did you do with it?"

"I put it on the table Daisy and the other speakers were using for home base," I said.

"And what was in the smoothie?" he asked.

"Strawberries, almond milk and a banana," I said, remembering that I had read the ingredients on the label stuck on the cup.

"Did you notice anything about how it smelled? Like an almond scent?"

"There was a lid on it, so I didn't really smell anything." This was starting to get kind of weird. "Why all the questions about the drink? Was there something wrong with it?" I looked from one man to the other.

Rick wasn't going to say any more, but Barry took over. "She might have been poisoned."

I wanted to ask why he thought that, but just then the people in white suits pulled down the yellow tape on the entrance to the bookstore and announced they were finished. The two detectives took their coffees and went to leave. Rick Carlson glanced back at me with a piercing stare. "We'll talk again," he said and went on into the bookstore. What did that mean? I wondered as I stayed behind at the table trying to process that whole thing.

Mr. Royal was busy clearing everything up when I finally went in. The chairs were already stacked and he was unrolling an area rug over a place where the carpeting had been cut out.

"The CSI people did that," he said before I could ask. "This will have to do in the meantime."

Even with the detectives and CSI people gone, the whole day felt off and I was relieved when the Hookers started to arrive for our happy hour session. At last, there was something that felt normal and routine. They were already around the table with yarn and sheets of paper spread out between them.

"It would have been different if I'd been there," Adele said, taking her seat at one end of the table. "For one thing, Eric would have been in the audience and been able to offer first aid," she said, reminding everyone that as a motor officer for the LAPD he was a first responder. She looked at CeeCee and Elise. "But there was no way I could be a mere observer to an evening that had a crochet theme." She tossed her head in a haughty manner that sent her beanie flying. She let out a loud sigh and went to retrieve it.

"You should have made it bigger," Rhoda said in her blunt manner. "You can see it barely fits over your hair. Any movement and it falls off." She had stopped mid-stitch as she talked. Adele stuffed the offending beanie in her tote bag.

"Adele, really," CeeCee said, shaking her head in dismay. "I can't believe you are making this about you. It's terrible that the woman died. It seemed like she had a seizure." She looked to me. "No need for you to investigate this time, dear," she said.

Then began the excuses of why the rest of them hadn't been there to support their crochet sisters. Rhoda had an event with her husband Hal. Shelia was tied up with preparing Luxe, the lifestyle store she worked at, for a special sale, and Eduardo had had a meeting about a commercial shoot.

For a few minutes they were distracted by his news and wanted details.

"It's for a cat food ad. You know the style of ads now is they're not really about the product. I would be a king going shopping in a grocery store," he said with a laugh. Part of his charm was that he didn't take himself seriously or was caught up in his looks.

Dinah Lyons came in at the end. She glanced over the group at the table. "Were you in the middle of something?"

"I was just saying that if I'd been included in the crochet evening, I might have saved the day," Adele said, fluffing her short dark hair now that she wasn't wearing the beanie.

"Saved the day? What happened?" Dinah said, looking at me. I felt bad that with everything that had gone on, I had not had a chance to call her and tell her about Daisy.

"You didn't hear?" Rhoda said, surprised. "I'm sure it was on the

---

late news."

"I tried doing it Commander's way and went to bed when he did." She let out her breath. "I couldn't fall asleep, and he has to have it pitch-dark and silent. No TV or screens of any kind."

I nodded with understanding and was going to give her the short version of what happened, but Elise took over and described the events of the previous night. Dinah's eyes grew wide and she looked at me, and I mouthed I would tell her later.

"Can we finally get to what we're here for?" CeeCee said. "This is a crochet group, after all." She glanced around the table and they all nodded in agreement. She handed sheets of paper to Dinah and me. "I thought about baby blankets, but I was thinking why not make something for now and the future. Something a child could keep." She picked up her copy of what she had given out. "These are basic instructions and then each of you can decide what size you want to make and what yarn you want to use."

"There's a diagram of the stitches," Rhoda said in an unhappy voice. "They just confuse me." She looked at the other page and seemed relieved. "I'm glad you included written instructions."

"I don't know," Elise said, picking up the sheet. "I think I like this. It's really clear what stitches go where."

"I thought I would give you both," CeeCee said. "They're called granny square striped blankets. Instead of making a square, there are long rows of the spaces and clusters. They're great for using up leftover yarn. Some people do rows of stitches with black yarn between the colorful ones. It's really your choice." She held up a small sample and they passed it around. She had used the rows of black yarn with double rows of color in between.

Rhoda had pulled out a skein of black yarn and started to make a swatch of the stitches but looked up frustrated as she showed off the small piece, which had uneven edges.

CeeCee took the floor again. "It's really very simple. Once you've done the foundation, there are two rows you repeat. The two rows look like they're the same, but there is a slight difference. Once you get it down, it's very easy. Each blanket will be unique and we can donate them for toddlers and older children or adults."

The idea was a hit and they all began talking about yarn they would buy or old yarn they would use. Some of them wanted colors that blended, others wanted contrast. And then they finally picked up whatever project they had brought with them and began crocheting.

Our get-together lasted around an hour. It was close to dinnertime and they all had someplace to be. Dinah hung back as I started to clear up the leftover bits of yarn and stray cups.

"You were going to tell me more about what happened. The cops must have come and I bet they questioned you." I knew where she was heading.

"Yes, it was Barry who questioned me," I said.

"It must have felt strange," Dinah said. "How did he act?"

"He was doing his cop thing, so it was barely personal. The door on that is closed forever—for both of us. He's back with Carol." We were interrupted as someone approached the table.

"So this is your yarn department," the woman said. She looked familiar, but I knew I was seeing her out of context and couldn't place her. It happened a lot. Someone would come in the bookstore I was sure I knew from somewhere, but wasn't sure from where. Did they work in a business I frequented? This woman didn't look like a grocery cashier or someone from the Tarzana Library. She had a polished aura and her clothes had a designer look. It was when she held up the paper bag in her hand and said she'd bought a book for Alexander that I realized she was Lily Langford from the mommy group and the wife of the man I was supposed to be investigating.

I introduced her to Dinah. "Lily has a company that makes a wrap she calls the Cuddle," I said. Lily picked up on it and did a whole pitch on the different fabrics it came in. "We cover everything from evening wear to something you would wear to the beach. I'm very excited that Bloomingdale's is going to carry them."

Dinah smiled with interest and then said she had to go. "Commander's cooking and he is very punctual about dinner," she said. "Nice to meet you." She nodded at Lily. She touched my arm. "Call me later."

"I heard what happened here last night." She glanced around. "It was so eerie since you had told the mommy group about the bookstore and that event. You must have been right there when it happened. Did she just fall over?"

"It was pretty bad," I said. "And yes, I was right there. I don't think the cause has been determined." I deliberately left it vague. By now I had talked about what happened to Daisy enough and I thought this might be a chance for me to find out more about Miles. "Is there something else I can help you with?"

"I've seen the bookstore but never come in before. I'm local." She waved her arm in the direction of the Santa Monica Mountains. "We live up in the hills. I was curious since you mentioned that you had a yarn department and that Hookers group. Once I got involved with making the cocoons, I got interested in different forms of making cloth."

"I never thought of it that way," I said. "But you're right. We do make cloth."

She had her phone out and had typed in the word *cloth*. "It describes cloth as a pliable material made by weaving, felting or knitting." She read it over again. "Funny that they don't mention crochet. I suppose they lump it in with knitting."

I looked around in a panic, afraid Adele might overhear and get in the middle of it. Worse, she might call me by my last name and blow my cover where it really mattered. I let out a breath of relief when I saw she was on her way out the front door. But something else I saw made me tense all over again. Someone was in my cubicle, and even from a distance I could tell they had their eyes on my computer screen. By now I'd discerned it was a man in a suit.

"If you'd like to stop by for one of our get-togethers, you'd be more than welcome. You can even get a crochet lesson if you'd like."

"Maybe I will," she said, and I gave her the schedule when we met.

I stayed with her while she looked around at the cubbies of yarn and the knitted and crocheted samples hanging off of them. I tried to get her to talk about her husband, hoping she'd drop something I could tell Peter so that he would see that I was on the case. All I really learned was that his family were builders, but he was in the entertainment industry. "We're really a power couple like Taylor and Andrew," she said. "I have my business and Miles is a producer." By the time she left, my cubicle was empty. I still went to investigate.

Mr. Royal passed me on the way to the front. "I hope you don't mind, but that detective with the sandy-colored hair asked if he could use your computer to look something up. I always like to do whatever to make their lives easier and I couldn't see the harm, so I said yes."

I knew he meant Rick Carlson and his request seemed a little odd. I made a stop at the computer and clicked it on. He hadn't done a good job of covering his tracks. He had left it on the screen that showed my recent searches. Why?

Chapter Twelve

This time when I got home there was no circus. My parents had already left, no doubt to make up for being stuck there so late the night before. Peter was the only one there and was anxious to leave. He hung back just long enough to ask me if there was an update in the assignment he'd given me. He seemed disappointed when all I had to give him were details about Miles Langford's wife. I gave him the rundown of Lily's visit to the bookstore and told him about her clothing business. His eyes were glazing over by the time I described the Cuddle. The only information I had about Miles was that the money he was going to use to invest in Peter's production company probably came from his family's business. "I don't know exactly what they've built, but they're developers."

Peter gave me a disgruntled look. "I knew that already. Miles's brothers are really the ones who run the business. They build outdoor shopping centers and tracts of houses. Miles isn't active in it. He just gets a share of the profits." My son looked at me. "I don't know why I'm giving you information. You're supposed to be the detective. He's using the money to buy his way into show business. If I take his investment, I'll give him an executive producer credit."

"Will he do anything on the project?" I asked.

"He might show up on the set occasionally, but he won't have any responsibilities."

The dogs, with the exception of Blondie, were gathered at my feet wanting to be let out. Marlowe was in the playpen beginning to whimper. Peter took it all in. "Time to go," he said. He looked at Marlowe and started to take a step in her direction, but stopped and gave her a wave. "I'll leave everything to you. Give her a kiss from me." I followed him to the front door with the parade of dogs trailing me. Just before he left, he told me that Gabby had texted him about Marlowe and wanted to know if I had gone to the mommy group. "She was worried that you might mess things up for her," Peter said.

"What did you tell her?" I asked.

"Nothing," Peter said. "I just sent her a picture of Marlowe in her new digs." And he was on his way out.

Marlowe was in full cry mode as I shut the door behind him. The dogs were getting feisty and were nipping at each other. Who did I deal with first?

I grabbed Marlowe and held her while I let the dogs out. She had what looked like applesauce in her hair. Her diaper felt heavy and probably had not been changed in a long time. She needed a bath and to be put in her sleepwear. On top of that, she was probably hungry. Peter was a throwback to how dads used to be when they were deliberately clueless about dealing with diapers, giving a baby a bath, or getting stuff out of their hair. He was just following in Charlie's footsteps. It was only when the boys got involved with sports that he knew how to deal with them.

I went across the house to get Blondie so she could join the others. All the activity had made Marlowe forget about crying and she giggled when I pretended to be an amusement park ride as I dipped her down with me and poured dry food in the cats' bowls.

We stood at the back window watching as the dogs ran around in the shadow-filled yard. I entertained her by telling the story of each of the dogs. "When I first saw Blondie, she was sitting at the back of her enclosure looking oh, so lonely," I began. "And now she has all these dog and cat friends." I wondered if I should add something about Blondie staying away from everything. Finally, I said that Blondie liked to sit in her chair and that it was okay to be different, and we loved her just the way she was. The black mutt ran in front of the window. "That's Cosmo," I said. "See how long his fur is. Sometimes it's hard to tell which end of him is which. He used to stay here but belonged to some other people. But now this is his forever home." I looked out into the yard, where Felix was barking at a squirrel. "His fur is gray and wiry," I said. "Your Uncle Samuel brought him home." I left it at that. It was too complicated to say that it was really Samuel and his then girlfriend who got the dog. "And that little white puff ball of fur is Princess." What to say about her? It was too much to explain that her owner had died and the dog was alone in the house when I had sort of broken in to rescue her. "She was all by herself and she needed a new family," I said finally. "And now she has one, including you." I gave the baby a kiss on her forehead and discovered more stickiness. The applesauce must have gotten there, too.

With the dogs back inside and fed, Marlowe got the full treatment. I stripped off her clothes and diaper and gave her a bath. While I was sudsing her hair, my mind kept slipping back to my computer at the bookstore, wondering why Detective Rick Carlson was checking my browsing history. I considered calling Barry and asking him what he knew, but it felt too awkward. "I'll just have to figure it out myself," I said to Marlowe. "With your Auntie Dinah's help."

Before I could call Dinah, she called me wanting to know the complete story about what had happened to Daisy. "There's lots of leftover Thai food," I said as a lure. "I'll tell you everything if you come over."

"Thai food and talk. How could I possibly refuse. It's like a tomb around here. Commander is one of those people who turns off lights when he leaves the room. He's already in bed reading. I can't do another night of going to bed when he does. It's not that he's said anything, but I feel uncomfortable even banging around in the kitchen when it's so quiet."

"Come over. No problem here. The lights are on and there's no need to tiptoe around here because Marlowe is sleeping." Dinah was on her way out the door as she clicked off her cell.

"She doesn't seem to be bothered by noise or the chaos around here," I said, pointing to Marlowe's portable crib, which I had moved from the living room into the den. The baby had zonked out as soon as I'd given her a bottle. The fact that the lights were on and the cats were running around after each other playing their nightly games made no difference.

"It looks pretty empty in there," Dinah said, peeking in the bed. "Should we add some stuffed toys?"

"And have Peter throw a fit?" I said with a laugh. "Ever since Marlowe started staying here, he's been doing all kinds of research about childcare and then giving me orders. They aren't supposed to sleep with stuffed toys and absolutely no bumper pads around the crib." I shook my head remembering all that Peter had said. "He's not so good at doing the ground work but excels at giving orders."

I waved Dinah away so we could move on to the food and talking. "The funniest thing is how upset he gets when he sees a baby picture of himself in a crib outfitted with the devil bumper pads. One of my favorite photos shows him surrounded by all of those stuffed toys that used to be considered company and now are suffocation threats."

"I guess he doesn't notice that he survived despite the bumper pads and toys."

I laughed. What she said was true, but Peter would probably say it was only because he was very lucky.

My parents' philosophy was better too much than too little when it came to food, so there was plenty of noodle dishes and skewers of chicken satay. Samuel had recently become a vegetarian, so they had even gotten him meatless chicken satay. Dinah and I both tasted it and decided it was delicious.

When we had our plates of food, we went into the living room and sat together on one of the soft leather couches.

"I'm ready for the details," Dinah said. "The story I saw online gave few details beyond that she appeared to have a seizure."

"That's true. It did seem like a seizure, but the cops are thinking it might not have been natural causes," I said.

"The cops?" Dinah said. "Did you get that from Barry? Tell me again about seeing him."

"Like I said before, the door is shut on that." I closed my eyes for a second and let out a sigh. "But I'd be lying if I didn't admit to feeling something. It was a whole mix of emotions. Remembering the Hawaii trip, which was all hot and dreamy. And then the reality when we came home. Getting up in the middle of the night with no idea where he was. Knowing that I was an afterthought to whatever he was working on. I couldn't live that way. But I said cops, as in more than one. Barry came with another homicide detective I'd never seen before. His name is Rick Carlson." We'd been sitting with our forks poised with the orangish sauce-covered noodles hanging off of them and we finally let them reach their destination. The pad Thai was delicious.

Since Dinah hadn't been at Shedd & Royal for the event, I wasn't sure how much she knew about Daisy's demands, so before I talked about the detective, I filled her in on the saga of the strawberry smoothies. "The first one didn't please her and I had to go back to get a different one," I said. I gave my friend a description of what happened after that, with Daisy starting her talk and then collapsing.

"Rick Carlson seemed focused on the drink, as if there was something wrong with it. Then Barry mentioned that Daisy might have been poisoned." I paused for a moment. "There's something else." I told her about the situation with my computer. "Mr. Royal made it sound like nothing. The detective just wanted to look something up. But then why was he looking at my browsing history?" I said.

"By asking Mr. Royal's permission, he bypassed needing a warrant," Dinah said.

"I already thought of that. If they think she didn't die of natural causes, do they think I'm involved?" I was incredulous.

"You better tell me exactly what happened and then we can play our Sherlock Holmes game and see what we can figure out." Obviously, we weren't close to being like the real Sherlock Holmes. Well, the real fictional Sherlock Holmes, anyway. He was a master of deducing things, like figuring out that someone was lying about being out in the rain because it was clear their umbrella had never been unfolded because it was still in the case. If it had gotten wet, the owner would have left it outside the slip-on case until it was dry.

I told Dinah everything I could remember about the evening. As I got to the part about the smoothie, I had an aha moment. I hadn't really been focusing too well when Barry Greenberg and Rick Carlson were talking to me. Rick had asked a lot about the drink—what the ingredients were and such. "What if it had something to do with the drink?" I brought up that the CSI people had cut out some of the carpet as I realized it was where the drink had spilled when Daisy fell forward, knocking the cup to the ground.

"And I brought her the drink." I thought back to how I had told them all about her demands for the drink.

"Did you sound annoyed about having to get the smoothie when you talked to them?" Dinah asked.

"Maybe. But hardly enough to kill her over. If I'd done something to it, would I have been so honest about getting it for her?" I said. "But it's impossible there was anything wrong with it. I had the drink freshly made and set it on the table with the water bottles right before I introduced them. How would anyone have even known the drink was for her?" I thought it over for a moment. "There was one person who knew about the drink—Leslie Bittner, Daisy's assistant."

"You said that the detective looked at your search history. Do you remember what was on it?" Dinah asked and I winced.

"It was after I talked to him, but I searched strawberry smoothies and poisons that smell like almonds."

"He must have noticed that it was after the fact when you did those searches," Dinah said, trying to be encouraging.

"Everything has been so scattered with Marlowe and my other investigation, this is the first time I have put all the pieces together," I said with a feeling of doom. "I don't want to talk about it anymore." Dinah gave me a reassuring pat on the arm and I brightened. "Let's play Sherlock with Lily Langford. She's the woman who came in the yarn department when you were leaving who makes those wraps." Dinah nodded, remembering her. "I'm not really investigating her, though I suppose if she did something awful it could cause Peter a problem."

"What do you know about her?" my friend said, going along with my request.

I cut to the chase and said that Lily seemed to want to have it all. "She has an identity as a business owner. I think she wants to be like Taylor Palmer and be part of a power couple. And at least in appearances, she wants to seem like an involved mom." I shrugged. "There's nothing problematic with any of that," I said.

Dinah nodded and let out a little laugh. "Not for Peter's business, unless she tries to make all the characters wear the wraps she makes." She ate the last of her food and got up for a second helping. "Let's get back to Barry. Are you upset that he's back with Carol?"

It was more comfortable to move back to talking about Barry and his relationship with the ER nurse than to talk about Rick Carlson and his questions.

"Maybe a twinge, but I'm resigned that we are done forever, and why shouldn't he be with someone who can deal with his lifestyle?" I said. "Even if it sounds like more of an arrangement than a love match."

Dinah nodded. "I'm sure you're right. Can you imagine their conversations. His about the blood and gore he saw and hers about the blood and gore that she fixed."

We went on talking about their life together and how they must be adrenalin junkies. I was glad to be distracted. It was far more upsetting to think that Rick Carlson might be considering me a person of interest, which was sort of a suspect, but not quite. It was sort of like being engaged to being engaged. I knew Peter would be upset, but circumstances had sucked me into investigating what really happened to Daisy. Now that I had thought over the questions Rick had asked me, along with what I'd found out on my search, if she was poisoned, it was probably cyanide.

Chapter Thirteen

When a number of days passed and nothing happened, I wondered if I'd been wrong about being considered a person of interest. In the old days, I would have been able to find out from Barry, but it didn't feel like an option now. I had other things on my mind anyway. I was taking Marlowe to another of the mommy group get-togethers. This one was at the Langfords' and I hoped to get some information I could pass on to Peter that he didn't already know.

They lived just below Dirt Mulholland, as the unpaved portion of the road was called. The houses were all built on pads that had been cut into the steep hillside. They lived on the kind of street where you had to be sure to point your wheels in the right direction when you parked so that if your car slipped it would go into the curb instead of tumbling down the hill.

The house was one of the farmhouse designs that were replacing older houses that were being torn down. There were several variations on the wood-frame houses, which made them seem like tract houses for the wealthy. Personally, if I had spent all that money on a place, I would want it to be a custom design. Most were white with black trim, but a few were a brooding shade of gray. Theirs appeared to be the bigger version and was all white. Without even going inside, I already had an idea of the layout from others of these houses I'd visited.

They were all two stories with flooring that looked like wood. All the common rooms on the lower floor flowed together. The central common area on the lower floor was what was called a great room. The kitchen was part of it, separated by a massive island. Folding glass doors led to a patio that had ceiling fans and a TV screen. The living room felt like an afterthought and was an open space near the base of the stairs. They all had a formal dining room with a narrow cabinet-filled wet bar that led to the kitchen. The only room that had a door was the powder room.

I put Marlowe in her stroller and wheeled her to the entrance. Kath greeted me and invited me in, explaining that she had taken over for Lily, who'd had a last-minute situation with her shop. "Her husband is here, too, but he seems a little overwhelmed by it all," Kath said. Not that I needed directions, but she pointed me to the great room.

I chuckled to myself as I noted that the rooms, or really areas, were exactly where I expected them to be as I went straight back to the space where everyone was gathering. Garth was already there with his twins. Plum was sitting on the floor holding a stuffed rabbit. Alexander went up to Plum and grabbed the rabbit, saying that it was his. I assumed the man in the middle of it was Miles. He was tallish with dark hair. His most outstanding feature was the downturn of his mouth, which made it look a little pouty. Taylor was walking behind Oliver as he toddled toward the others.

A woman came in dressed in a colorful skirt holding a guitar and a box of instruments. "The kids are going to do music," Kath said to me. "The plan is that they'll have their entertainment out on the patio."

Taylor had Oliver by the hand and was attempting to get him to join Edgar and Lucy. She didn't seem happy with the situation.

Kath looked at Marlowe still in her stroller. "You can let her loose. Miss Merry Music will take charge of the kids with the housekeeper's help. The kids have juice boxes and pinwheel cream cheese and jelly sandwiches. And there is coffee and bagels on the island where those two nannies are sitting," Kath said with a note of distaste. "I think Taylor is right about removing them from the group." The two plain women were sitting on the stools appearing indifferent to their charges, who were wandering with the others.

I handed the baby off to the housekeeper, who seemed placid despite all the commotion. She held on to Marlowe as she and Miss Merry tried to lead the kids out to the patio, but they all resisted. Accepting defeat, they got them into a portion of the large room. There was a positive in all the confusion for me. I thought of my mission and realized it might be the only time I could check out Miles's surroundings. I used the most obvious cover and asked Miles for directions to the powder room. He pointed toward the front and said it was on the right before going back to his conversation.

I checked that no one was watching and I went left instead. In addition to knowing the layout of the common rooms, I knew about the private area and went past the stairs to a hallway. Unlike the other side of the house where everything was open, there were closed doors off the hall. I wasn't exactly sure of what was behind each door and began opening them. The first one led to a garage. It was dimly lit and all I could make out was a large black SUV. It seemed like there was nothing there for me to see, so I moved on. I did spend a few moments admiring the laundry room. I had just a washer and dryer crammed in a space off my kitchen. This was an actual room with a window. There was a sink and a counter for folding. After that I found a closet and finally what I was looking for. I knew there was a room that could be a guest room or office. It was obvious by the two desks and two computer setups that they used it for an office. I checked out the doors in the room. I'd barely opened one a crack when I saw that it led back to the great room. Miss Merry Music had just started singing the rainbow song and the kids and adults seemed caught up in the music.

Another door led to a full bathroom. I stopped to give it the once-over. It had a freestanding soak tub that was the style now. It looked like taking a bath in a bowl to me.

The last door went to a walk-in closet and yes, I did go in there to see if there were any skeletons. There weren't.

Back in the office, I noticed one wall had a lot of photos, but I was more interested in the desks and wondered which one was his. I saw a receipt on one of them and realized it was from Shedd & Royal, which meant that desk was hers, as I knew she'd bought a book for Alexander the day she came into the yarn department.

I went to the other desk and was contemplating what to look at when the door to the great room opened and Miles Langford walked in. I swallowed a gasp as he gave me a surprised look. I didn't give him a chance to say anything and offered an explanation. "I made a wrong turn looking for the powder room," I said, trying to play the part of the ditzy grandmother and added quickly that I'd been fascinated by the photos. I had not actually looked at them until I had said that. A large frame held a screenshot of his credit as an executive producer for something. I remembered what Peter had said about trading investing on a project for getting that kind of credit. I deduced that Miles had done before what he intended to do with Peter. Obviously, nothing horrible had come out about Miles during that production, which I took as a good sign.

Miles had no idea about my thought process and started talking about the photographs. "They're all from *Back Home on the Range.* We filmed up in Chatsworth." He seemed extremely proud of the photos and also seemed to have forgotten that he found me wandering in his office.

He went over them one by one. The first had Miles sitting in a director's chair with a pair of headphones hanging around his neck. A tall man was next to him wearing a baseball cap and jeans that seemed like the uniform for a movie crew. "That's me and Rance," he said. "He was my buddy on the set." He pointed to another picture. "I love this one," Miles said, gazing at a picture of him sitting on a horse wearing a white cowboy hat. The same tall man was next to him in this shot, too. "Rance was great. He made sure I was good on the horse so I could do this." He indicated a group shot of men wearing jeans and cowboy hats with a rugged background. "Not only was I an executive producer, but I got to be an extra along with those guys." He laughed. "We were the posse going to stop the bad guys from robbing the stagecoach. It was a grown-up version of a little boy's dream." He moved down to more of the pictures. This time they were all dressed in western-style formal wear on a stage. I looked over the crowd and recognized the tall man who'd been in the other shots with Miles. This time he wasn't wearing a baseball cap. He noticed who I was looking at. "He cleans up pretty good. We were collecting our award. We won a Westie for Best Old Style Western Movie." He went to the credenza against the wall and grabbed a statue of a horse with a plaque on it. "This is it."

I pretended to be impressed and asked what his actual job had been aside from being an extra. "Oh, you know, this and that," he said, being vague. "It's very exciting being part of it all. Who knows what I'll get to do next time." He let out an unhappy sigh. "I hope this guy hurries up to finalize our deal. I can't understand what the holdup is." I knew he was talking about Peter and it felt strange, like looking at a scene from the other side of a one-way mirror.

"Is that a western, too?" I asked. I didn't actually know much about what Peter was putting together other than I thought it was for a streaming channel.

"No. It's a touchy-feely drama that I have a feeling could be another *This is Us*." I was sure he would have said more, but Lily came through the open door.

"What are you doing in here?" she asked and then she saw me.

"Miles was telling me all about being a cowboy star," I said.

He put the horse statue back as his wife had us rejoin the others.

Miss Merry Music had corralled all the kids in one section of the big room. They seemed fascinated by her singing and guitar playing. Garth's twins had helped themselves to the bag of instruments and were shaking maracas not exactly in time to the music. The house-keeper was standing guard to make sure there were no wanderers. Lily led us to the dining room, explaining she had moved the adults there.

"I found them," Lily said, pointing at us as Miles and I came in. I took one of the chairs, but he begged off now that she was back. Then she followed her husband out of the room. Taylor was looking at her phone and went to the other room to make a call. The nannies were still sitting in the great room at the island. The only ones left at the table were Garth and Kath.

The food had been moved and was set out on the table. I went to snag one of the bagels and get a cup of coffee. They were from a new trendy bagel shop that supposedly had lines waiting when they opened at six a.m. The bagel had all different kinds of seeds on the outside, including pumpkin and sunflower seeds. There was a selection of cream cheese, but I went with the plain.

"We were just talking about what happened to Daisy Cochran. You must know all about it. Give us the inside dope, the behind-the-scenes story," Garth said.

I had a mouthful of bagel, which was delicious, but I didn't want to be rude and talk with my mouth full so I held up my hand to beg off. Kath said, "I'd forgotten but Michael reminded me that Daisy had interviewed him about what sort of plastic surgery his celebrity clients were getting. He didn't name any names. Doctor-patient privilege and all, but I think she figured out who he was talking about. He was not happy about it."

"Maybe you should burn some sage in the bookstore to clear out any bad vibes," Garth said.

Kath seemed unconvinced. "I'm not so sure anything like that works. Taylor can have all the psychics do their chants and burn wads of sage, but it doesn't seem to change anything. Every time I go there, I feel like someone's spirit is still hanging out there."

I was hoping for more details, but then Taylor returned and Kath stopped talking. Taylor glanced over the three of us. "Did I interrupt something?"

Garth shook his head. "Molly was just telling us about what happened to Daisy Cochran."

"It was quite a night," I said. I glanced at Taylor, expecting her to say something about being there and taking over the conversation to give her take on what happened, but she seemed more interested in the bagels and the trendy place they'd come from and went on that it was quite a coup to score them. Kath and Garth listened to her politely, but quickly turned their attention back to me. Given a choice between bagels and a woman they know of collapsing and dying in front of a crowd, no surprise which they were more interested in.

"I heard it was a seizure," Kath said.

"I don't think they have determined it for sure," I said.

"Did Daisy say much about the podcast?" Garth asked.

"I think she'd just started talking about it. There was a lot going on so I wasn't paying that much attention," I said.

"But then she probably told you about what she was going to cover in the podcast," Garth said, making it sound like a question.

"Not really," I said. "She never told me much other than she wanted to give a tease to get people's interest."

Lily came in the dining room flush with excitement. "I just got off the phone with a national morning show. They want me to come on and talk about the cocoons and show off the different styles of them."

I waited for Lily's excitement to calm a little and then I approached Taylor. "I guess you managed to slip out before the police arrived the other night at the bookstore." When she gave me a blank look in response, I continued. "When Daisy Cochran died. You were there for her author event," I added.

"I don't know what you're talking about," she said. "The only time I came to the place you work was when I brought my son."

What?

Chapter Fourteen

"Do you think she was lying about not being there for Daisy's demise?" Dinah said. We were sitting at the table in the yarn department waiting for the rest of the Hookers. I had told her about my morning at the Langfords'.

I had taken out the blanket I had started and just begun a row with black yarn. I still had to pay attention to what my hook was doing so had stopped working at Dinah's question. "She was so adamant that she wasn't there. Maybe I was wrong. There was a lot of commotion."

The Hookers had begun to come to the table, and as soon as CeeCee arrived I asked her if she remembered seeing Taylor at the event. "You said you knew who she was—Andrew Palmer's second wife."

"Dear, there was so much going on that the crowd was a blur to me. And honestly, while I know who Taylor Palmer is, I can't say I'd recognize her." Then came the obvious question of why I was asking.

I told CeeCee about the mommy gathering and how when I'd mentioned Daisy and the bookstore event, Taylor had said she wasn't there.

"Hmm," CeeCee said. "Maybe she was there and wanted to distance herself from what happened. Did the woman you saw give a statement to the police?"

I thought back and shook my head. "A lot of people took off as soon as Daisy collapsed and I don't recall seeing her when the police were there."

"Have you heard anything more about what exactly happened to Daisy?" the actress asked. "It certainly was a disastrous evening."

"You can say that again," Elise said as she pulled out one of the chairs. "I never even got a chance to talk about the kits."

"Really? You're bringing up not selling kits to crochet vampire scarves, when a woman died?" CeeCee said, shaking her head. "How about me. I was all dressed up as Ophelia and had to sit in that uncomfortable dress for hours until the police let us go."

Adele had joined us by then. She plopped in her usual chair at the end of the table. "I wouldn't know because I wasn't there," she said in a disdainful tone. "Maybe next time you plan an author event that includes crochet, you'll include me." We all ignored her comment.

"To answer your question," I said, going back to what CeeCee had said. "I haven't heard anything for sure, other than I know they took a square of the carpeting where Daisy's drink had spilled." As I was debating whether to mention that I thought Rick Carlson had been looking at my search history on my work computer, Adele continued to be difficult.

"It'll be hard for you to investigate now that you're not with Barry anymore," Adele said as the rest of the group rolled their eyes. "I was just stating facts. Of course, I'm sorry that Pink is single again." She gave my arm a sympathetic pat. "But I still have a door to the inside," she said. "As a motor officer, Eric has his ear to the ground. All I have to do is ask him and he'll tell me everything." Adele glanced around the table. "I can see what he knows about what happened the other night." Despite what Adele said, we knew that Eric wasn't likely to know about a death investigation unless it had to do with traffic.

Rhoda Klein had joined us and she gave me a squeeze on my shoulder before she sat down. "Molly, I have someone I could fix you up with. We met with our CPA yesterday and we got talking. He's a widower and lonely. He has a house and a nice business. He'd be a good catch."

"But does he like having fun? Or being surrounded by dogs, cats and chaos?" I said

Rhoda's expression flattened. "When you put it that way, maybe you're not a good match."

Eduardo heard the interchange and joined in. "If Molly is looking for a boyfriend, I have friends—" I stopped him before he could say more.

"I am not looking for male company," I said. I thought it sounded silly to talk about boyfriends when you were in your fifties. "I am not lonely. Just the opposite. Between everyone being at my place and having to take Marlowe to the mommy group, I'm glad for some time alone."

"You could always sign up for one of those online dating sites," Elise said, totally ignoring what I'd just said.

"No, thank you," I said. "Not only do you have to worry about being scammed or worse, the idea of getting all dressed up to go on a date with a stranger who may or may not be a serial killer or scam artist is not for me."

"And you'd have to get all dressed up, with heels and all. But not for the CPA. We actually talked about high heels. He said his late wife wore them and she ended up getting her heel stuck in the dirt and falling in the mud. When I told him about you, his first question was about your shoes."

"I don't know about that," CeeCee said, looking under the table at her footwear. "These flats are nice for coming here, but I certainly wouldn't wear them with an evening gown. I wore kitten heels with Ophelia's dress for the event."

"Any heels can be deadly," Rhoda said. "You must have heard about that woman who fell down the stairs at that big house. She was wearing heels and she died."

"You're saying the heels killed her?" Dinah asked.

"You could say that. She wouldn't have fallen if she wasn't wearing those shoes. Though what really killed her was she hit her head and was home alone," Rhoda said. "But if she'd been wearing sneakers or even flats, she probably wouldn't have fallen in the first place. I think the article said something about they thought her heel caught in the carpeting. There was a photo of the house. It looked huge. It was kind of sad that she was there all alone. You'd think she'd have a housekeeper."

"Maybe it was their day off," CeeCee said.

"Or maybe she wasn't alone and it wasn't the stupid shoes that killed her. Maybe somebody pushed her." Elise looked around the table with an intent expression. "It sounds pretty suspicious to me," she said in her bird-like voice.

"I still say if she'd had any sense and worn something like these, she'd still be alive and living in that fabulous house." Rhoda stuck her foot out from under the table and showed off her silver Crocs. She wasn't finished with her rant and we all listened politely as she continued.

"I'm telling you they should outlaw those shoes. Well, they do in Carmel, California. You have to have a permit to wear them because they have all those pushed-up sidewalks from tree roots. They don't have street addresses either," she added as a non sequitur. "Not only are those shoes death traps, but they destroy your feet. People are finally wising up. Crocs have become stylish. My teenage granddaughter wanted to borrow these." She stuck her foot out from under the table again and showed off the silver plastic shoe with the jeweled decoration stuck in one of the holes that covered the top.

"How about we get down to crocheting," CeeCee said. "If we're going to donate blankets we have to make them first." She looked around the table and nodded at Sheila, who had slipped in unnoticed. "Okay, folks, it's hooks up."

I was glad that it was a simple pattern with two rows that kept repeating. The only thing that changed was the colors. I had chosen to have two rows of black and two rows of colors. It was a good way to use up all the partial skeins of black worsted-weight yarn I had and the leftovers of bright-colored yarn. The talk died down as we all began to work on our blankets. CeeCee, Eduardo and Adele could have easily carried on a conversation while moving their hooks through the yarn, but the rest of us needed to pay attention to what we were doing. But that didn't mean I couldn't think about something else. I wondered if I really was being considered a suspect in Daisy Cochran's death.

Adele was right. In the old days I would have called Barry. He had always objected to giving me any inside information, but I always got it out of him. I wondered if Barry had told Rick Carlson anything about our past.

I looked up from my work. "CeeCee, you and Elise where there. Did you see anything happen to the smoothie I'd gotten for Daisy?" It was a bit of a non sequitur and they both gave me puzzled looks for a moment until they realized what I was talking about.

"The only thing I noticed, dear," CeeCee said with an edge in her voice, "was that all you had for us was water."

"Yeah," Elise said. "You could have at least gotten us some of that fancy water instead of store brand. It was pretty clear who was important and who wasn't."

"Really?" Dinah said. "Considering what happened to Daisy, you should be glad you got sealed bottles of water."

CeeCee looked stricken. "You mean you think there was something in her drink that made her have a seizure?"

"There might have been poison, though I can't figure out how," I said. "I watched them make it and I put it on the table. It was covered with a straw sticking through the lid."

"Covered and a straw? I don't think so," CeeCee said. "Though I suppose she could have taken the lid off. I remember seeing her pick up the cup and take a sip out of it. It smelled really good of strawberries and something else." She paused to think a moment, never stopping her hook action. "I know. I thought she might have spiked it."

"You mean with alcohol?" I said, and CeeCee nodded.

"It reminded me of a liqueur."

"Whoever it was would have had to get the poison in the drink in front of everybody." When I looked around the table, I saw that Lily had sat down with the group and I greeted her.

"So this is your Hooker group." She looked around the table as I explained who she was and her business of making the cocoons. She was wearing a red one over a pair of black leggings and black top. She got up and a did a model twirl to show it off as she explained the combination of fibers the cloth was made of.

"Since I'm into fibers and cloth, I thought I'd see what crochet was all about." She'd barely gotten the words out when Adele stood up.

"Anything you want to know I'm your crochet ambassador." Adele turned to me and I knew she was going to call me Pink, so when she'd barely gotten the *P* out, I interrupted and told Lily that Adele was our well-loved story-time leader who would be handling the mommy group event I put on. "In addition, she is starting a new business of putting on kids' birthday parties."

Adele forgot about whatever she was going to say to me and turned to Lily and started to pitch the parties. Adele, as usual, was very dramatic as she popped out of her seat.

"Imagine a children's party like there's never been before," Adele said. "Starring me, Queen Adele, as I'm called." She went on how there would be food, unique entertainment, decorations and party favor bags without Lily saying anything.

The rest of us were all rolling our eyes, but Lily seemed interested. "I like the idea that it's something different and I'm in a bit of a bind. The venue I was going to use for Alexander's fourth canceled out. A pipe burst and the place is a wreck. It's too late to find any spot worth having, and I'm going to have to do something at my house." She took one of Adele's cards and said she would definitely be in touch.

She glanced around the table and asked what they were all making. After Elise showed off the granny square striped blanket she was making, the rest of them showed the personal project each had stashed in a tote bag. When Sheila pulled out the piece she'd brought, Lily oohed and aahed. The rest of us were used to the reaction by now.

Sheila's specialty was using a number of strands of mohair yarn in shades of blues, greens and lavender. The colors ended up with a soft hazy look that reminded people of an impressionist painting. She had pulled out the beginning of a knitted blanket and with an anxious eye on Adele shoved it back in the bag and took out a crocheted one.

Lily took off the cocoon jacket and showed how it was constructed. "Could you make something like that?"

I knew that Sheila would be self-effacing and probably say she couldn't make anything like the Cuddle because she was worried it wouldn't measure up. I spoke for her and said she could make anything, mentioning the display of her pieces at Luxe, which happened to be just up the street. Lily seemed interested in the mention of the store.

"I'm glad I stopped here and got to meet you all." She thanked us but turned down the offer of a crochet lesson this time, and I went to walk her to the front. She commented on how the group was more than she expected.

"I know you thought we'd all be sitting in rocking chairs, wrapped in shawls." She laughed at my description then admitted it was true.

"You know, I overheard some of the conversation before I sat down, and it's no surprise that someone wearing Crocs would be hostile to heels," Lily said with a laugh. "You do know that the house the woman in the Crocs was talking about is Taylor's. You saw the staircase for yourself. I heard the first thing she did when she got the house was to rip out the carpet."

With that Lily rushed off, saying she wanted to have a look at the lifestyle shop. It sounded like a perfect place to carry a selection of her cocoon wraps.

Chapter Fifteen

I was anxious to call Dinah, but I got home to more chaos again. Without any input from me, Peter had decided that Marlowe should have a real crib instead of the portable one. He'd ordered one from a trendy baby boutique and had it delivered, not realizing it had to be put together. Peter was not a do-it-yourself type, to put it mildly. Samuel wanted to help, but he had to leave for a gig in Ventura. It wasn't my father's forte either. The She La Las were done with their practice and were enjoying the platters of Israeli food my parents had gotten at a local place.

Also without any input from me, they'd decided the location of the crib should be in my bedroom. "It's not as if you're sharing it with anyone," my mother said.

"I get it. You're still upset that things didn't work out with Mason," I said, watching as Peter and my father held the sides of the crib up and tried to line up the screw holes. "But you need to let it go," I said to my mother. "Time for us all to move on."

"At least you're not with the detective anymore," she said. She had never been a fan of Barry's and I sometimes wondered if that had been part of his appeal. I thought, but didn't say, that they would have been very grateful to have Barry around just now. He knew how to fix everything, except maybe our relationship. He would have had the crib together in the time my father and Peter put in the first couple of screws.

Having the crib in my room did seem like a good idea. The room was large enough to easily fit it along with the furniture that was already in there. With the hallway, dressing area and bathroom, it was separate from the rest of the house and I would worry if the crib was in one of the bedrooms on the other side of the living room, even with a baby monitor.

Peter insisted that I stay in the room while they worked. It was partly to have another pair of hands to hold some parts together and partly so he could grill me about what I'd found out about Miles Langford.

I told Peter about what Miles had said about working on the western without mentioning that it came up when he had caught me snooping. "He certainly liked being on the set. I surmised that he had a handler who got him the chance to be an extra and ride a horse. He really liked being onstage when the movie got an award and I'm pretty sure Miles wanted to believe his input had made the difference and contributed to the award."

"I get it. In a way he's right. I'm sure whatever he invested in the project helped get it made. It's hardly a skeleton," Peter said. "And no reason to turn down his investment." He sounded happy at the news. He looked at me just as the side of the crib he was holding fell loose. "But keep on it and see if there's anything else. I hope there isn't, but I can't afford to take him as a partner and get sabotaged later."

I told him about Lily coming by the bookstore and Adele's party business. Peter looked stricken and hit his forehead with his hand to demonstrate his upset. The other piece of the crib fell loose and the pieces fell to the floor. "Now she's got a party business? You've made her sound like some kind of crochet maniac and nothing but trouble. You can't let Adele get involved with Lily. It'll be a disaster." He stopped abruptly. "Lily doesn't know who you are, right?" I nodded and he relaxed and then tensed again. "Didn't you say that Adele likes to call you by your last name? There aren't a lot of Pinks. It'll be embarrassing if anybody finds out that I'm using my mother as an investigator."

"Nobody's going to find out anything," I said. "And if Adele did do a party for them, it would be more of a chance for me to find out stuff." Peter still looked distraught. "She's already set it up that she thinks I'll be helping her with her business."

"Now that I hear you are bringing crazy Hookers into it on top of having someone die at that bookstore, maybe we should forget the whole thing and I'll just assume there's nothing terrible to come up."

"You must know who Daisy Cochran is, or was," I said to my son.

"Of course I do. But when her column ended, so did her power," he said. I mentioned her plan for the podcast and he nodded with understanding. "She must have had a lot of dirty laundry she never aired. But now no one will ever know."

"And it could be that what she knew got her killed," I said.

Peter's eyes narrowed as he looked at me. "Don't tell me you're investigating what happened to her." He said the word *investigating* with such horror, I almost laughed. But I also realized it was better not to talk to him about any of it, most of all that I might be a person of interest or worse. I changed the subject back to Miles Langford and Peter's desire to end my search for dirt on him. I probably should have thrown my hands up and agreed to let it go, but my pride was involved. I had barely scratched the surface and I wanted to finish the job.

We went back and forth and agreed on a time limit. If nothing bad turned up by then, he'd make the deal with Miles and take his money.

I finally called Dinah and had to tell her there was too much going on at my place to invite her over. Instead, she told me to bring Marlowe to her place. "Commander is trying to change his habits and stay up later. He drank some coffee at dinner and now he's too awake. I'm sure that he would love to play grandfather for the evening. Bring the stroller and he can take her for a walk."

• • •

Commander Blaine was sitting in the living room when Marlowe and I arrived. The house he shared with Dinah was a short walk from the bookstore in an area called Walnut Acres. The tall old walnut tree in the front yard was a reminder of the grove of them that had been there once.

He was still dressed in his work clothes. He had made a Mail It uniform for himself of a blue dress shirt and belted khaki pants. I knew he had been at the store from opening to closing, but he appeared neat and fresh. Only his expression seemed a little tense.

"I'm not so sure the coffee was a good idea. I feel like I'm buzzing on the inside. I'm going to have to figure out another way to stay alert," he said to Dinah.

"A walk will help," his wife said. "And you'll have a chance to spend time with Marlowe."

He looked at the baby with a glowing smile. "It'll be good practice in case my daughter ever produces any offspring," he said. He spent a few minutes introducing himself to Marlowe. He had totally softened and started playing peek-a-boo with her. It was funny how with all the changes in everything, the simple game was still a hit and the baby giggled with delight. He got a jacket and his phone and studied how the stroller worked and then left for the walk.

Dinah let out a sigh. "Remember that thing about being careful what you wish for?" She glanced around the living room. "It didn't occur to me that having him stay up later would mean he thought we should spend every minute together." She shook her head with a confused expression. "I don't know how anybody manages to get married, especially when they're older. He has his ways. I have mine. Both of us think we're right."

"You're not regretting it?" I asked.

"Maybe we shouldn't have messed with something that worked. We had our own places. His daughter didn't resent me. We didn't have unreal expectations of each other." She let out another sigh. "He is a totally good guy, but I don't know if I'm meant to be married."

"Tell me about it," I said with a laugh. "It's so much easier when you're young and believe that everything will just work out." We both laughed, thinking of the Hookers trying to fix me up. Now that we were talking about the Hooker meeting, Dinah wanted to know all about Lily. We went back into her she-cave and I went to lounge on the chartreuse sofa. "Do you think Commander will ever be ready to have this back in the living room?" I asked.

"I don't think so," she said. "But it's hardly an issue like our conflicting habits." She was already making tea and brought over a tin of cookies.

I reminded her that Lily was married to Miles, who was the one Peter had me investigating. "Or almost had me stop investigating. When he heard about Adele possibly doing a party for them, he wanted to pull the plug. He got upset, thinking I might be investigating what happened to Daisy, and that's without him knowing the whole story."

She wanted to know how I'd handled it and I laughed. "I glossed over it and he was having so much trouble with the crib and wondering about Miles, he forgot about it."

"Adele putting on a party," Dinah said, shaking her head with disbelief. "You know it's going to fall on you. But at least you have your own purpose for helping her on this one." Dinah brought the teapot over and poured us each a cup. "So what do you know so far? Let's see what we can deduce from it."

I accepted the invitation. She went and got her laptop. "We have an advantage over the old-time detective. We have Google."

I mentioned the name of the movie that Miles had worked on. We were reading about it when Commander returned with Marlowe. The motion of the stroller had lulled her to sleep and he wheeled the stroller into Dinah's she-cave.

"How about you?" Dinah asked, looking at her husband with concern.

"It mostly calmed my coffee jitters, but I don't think I'll ever be able to fall asleep."

Dinah left me with the sleeping baby and took Commander into the main part of the house. She returned alone a few minutes later. "I gave him a cup of chamomile tea. I bet he'll be off to la la land almost at his usual bedtime. He gets an A for effort, but I don't think he can change his body clock."

In the meantime, I had done a search on *Back Home on the Range* and saw it was available for streaming. "I am not sure what clues might be in it, but it seems worth watching. Having more information is always better," I said, and Dinah agreed.

The movie went directly into the first scene without even displaying the title. A stagecoach rumbled over a rocky road. "It really is an old-fashioned western," Dinah said. The scene cut to a steep hillside with slabs of golden-pinkish stone. Three men on horses watched the stagecoach as it tried to make it up the precipitous incline.

As expected, they robbed it. They got a sack of mail along with gold. It turned out that the mail bag had documents that were so valuable that the local lawmen plotted to get them back. The modern touch was that one of the sheriffs was a woman instead of working in a dance hall. The good guys won and the credits began to roll. I went to stretch, knocking over my teacup as I did. Dinah rushed to wipe up the liquid before it poured onto the carpet. I looked up just as the last of the credits went by. I grabbed the remote and stopped it. "I wanted to see Miles's credit," I said as I went back through them. It took some doing of going back and forward, but I got to the screen that listed him as an executive producer. It looked just like the photograph that I had seen. I was curious if he got a credit as an extra and read through all the rest of the crawl. There were a bunch of supervising producers and I recognized the name of the man that Miles had said was his buddy on the set. The list of credits seemed to go on forever, listing the caterer, greenery handler, public relations firm and even the drivers. Finally, there was a short list of featured extras and Miles's name was included. As soon as I saw it, I stopped the crawl.

"I'm afraid there's not much to deduce from the movie other than what I'd already figured out," I said. I told Dinah that Miles had been an investor in the movie, which got him the executive producer credit, and that he'd been on the set and got to ride a horse and be a background person. "I already told Peter that I thought that Miles wanted to be more than just a money person and the people who made the movie must have humored him."

"We don't need Sherlock Holmes to figure out that Rhoda is nuts when it comes to high heels," Dinah said, changing the subject to the conversation during the Hookers meetup.

"It turns out that I was in the house Rhoda was talking about and saw the staircase where the woman fell. It was the first time I took Marlowe to the mommy group at Taylor Palmer's house." I stopped and let everything swirl around in my brain for a moment. "Here's something Sherlock would latch on to. I thought I saw Taylor at Daisy Cochran's author event, but when I said something to her about it, she said she wasn't there. There was a lot of confusion and people milling around, but I really thought it was her."

"I know you," Dinah said. "And if you said it was her, I'd bet on you being right. Why would she want to deny being there?"

"Taylor might have been curious what Daisy had to say since it was about the world she's in, but she wanted to be anonymous. When Daisy collapsed, she could have fled like a lot of other people," I said, remembering how much smaller the crowd was when the police were taking statements.

We spent a little time after that seeing what we could deduce about Taylor and decided that since she viewed herself as being part of a power couple, it would be embarrassing to admit that she wanted to hear what a has-been columnist had to say.

"Can't you tell the cop about Taylor?" Dinah said.

I shook my head vehemently. "I'm afraid that Rick Carlson would look at it as me trying to distract him and get myself out of the spotlight. And if he did actually pay attention to what I said and talked to Taylor and it came out why he was talking to her—and you know it would—I'd get kicked out of the mommy group and my cover would be blown."

"I see your point," Dinah said, yawning. "And I think it's time for Sherlock to sleep on it."

When Marlowe and I finally left, it seemed like the chamomile tea had worked. The house was quiet and Commander had turned off all the lights. Dinah made a grrr sound and flipped the living room lights back on.

I was glad that the top of the stroller was the car seat and that it had a handle like a bucket's. I was able to put the baby in the car and carry her into my house without disturbing her. I set down the seat while I let the dogs out into the yard and went across the house to get Blondie. It appeared Marlowe would be spending another night in the portable crib.

I looked at the pieces of the new one leaning against my bedroom wall and wondered what would come first, the crib being together or Gabby's return.

Chapter Sixteen

It was one of those mornings when I didn't even have time to make myself a cup of coffee. Peter barged into my bedroom with a handyman in tow that he'd found on an app. The guy was on a schedule and I had to rush to get myself together and vacate the room so he could do his work putting together the crib. The dogs made a ruckus at the arrival of the invader. Even Blondie got out some barks from her chair. Samuel heard the noise and came in half asleep since he'd played a gig the night before. He got in an argument with his brother, saying he would have put the crib together.

I think Peter took his inability to assemble the crib himself as a blow to his manhood and argued back that Samuel was all talk and that getting it done was all that mattered, not by who.

Considering the start to my day, it was no wonder that I rushed into the bookstore café without checking out who was in there first. If I'd seen Rick Carlson sitting by the window with a cup of coffee, I would not have gone in. Why offer myself up?

But I was already at the counter when the homicide detective came up next to me, telling Bob my order was on him. It was a bad sign when he urged me to get something to eat as well.

"I hate to drink alone," he said when my order was ready. "Join me." His manner was all friendly and casual. Even so, I didn't want to sit with him, but if I made an excuse, it would look like I had something to hide.

I had been around the block a few times with being questioned and felt pretty certain I could hold my own, and I followed him back to his table while he carried my coffee and a cookie bar.

His manner didn't fool me. I knew that anything I said wasn't off the record and could be used against me.

He made small talk about how good the coffee was at the café, making it seem that was why he was there. "I know that you and Greenberg had a thing," he said, moving into something a little heavier than what kind of coffee roast the bookstore used. "He really likes the coffee here, too, but he was afraid it would be awkward if he came with me. For you."

"You can tell him I have no problem with him enjoying Bob's drinks," I said. I was going to leave it at that, but he was just using it as an opening.

"Greenberg told me that you are kind of an amateur detective. He said you might have some insight into what happened." He didn't have a blank cop face, but instead a relaxed expression. Like Barry, he appeared to be in his fifties, but had a softer build. The clothes were the same as what Barry wore, a nondescript suit that never wrinkled and a dress shirt and tie.

I knew what he was doing. Flattering me so I would be caught off guard. I wondered if Barry had also told him that I could hold my own. "I'd hardly call myself a detective like you," I said. Two could play the flattery game. "I'm just like everybody else these days, fascinated by true crime programs. Did you know that the victim was going to do a true crime podcast?"

"No," he said, looking suddenly uncomfortable that I'd asked him a question instead of falling for his flattery. "Then you must have known Ms. Cochran pretty well," he said, trying to recover his upper hand. "I'm sure you deal with all sorts of authors, but Ms. Cochran with her Hollywood connection and this podcast you mentioned was different, wasn't she? Maybe more of a prima donna than most?"

He left an opening for me to say something. "I certainly know about prima donnas," I said. He leaned a little closer in anticipation of what he thought I was going to say. "If you really want to see one in action, I can introduce you to Adele Abrams Humphries. She works here at the bookstore in the children's department. Do you have kids?" I gestured toward the entrance, and he pulled back into his seat.

"Ah, no thank you for the introduction," he said simply, not answering the personal question about his family situation.

"Have you gotten any test results back for Daisy? You seem to be looking for a motive. Does that mean her death is considered a homicide now?" I asked.

He ignored my questions. "I understand there was an altercation between you and Ms. Cochran about the drink."

I drew a blank at first and then it came back to me that there had been an issue about the smoothie. "I'd hardly call it an altercation. There were two drinks called strawberry something and I had gotten the wrong one."

"But a witness said they heard her accuse you of trying to kill her."

I'd totally forgotten about that part and suddenly found myself on the defensive. "It was hardly serious. She overreacted. She was just nervous about the crowd."

"Nobody likes being treated like that, particularly in front of other people. And it wasn't the first time, was it? She was difficult all along. Maybe you got tired of all of her demands." He stopped for a beat before continuing. "You're surrounded by all these books. I suppose you learn about all kinds of things. Or you could just do a search on a computer. I noticed a book meant for mystery writers in the reference section that was all about poisons. Did you know there was a mention of one that could easily have been hidden in a fruit drink?" He took a moment to sip some of his coffee, which really seemed more about letting what he had just said sink in.

"Really?" I said. "We do have so many books here. Are you saying that you think Daisy was poisoned for sure? Did you find something in the carpet sample your people took?"

The set of his mouth looked frustrated. He must have expected to be the one asking the questions, but I kept turning the tables on him. Finally, he picked up his empty cup. When he looked at me, he was back to the blank cop face expression. "Thank you for your help. I hope we can do it again."

I got it. He was setting me up to know that he was going to do a Columbo and would keep stopping by with a question or a comment, hoping he could catch me on something. I waited until I saw him get in his Crown Vic and drive away and then I went to the reference section and looked through the books until I found the one I thought he meant. There was a section on cyanide and its almond-like fragrance. I could see why it looked bad for me. Daisy had made a fuss over the wrong drink and she had yelled something about me trying to kill her. I had the most access to her drink. But it had been left on the table. I know I'd left it with the lid on and a straw sticking through it. But CeeCee had mentioned seeing the lid off the cup, so someone could have tampered with it. Still, wouldn't someone have noticed if someone poured something into the drink?

I really wanted to focus more on the job that Peter had given me checking Miles out, but since it was obvious that Rick Carlson was going to keep hammering me, I needed to find a way to get the heat off of me. The best way was to find out what really happened with Daisy. Mrs. Shedd and Mr. Royal had told me they hoped that Daisy had died from natural causes. Having a murder committed at an author event wasn't the kind of notoriety they were looking for to draw people into the store. I was kind of hoping for natural causes too, but it seemed like that boat had sailed.

I went back to my cubicle to work on the newsletter with a list of upcoming events. Adele had tried to talk me into adding a pitch about her party business. Not only would it have been inappropriate since it wasn't really part of the bookstore's business, but until she put on a successful party, it was nothing more than a vague plan. I was adding a write-up about a romance book club that was having a meeting when Mrs. Shedd brought Leslie Bittner to my cubicle. Daisy's assistant and self-proclaimed podcast producer was holding a box of books.

"It's a sad state of affairs when someone dying ups book sales, but it is the truth," the store owner said. "We're almost sold out." Leslie put the box on the counter that surrounded my enclosure and I noticed something different about her. She seemed to hold herself a little higher and her manner was more confident. Mrs. Shedd pulled out a box cutter and opened the top. She pulled out a copy of the book and looked at the black cover with *More than Glitter* in gold letters. "Molly, we should create a special display for Daisy's book. Maybe you can say something, like *from a recent author event.*"

Leslie left to get another box of books and Mrs. Shedd mentioned that she and Mr. Royal would be gone for several hours. They were off to the Huntington Garden for afternoon tea in the Rose Café. I envied them. Mason had taken me there more than once. It was his style to show up and spirit me off to someplace wonderful. I missed the romantic surprises more than I let on. I missed him more than I let on. After the encounter in the pet store and his cold expression, it was clear that he was over me. But what did I expect after what I had done. I shut down the ruminating and put on a smile, ready to deal with Daisy's assistant.

I thought of my encounter with Rick Carlson and his mention of Daisy being a prima donna. His implication was that it was a motive for me to have killed her. Wouldn't that make Leslie an even more likely suspect? She certainly was aware of Daisy's drink demand. I'd only dealt with Daisy a short time, the assistant might have been mistreated for much longer. After she delivered the books, I did a Rick Carlson and invited her to have coffee.

"Thank you," she said when I set down her coffee and some of Bob's famous oatmeal raisin cookie bars. "I've been running around all morning trying to get things together. I want to carry on what Daisy started."

"You mean her podcast?" I said.

"Yes. She left notes and an outline for each of the first couple of cases. I just need to figure out where she filed them on her computer. I can turn them into programs. I just need to find a host."

"You don't want to do it?" I asked and she shook her head.

"I do the technical stuff. Besides, nobody knows who I am. I need to get a name. Thanks to her column, Daisy was well-known. It was kind of a double-edged sword though. When the column ended, she needed money and did some PR stuff, but kept it under wraps since she felt it was such a big step back after the power she had with her column."

"Daisy made it sound as if she was going to give out some information that might cause some problems," I said.

She nodded. "That was the point. And a way to attract listeners. All the time she had the column, she was always discreet about anything negative. Because of that she was privy to a lot of stuff. It turns out that she kept a lot of notes."

"Aren't you worried after what happened to her?" I asked.

"I'll just be more careful. I want to finish what she started. I know that's what she would want," Leslie said. She sounded very confident, and I wondered if it was more than youthful bravado and she had another reason not to be concerned.

Chapter Seventeen

"Am I glad to see you," I said to Dinah, giving her a hug. "It's been another one of those mornings." She was wearing one of her many linen pants and tunic-top outfits, always with one of her trademark long skinny scarves. She had started winding more of the scarf around her neck and leaving less to twirl in the breeze. She said it was to hide the signs of crepey skin. I couldn't see what she was talking about, but she assured me that it was there. She had dropped in the bookstore on her way back from the community college.

The effects from the earlier coffee drinks had worn off and I was ready for another jolt of caffeine, but even more important, someone to talk to.

"Your welcome was just what I needed after my morning," she said as we headed to the café. "All I can say is that I'm glad the semester is almost over. This bunch of freshmen have been the most difficult. They argue about everything and have asked for do-overs of tests when they claimed they'd had a late night. And speaking of late, they take the start of class as a suggestion and wander in over the whole hour. But the most difficult thing is that they're sure they already know everything and what I'm teaching them is outdated. They should be able to make up words, use emojis in their papers and write in text talk. Writing is another issue. When I insisted that they turned in a handwritten assignment, they argued that nobody handwrote anything beyond an autograph anymore. Their papers were illegible. Thank heavens I have one student in that class who actually listens and has handwriting I can read." Dinah looked around the interior of the café as we went to the counter. "She may stop in here. She wanted to drop off an extra-credit essay. Extra credit," Dinah exclaimed. "Who hears of that anymore." She turned to me. "She's older than the rest of them, which probably explains it. She wrote a paper about a film she worked on."

We took our drinks to a table in the corner, where we had some privacy. I'd barely hit the seat of the chair before I started to vent about my morning.

"I was chased out of my bedroom by a guy in shorts waving a screwdriver. Peter hired him to put together the crib and the guy was in a hurry. Peter and Samuel were fussing. At least Samuel took over Marlowe's care until Beth got there so I could rush to the bookstore," I said.

"Too bad Barry's out of the picture. He would have had it together before your two sons finished arguing."

"Don't even say that," I said with a sigh. "Even though it did cross my mind." I took a sip of my drink. "But that was only the beginning." I mentioned Rick Carlson stopping by.

"He doesn't really think you oopted Daisy," Dinah said.

"*Oopted?*" I gave her a puzzled look.

"Sorry. It's their new word for killing or dying. I think it comes from video games." She let out a disgruntled sigh. "I tried researching it and couldn't find anything, but several of my students persist in using it anyway. Now they've got me using their made-up words." She poured some more of the steamed milk and coffee into her cup. "The point is he can't really think it is you. What's your motive?"

"He seems to think I lost it because Daisy was a prima donna," I said.

Dinah let out a laugh. "If that were true, you would have oopted Adele long ago."

I chuckled as I nodded in agreement before getting serious. "He brought up that Daisy had been overheard saying that I was trying to kill her. It was all because I got her the wrong smoothie. Her assistant told me which one to get and I must have gotten it mixed up."

"Oh," Dinah said, wincing. "I'm sure Daisy just meant it as a euphemism and it probably showed in her voice, but hearing just the words without her intonation is different. So they really are investigating it as a homicide."

"I think Rick Carlson is going by his cop gut," I said. "I'm worried that his instinct has decided it's me and he's going to keep badgering me, thinking I'll confess." I took a sip of the coffee. "I'm not sure if they have proof there was poison in her drink."

"Cop's gut," Dinah said with a disparaging shake of her head.

"It's ridiculous how even Barry would decide he knew who a killer was without hard evidence. He said it was based on all his years of being a homicide detective and that he'd developed an instinct." I let out a chuckle. "It sure bugged him when I ended up proving his gut was mistaken." I glanced toward the entrance of the bookstore to make sure nobody was looking for me. "Actually, I have found a much better suspect for Detective Carlson," I said, and Dinah leaned forward in anticipation of what I was going to say next. I told her about Leslie Bittner.

"She's got motive," I began. "I'm sure it was no picnic working for Daisy. But what struck me was how excited she was about taking over the podcast. She wants to hire a host, but the podcast will belong to her. She expects to use Daisy's notes and outlines. She also had opportunity. She's the one who reminded me to get Daisy's smoothie. Maybe it wasn't that I got things mixed up, but that Leslie deliberately told me to get the wrong smoothie." I paused for a moment and considered what the problem could have been with the first smoothie, remembering how Daisy had reacted. "I bet Sherlock would deduce that Daisy was deathly allergic to something in the first one I got, like maybe soy." I thought back to the night of. "Leslie was milling around with the others when the cup was sitting on the table and could have dropped something into it when she realized I had gotten Daisy the right smoothie."

"You mean like a pill or something?" Dinah said and I shrugged.

"I wonder if a pill would dissolve fast enough," I said. "But pouring in a liquid would be pretty obvious. I'll have to think about it." I felt much better talking about it to someone. "And now I have to create a display of Daisy's books. Mrs. Shedd tried to soft-pedal it, but Daisy's death has kicked up the demand for her book. It's my job to figure out a sign to go on the table that reminds people that she just died at the bookstore, but without saying it."

"I should turn it over to my students. They'd probably say something liked *Oopted Here* and point an arrow toward where it happened and then stick in some emojis of a coffin."

"There's a coffin emoji?" She took out her phone and showed me one.

When we parted company, we both felt better for having been able to vent. I put together the display table of Daisy's books and the sign simply gave her name and said *Recent Bookstore Guest.*

By late afternoon I needed to recharge and went back to the yarn department for some crochet therapy. Anyone who needed me could find me, and since handling the Hookers was really a bookstore event, crocheting really counted as working. I had taken out the granny square striped blanket. I was working it the long way and it took up a lot of space. But since I was there alone, it was no problem.

The being there alone did not last long.

"Pink, there you are," Adele said, seeming agitated as she came up to the table. "You have to help me." I let out a sigh and prepared for the rest of it. I never knew with Adele. She was so overly dramatic about everything. "I got a call about someone interested in Queen Adele putting on a party." I assumed she had pitched the parents when they'd picked up their kids from story-time. Before I could say anything, she continued. "I have to go to her house and tell her the details of the party."

"That sounds like good news to me," I said.

"Of course it's good news, but other than my costume, I don't know where to start. Probably some food." She was half talking to herself but then she looked at me. "You're the event specialist, what do I need?" There was a definite dig when she said *event specialist.* Even after all this time, she was still upset because I'd gotten the position and she hadn't. At the same time, she expected me to rescue her. I was considering leaving her to deal with it on her own, but then she told me who had called her. "It was that woman who came to the Hookers the other day. She said she was part of that mommy group you're going to."

"You mean Lily Langford?" I said.

"That's the one. You probably know what their house looks like." Adele looked at me expectantly and I knew I had to come up with something.

"Yes, you'll need food, decorations and something for the kids to do," I said. "You need to have a theme. Let me think about it for a moment." Adele's expression had brightened.

"Get back to me when you figure out something. You probably should write it all down and figure out how much everything is going to cost. Then I can add on my profit." Adele prepared to make a dramatic exit. I was trapped and had to help her seem professional.

I looked down at the crochet project regretfully as I packed it up to work on later. Adele had set the meeting with Lily for two days from now. I had the next day off from the bookstore and added coming up with a plan to the list of things I had to take care of.

Chapter Eighteen

I came home to relative quiet. The dogs and cats were waiting for my attention, Beth was getting ready to leave after looking after Marlowe. I was pleased to see that Peter was there and seemed to be taking an active role in Marlowe's care. He had her sitting in the high chair that had appeared shortly after she came to stay and he was feeding her something out of a jar. He looked up as I went through the kitchen with the dogs in tow.

"It's not the same as when I was little," Peter said, wiping a dribble of puréed peaches off his daughter's chin. "Did Dad ever do diaper duty or this?" He had a spoonful of the peaches and pretended it was a plane coming in to land in her mouth. "I saw this move on a TV show." She giggled and he tried to hand the spoon to me.

"Nope," I said. "Finish what you started." I did a pitch on how he should be so glad to have a relationship with his daughter.

He let out a tired sigh. "I think I like the old way better when all that was expected of dads was taking them out for a pony ride." Peter told me that his brother had fed the whole crew of animals before he left. I let them out into the backyard and went to check the refrigerator to consider my dinner and asked Peter if he was going to join me.

"You know I'd love to," he said in the tone he used in his business. "But I have a dinner meeting." He tried to feed Marlowe some more, but she was done with the peaches. He put the cap back on the baby food and dropped the spoon in the sink. "Any update with Miles?" he asked.

When I said there was nothing new yet, his expression changed to displeased and he brought up ending it again. "Maybe it's one of those things where there is no there, there," he said. "You could just drop out of the mommy group until Gabby gets back."

"Not exactly," I said and told him about Adele's call from Lily. If he looked displeased before, he was really upset now.

"She's sure to let on who you really are and it would be so

embarrassing to have it out there that I was using my mother to check up on potential investors. I'm sorry I listened to—" He interrupted himself. "You have to go with her when she goes to their house and make sure they don't decide to use her for the kids' party."

He went off to his business dinner and I made an omelet for myself as Marlowe watched from her high chair. She eyed it as I was eating and I put some pieces out for her, which she ate on her own. I thought over what Peter had said and came up with a solution.

• • •

Adele was waiting for me when I came to the bookstore the morning of the party meeting. She was dressed in her queen outfit for story-time. "I thought it would be good for the meeting," she said, swirling the red velvet cape she wore over a long dress before adjusting the crocheted silver crown that was a little off-kilter. She wanted to know the plan I'd come up with since she was going to be the one to present it. I had written something up and handed the folder with the pages to her while admonishing her not to use my name, but instead refer to me as her associate. I got her to agree by convincing her it would put too much of the spotlight on me to use my name. "Absolutely. I will call you my assistant. Queen Adele is the one in charge."

Since I knew the goal was not to get the gig, I was more than happy to let Adele run the show.

She insisted on driving even though I knew the way. We made quite a pair as we walked up to the house. She had the cape and crown and I was wearing my usual khaki pants and white shirt with a sweater over it that had become like my work uniform.

The housekeeper did a double take as she let us in and sent us back to the great room at the back of the two-story pseudo farmhouse where the mommy group had met.

Lily joined us after a few minutes. There was no semblance of it being a social call as when I'd been there before. No offer of a drink or elite bagels meant to impress. She clearly viewed us as the help. Adele went overboard with referring to me as her assistant and actually made me stay a step behind her, which worked out in my favor. The only time I stepped out of the background was when I asked if Miles would be joining us. Lily dismissed the idea.

"I'm the one making the arrangements. Even with being CEO of my company, I still have to take care of everything." There was a strong emphasis on *everything*, which led me to believe she had to clean up his messes, like maybe pick up his socks. Adele took out a storyboard from the oversized portfolio she'd brought in. She'd created a whole presentation from my notes. The one thing for sure about Adele was that she knew how to command a room. She'd brought a laser pointer and was busy describing the setup for the party as she pointed to the board. I slipped further into the background and mumbled something about using the restroom, which went unnoticed. I couldn't pass up the chance to have one more look around. I thought it was too intrusive to try to look upstairs and figured the best place to find anything about Miles was in the office where I'd been interrupted by him when I had looked before.

I was beginning to think that Peter might be right about there being nothing to find. Or if there was anything to find, it wouldn't be there. As I looked around the pleasant room with a view of the side yard, I went over what I had found out about Miles. His two brothers were the principals in the family construction business but he got a share of the profits. He was trying to buy his way into show business and seemed to want the image of being a producer. I looked at all the pictures on the wall from the western and Miles appeared to be having the time of his life.

I guessed he would probably want to do the same with Peter's production and I ought to make a point of that to Peter again. Maybe it wasn't anything terrible, but having Miles in the middle of things might be annoying. I glanced at the desks. His appeared unused, but the receipt I'd seen before on her desk had been joined by some others.

I didn't dare stay gone too long and went back into the large open space. Adele was still using the pointer and the storyboard. Lily had a flat expression and I expected her to interrupt Adele at any moment and tell her she'd changed her mind.

My absence didn't seem to have been noticed. Adele had gotten to the list of what she would provide, which I knew was the last part of the proposal I'd created. I let her finish and got ready for the rejection.

"Let me see if I understand this," Lily said. "You are proposing putting on a vintage-themed party with games such as pin the tail on the donkey. The food would be a lunch of hot dogs, French fries, Jell-O, a grocery store sheet cake and cups of grocery store brand ice cream. The decorations would be streamers, a banner with a personalized happy birthday, and balloons. There would be party hats and party favors, which would be paper baskets filled with bags of something called penny candy. The entertainment would be you reading some special stories."

I listened, almost mouthing the words, imagining what she was thinking of the plan. There was no ice cream truck offering an assortment of treats, no pony rides, goody bags with real jewelry or a fancy menu of goat cheese pizza and fruit parfaits or a cake from a trendy bakery. There was nothing elite about the party.

Lily got to the end of her roundup of what Adele had said and I took a step toward the door.

"I love it," Lily said finally. "The whole vintage concept is so fresh and nothing like the parties we've gone to. I'll be a trailblazer." Then she gave the date when she wanted it and my mouth fell open at how soon it was. I also understood why she was willing to hire Adele. She had no other options.

All I could think of was that Peter was going to throw a fit.

• • •

Adele was still high from giving her presentation when the Hookers met in the late afternoon and I realized I had created a monster. "It's just the start," Adele said, pacing up and down next to the table where the rest of us were sitting. Adele's over-the-top behavior had affected Sheila the most and she'd pulled out her emergency string and crochet hook and was frantically making a long string of chain stitches.

Rhoda laughed that Lily had found the idea fresh. Elise was upset that she'd been left out since she thought her real estate expertise would come in handy. Eduardo suggested adding a pinata.

While Adele was going on about her triumph, I had leaned in to Dinah and told her how my plan had backfired. "And now I have to help her do the thing," I said.

Elise made another pitch to help, but Adele refused again. "I know what you're up to," Adele said. "You want to pitch the parents on listing their houses with you." Adele shook her head for emphasis. "Molly is my helper." Everyone looked up at her not calling me by my last name. Adele glanced over the table. "Why are you all so surprised? Molly asked me not to call her Pink anymore." I choked back a laugh. Was that all it took? Just asking her?

Just then, Leslie Bittner walked into the yarn department and looked around at the table full of people and the cubbies filled with colorful yarn arranged by type.

"Are you interested in joining us?" I asked, indicating an empty chair. Leslie turned her gaze to the table. "No, thank you. I wanted to talk to CeeCee Collins," she said, looking directly at the actress. Eduardo got up from the chair next to her and gestured for Daisy's assistant to take it.

Leslie shook her head. "I was hoping for something a little more private." CeeCee got up and the two of them walked back into the bookstore and stood near the reference department while we all watched.

"What do you think she wants?" Dinah asked.

"After talking to her the other day, I have a pretty good idea," I whispered. I was going to say more, but CeeCee returned and Rhoda in her direct way asked what it was all about.

"She wanted me to host the podcast that Daisy Cochran was going to do. She's taking it over now," CeeCee said with a disapproving sound. "She said I would be the perfect host and tried to sell me on what a great opportunity it was for me. She seems certain the podcast is going to be a hit. She went on explaining that Daisy had left outlines for the shows and the reveals were going to be pretty shocking. She said that some people who thought they were home free might be in for a surprise. She didn't name names and once she understood I wasn't interested, she stopped cold."

"I suppose whatever information Daisy left could get the police to take an interest," Eduardo said. "Maybe even bring a charge for murder."

"Someone who thought they were home free could freak if they thought they were in jeopardy," Rhoda said. "I wonder how far they'd go to keep things quiet."

Elise looked at me. "You're the detective here. What do you think?" Adele let out a groan at the comment.

"I do think it could have gotten Daisy killed," I said. "I keep hearing about all the dark stuff she knew. Hearing that she was going to put it out there now must have made some people nervous."

"I thought she died from a seizure," Sheila said, making awkward stitches on the row of chains.

All but Adele's head swiveled back to me for an answer. She seemed to be purposely not getting involved and was staring down at the crochet project in front of her. "Maybe, maybe not. The homicide detective I talked to seems to be investigating it as foul play even though they don't seem to know for sure if it was," I said.

"Homicide detective?" Rhoda said. "Then you are talking to him again."

"No," I said decisively. "It wasn't Barry. I told you all that is over, as in no contact."

"What about this one?" Rhoda said. "What does he look like?"

"It doesn't matter," I said. "He was strictly investigating, playing Columbo with just one more question."

Betty Hechtman

"Or maybe he's just looking for an excuse to see you," Rhoda persisted.

I shook my head. "No. It's because I'm pretty sure he thinks I'm a suspect."

They all seemed shocked and I brought up the drink and that Daisy was overheard accusing me of trying to kill her.

"That's nonsense," Dinah said.

"I agree," I said. "But it's another case of a cop following his gut reaction, so sure that he's right."

"What are you going to do?" Sheila said in a worried voice.

"Find out the truth," Dinah said. "With my help."

Adele finally looked up, rocking her head and rolling her eyes. "Here we go again. P—" She started to say Pink, but stopped herself. "Molly is going to do her Sherlock Holmes–Nancy Drew–Miss Marple thing." I didn't dignify it with a comment.

"The CPA is still available," Rhoda said, going right back to her matchmaking efforts. "You could do worse."

"Or I could do not at all," I said. It seemed like I had enough on my plate without being worried about romance.

We'd been so I intent on our conversation that I hadn't noticed that someone was sitting in one of the easy chairs in the yarn department. It was only when Dinah got up to leave that I looked around the area and saw him.

"Garth?" I said, surprised at realizing he was the one occupying the chair. I felt all their eyes on me as I took a couple of steps toward the chair, prepared to talk to him. I decided to be proactive and not let the Hookers assume that the writer was some secret lover of mine. I retraced my steps and hung over the table. "He's from the mommy group I'm taking Marlowe to," I said in a low voice. "That's all."

I heard some chuckles as I walked away and someone said something about me protesting too much.

"Hey," Garth said as I approached. He was wearing jeans and a green T-shirt under a leather jacket. Hard to tell with a writer if they were his work clothes or his casual wear since they were probably the same. He stood when I got closer and glanced back at the table. "Is that CeeCee Collins?" he asked, looking at the petite blondish woman.

I nodded and explained who the group was.

"Tarzana Hookers," he said and chuckled. "I bet that gets a laugh every time." He wanted to know what we were making and the difference between knitting and crochet. I considered bringing Adele over and letting her loose on him, but I decided to spare him her dramatic show and told him.

"Good to know. Seems like you have some interesting characters." He paused for a moment, as if an idea had struck him and he was thinking it through. "I think I'm going to write a concept for a sitcom about a group like yours. Did I hear right that you investigate crimes?"

"That was Adele. If you need a character for your concept, she's the one to use. Though you'd probably have to tone her down. She was just teasing me," I said.

"I also heard you say you might be a suspect," he said with a question in his voice. "It sounds like something I could use. I could make it a comedy crime show."

I brought up Daisy and her author event. "It's ridiculous. All because someone overheard Daisy say I was trying to kill her because I got her the wrong fruit smoothie."

He laughed. "That's even too ridiculous for me to include in a script. I'm sure there were people with real motives. Daisy had been tossing around hints that she was going to release some stunning information. She talked to me about writing something for the podcasts. Not a script really, more of filling in an outline and organizing the information so suspense would build and lead to a final reveal."

"So then you must know about the information she had," I said and he shook his head.

"It never went further than her talking to me about how she wanted to organize the podcast. I wondered if it was all hype anyway. I guess we'll never know."

"Her assistant has all the notes and she's planning to go ahead with the podcast once she finds a celebrity to host it," I said.

"Oh," he said, surprised. Then he muttered something about thinking that the whole project was dead. He looked up at me and smiled. "Next time the group meets, it's our place. There won't be the splendor of Taylor's house." He let out a tired sigh. "She always makes such a big deal about the place and being Mrs. Palmer. I wonder how she's going to react if, like her husband's other marriage, theirs ends." He caught himself. "I shouldn't really gossip about the others in the group."

"Feel free to talk all you like," I said. "What about Lily and her husband?" I tried to appear nonchalant, but I was hoping for some inside information I could pass along to Peter.

"You've probably noticed that she's a bore going on and on about her cocoon jackets and how she's CEO," he said. "As for Miles, I'd say he's just what you'd expect from someone with two older successful brothers. He puts on a big act of being important, but I think he's pretty thin-skinned." Garth shrugged.

"I'm assuming you're here for a reason besides talking about the mommy group," I said. "Can I help you with something?"

"I had forgotten about this place until you talked about it with the group. I had some time to kill and I love bookstores. So here I am." He pointed at a stack of books next to him. "That's what happens when you browse in a real store instead of buying online."

He started to gather the books. "The woman in the front said you were back here and I didn't want to leave without at least saying hello."

It was the first time I'd ever talked to him without the group there and I asked him how he felt about being a guy in a mommy group.

"Well, since you asked," he said. "I don't really like it, but I do it because it's networking. The meeting I had today is because Kath thought of me when they decided to do an infomercial about her husband's plastic surgery clinics. I'd much rather work on something about your group, but in the meantime writing a script about the magic they perform pays the bills."

I asked if it was hard to write and he let out a sigh. "Yes. There's no storytelling. It's all about painting a picture full of promises and at the same time adding that there are no guarantees. I gather they had some unhappy patients."

Chapter Nineteen

Mrs. Shedd and Mr. Royal left me to close up the bookstore. Once the customers and other workers were gone, I went through the place and did a little straightening, picking up stray books and abandoned coffee mugs It was dark when I locked the front door and Ventura Boulevard was quiet. I had the sidewalk to myself as I walked to the corner on my way to the parking lot in the back. I was thinking ahead to going home and wondered what would greet me this time. Out of the corner of my eye, I saw a dark car pull to the curb. I was going to dismiss it, but it kept creeping along the curb. Was the driver looking for a parking meter that still had time on it? But it was past the time that you had to pay. I avoided looking directly at the car and picked up my speed as I turned the corner. I heard a car door open and close and then footsteps on the pavement. The parking lot was empty and I walked on an angle with my keys out, both to open the car door—wishing that the vintage Mercedes didn't predate clickers with panic buttons—and to use as a weapon if need be. I took a quick glance back and saw no one. Maybe I was getting paranoid and imagining things. I wished I hadn't parked at the far end of the lot, but it was the area set aside for employees. I checked my surroundings and was annoyed once again about the dimly lighted area. Was it real or my imagination that someone was hiding in the shadow of the lamppost?

I hurried toward my car, anxious to get inside, but when I got to it saw there was a note stuck under the windshield wiper, blocking the driver's line of sight. By the time I'd pulled it free, I sensed there was somebody nearby.

"Don't come any closer," I said in what I hoped was a gritty voice. "I have sharp keys." And then a man stepped out of the shadows.

I shoved my hand out with the keys visibly poking through my fingers, showing I was ready to do damage, but the voice stopped me.

"Barry?" I said, surprised. "What the . . ."

"I was driving by and saw you. The street looked dark," he said. "I was just going to make sure you got to your car. You weren't supposed to see me." He looked at my hand. "What's that?"

I did an imaginary punch with my hand and he reached out and grabbed my wrist to show how weak my "weapon" was. "Pepper spray or mace would be better." He let out a low laugh. "Though I'm glad for me you didn't have either."

"I thought you homicide detectives were supposed to be stealthy," I said. "I saw the car pull to the curb and follow me. And you ought to start wearing sneakers with your suit if you're planning to follow people." I shook my head in a scolding manner.

He hung his head in mock shame. "Maybe I better go back to detective school for a refresher course."

There was an awkward moment and I tried to cover it with ordinary conversation. "How's it going with Carol?" I asked. He seemed surprised by my comment and I felt I had to explain. "We had a conscious uncoupling," I said, giving my own twist to how Gwyneth Paltrow described her divorce with Chris Martin. "No yelling or broken hearts. We just faced that we were not meant to be."

"Maybe your heart wasn't broken," he said. He sounded like he was joking, but I wasn't sure. "But it's going okay with Carol. My lifestyle works for her. It turns out she really doesn't want a full-time partner anyway. Jeffrey likes her kids." He looked at the paper in my hand. "Aren't you going to look at it?"

"It's probably just a flyer for an oil change place," I said.

"Then let me throw it away for you." He held out his hand.

"I'll just use it for scratch paper." I stuffed it in my pocket.

"C'mon. We both know it's not a flyer and I stopped to see that you got in your car because I know you're probably mixed up in investigating." He paused as if considering what to say. "I shouldn't say anything, but then you probably have figured that Rick Carlson has you pegged as a person of interest."

"You could tell him that it's ridiculous. You know that I wouldn't kill anybody. I take spiders outside and let them go instead of squashing them."

"He knows about us, so anything I say will be taken wrong. He got me off the Cochran murder because he thought I'd be biased—that I'd be hostile toward you because we broke up."

"If that's the way his mind works, I'd never want to be involved with him," I said in a facetious manner.

"Good. Because I understand he's been hanging around and I know that you're single and he just went through a divorce."

I laughed at the thought. "I know it's a plan. He thinks if he keeps showing up, he'll wear me down. You can tell him he's wasting his time because I have nothing to confess to. And as for a relationship." I shook my head vehemently. "You filled my cop quota."

"Now that we're past all that—" He looked at the paper sticking out of my pocket.

I gave in and pulled it out, unfolding it. One side was an ad for a nail salon, but on the blank side there was a note in red pen. "Mind your own business or you will be pushing up Daisies with Daisy." I read it over again. "It seems like someone was trying to be menacing and clever at the same time."

Something that a writer would say.

• • •

Barry went home to Carol and I went home to the circus. He had wanted to give the note to Rick Carlson but realized that it would cause all kinds of problems, like what was he doing with it since we were broken up and he was off the case. And why would someone send me a threatening note? I thought it might indicate that I wasn't involved since it was threatening that I'd end up like Daisy. In the end, he let it be and said he knew it was useless to tell me to stay out of the investigation, and just admonished me to be careful.

I'm sure that even with Carol's kids, it was probably quieter than my house. The dogs were hanging by the glass kitchen door when I walked across the patio. I had a piece of latticework put across the bottom of the glass panel a long time ago, concerned with all their jumping around the dogs would break the glass. I could hear their yipping and barking above the music coming from inside.

They ran outside when I opened the door, and when I went across the house to get Blondie out of her chair, I passed through the living room. My mother and "the girls" were practicing a new song and the dance moves that went with it. My father was holding Marlowe and dancing along with them, or trying to. Marlowe was giggling and kicking her feet in time to the music. There were paper plates with sandwiches missing bites and mugs scattered on the coffee table.

Before I got as far as the den, the doorbell rang. It was kind of late for package deliveries, but I went to check. When I opened the door, Mumsy, as Gabby called her mother, Ilene Alter, was standing on the porch.

"I was just going to drive by, but when I saw all the people in your living room, I wondered what was up." She looked me up and down with a critical eye. She had at least ten years on me and was dressed flawlessly in slacks and a sweater set. "I just got back from my river cruise and Gabby wanted me to check on Marlowe," she said, pushing past me. "She wanted me to make an impromptu visit so I could see how things really are."

I could barely keep up with her as she rushed into the living room and all the commotion. They were all lost in what they were doing and didn't notice her. She turned back to me with a look of horror. "Gabby told me anything goes with you people. What are you feeding her?" She looked down at the half-eaten sandwiches.

"Then you're here because you want to take her home with you?" I said.

Mumsy shook her head. "No. I am just here to report to Gabby and I suppose advise you of what you're doing wrong. I would think your son would have hired a competent nanny instead of this." As she said it, the dogs came running in, having pushed open the door. Cosmos put his paws on the coffee table and snatched one of the partial sandwiches.

"And Gabby told me that someone died at the bookstore where you work, during an event you arranged." She said *bookstore* like it was a bordello, maybe because she knew about the Hookers, I thought with a laugh.

I asked her how Gabby knew what was going on here. "I don't know what she does, but she has her ways." Ilene put her hands up as if to dismiss my questions. "You need to get Marlowe proper care."

My father gave the baby a snuggle and a kiss on the forehead. "I think she has better than proper care," I said. The dogs had now noticed a stranger had arrived and were giving her shoes a strong sniffing.

"And all these animals," she said as Blondie came into the room along with the two cats.

Samuel turned off the music and the She La Las and my father noticed we had a visitor. I introduced her and said, "Ms. Alter is concerned that Marlowe is living in a crazy house."

I watched my mother's eyes flicker with anger and she marched over to us. My mother's silver bangle bracelets jangled as she approached Marlowe's other grandmother.

"Your daughter left her here. She practically abandoned her on the porch."

"The nanny she hired quit," Mumsy said, as if that was a defense. "I was cruising on the Danube. What could she do?"

"Molly took her in even though she had to go to work. She took Marlowe to work with her and made arrangements for Marlowe's family to take care of her. As you can see, we have a lot going on, but it hasn't kept us from looking after her because we are her family."

It was then that Mumsy recognized my mother. "You're in that singing group. I loved that song, what was it called?"

"Yes, we're the She La Las." My mother took a bow and pointed to the other two women. "Originally It was called 'My Man Dan,' but we made a new version called 'My Guy Bill,'" my mother said, losing her hostile stance.

My father offered to let her hold Marlowe and asked her if she was hungry. The next thing I knew she'd found a spot on one of the couches and my father was making her a sandwich. She waved me over. "I understand you're taking Marlowe to Gabby's mommy group." Her tone made it sound like Gabby wasn't happy about it. I didn't want to let on that Peter had put me up to it in an effort to get information about Miles Langford, so I simply said that I was trying to keep things normal for Marlowe. I looked at the baby, now in the playpen, hugging her toy giraffe. As if she'd even notice if we didn't go.

"Have you been to the Palmers' yet?" Ilene asked. I was caught off guard by the question and told her the truth that it had been my first introduction to the group.

"That's the one that Gabby is most concerned about you not messing up. Gabby has known Taylor for a long time. They both worked as production assistants. They were close until Taylor got involved with Andrew Palmer. He was still married, but she used the old trick of getting pregnant, knowing that he would marry her. He's very possessive of his offspring, particularly sons. Gabby said Andrew would do anything for Taylor."

"What happened? How did Gabby reconnect with her?" I asked.

"They met at the pediatrician's office and realized they could help each other. Andrew Palmer is much older than Taylor and she wanted a friend who was close to her age who she had a history with and who she could lord that house over. Gabby knew that a connection to Andrew Palmer could help her relaunch her career after your son's disaster." Mumsy made a *tsk tsk* sound before she continued. "Gabby is very ambitious."

I ignored the dis of Peter and considered what else Mumsy might know. Since it was obvious that Gabby gossiped about the mommy group, I wondered what she knew about Garth since the timing of seeing him at the bookstore and finding the note seemed suspiciously close together. She drew a blank, other than to say that Gabby thought his house was cute. I wondered if she knew anything about Lily and Miles. She leaned close, as if the couple was somehow in the vicinity.

"Gabby bought me one of those cocoon jackets Lily sells. As for her husband, Gabby hasn't said much about him except that he comes from money and seems to be easily offended.

I brought up that it was nearing my turn to host the group. "What did Gabby do when it was hers?" I asked.

"They're all very judgmental so there was no way that she was going to have them come to her apartment and I didn't want a crowd coming to our place. I'm not really a baby person. She organized something at a park in Encino and brought a picnic. Nobody can compete with Taylor and that house, so Gabby went for something different. What are you going to do?"

I told her about the bookstore and story-time. She gave me a look that said she wasn't impressed and they probably wouldn't be either.

"I think it might work out," I said defensively. "A number of them have come in the bookstore since I started taking Marlowe to the group and our story-time is famous. I'll have the café supply some of their special treats for the parents." I was thinking out loud now. "I'll have Bob make some of his wonderful Eggy Squares and the coffee is wonderful."

"Good luck," she said as my father approached with a plate of food. She eyed the thick corned beef sandwich and generous amount of potato salad. "I really shouldn't. There must be a million calories. But since you went to so much trouble." She took the plate and inhaled the scent of the food with pleasure.

Chapter Twenty

"You got her to come over to the dark side," Dinah said with a laugh as I finished describing Ilene "Mumsy" Alter's visit. "How'd you leave it?" I had called my friend to give a report.

"I don't think she intended to do anything but pacify her daughter by saying she had checked on Marlowe. She even said to me that she wasn't a baby person. But what she is is a gossip person, and she repeated some of what Gabby had told her about the others in the mommy group."

"I hope she came through with something about the people Peter is having you investigate."

"Not much really. She kept going on about Taylor's house," I said. Dinah asked if I wanted to play the Sherlock Holmes game. "Okay, but let's use Google."

Dinah laughed. "I don't think Sherlock would approve."

"That's only because he didn't have a computer or Google, or I bet he would have used it. Besides, it's our game and we make up the rules."

"Then computer it is," she said. "Your place or mine? Commander did his best to stay up, but he was out at nine thirty."

"I'd love to come to you, but the troops have all left and I have Marlowe, plus the mess they left behind. You can man the laptop while I clean up," I said.

I'd barely given the dogs some time outside when Dinah came across the back patio to the kitchen door. She walked in and looked around. There was stuff everywhere. "Every time my parents come, they bring all kinds of food. There's the take-out and then bread and cookies. Marlowe has enough baby peaches to last until she's a teenager."

I helped Dinah set up at my kitchen table. It was a built-in small booth next to the large windows that overlooked the backyard. The dogs were running around and Blondie was sitting on a chaise lounge.

Dinah looked at the terrier mix sitting aloof from the others. "That is one lucky dog," she said.

"We were both lucky to find each other," I said. Blondie was the first of the menagerie. It was right after Charlie died and I was feeling low and making too many bowls of caramel corn and then eating it. I found Blondie at a private shelter. She'd been at the shelter for a year and a half. Adopted once and returned. I had no doubts that it had to do with her personality. Whoever thinks of a terrier being anything but feisty? She was more like a cat. I'm not even sure she knew she was a dog since she mixed so little with the others.

Cosmo, the black mutt, was at the door, trying to push it open. Barry and his son had adopted him at an animal fair. Since they didn't have a yard and didn't have regular hours, the dog had stayed with me. The dog finally got the door open and came in, followed by Felix.

"You know who you are," Dinah said, laughing at the gray terrier mix, who was running around the kitchen barking at nothing. "You're a lucky dog, too," she said as the dog came up to her. "I don't get people. How could Samuel's girlfriend just leave the dog to never see him again when she broke up with him?" Felix abandoned Dinah when Princess ran in and started trying to get the white puff ball to play with him.

"I know—she's a lucky dog too," I said, watching the dogs move around the kitchen and knock into their water bowl. When I'd found her at the house of someone who'd died, I couldn't bear the thought of her going to the pound or worse, so brought her home with me. "She adores Peter. And though he tries to act indifferent, I know he loves the dog. But he can't quite manage keeping her at his place."

"They are all lucky animals," Dinah said as the two cats sauntered in. Mr. Kitty was black and white with markings that made him look like he had half a mustache. Cat Woman was grayish with markings that made her look like she was wearing a skirt. Samuel had brought the cats home. He'd seen them at the SPCA, labeled "hard to adopt" because they were older. Who wouldn't melt hearing that their owners had coldly dropped off the eight-year-old and ten-year-old cats who were both sweeties.

I had too many pets and Dinah had none, so we figured things averaged out.

I gave the dogs a round of treats and made sure the cats' bowls were full and located where the dogs couldn't get to them. "Okay, let's begin," I said, coming back in the kitchen. Dinah had the laptop open and had signed on to my Wi-Fi and was doing random searches based on curiosity.

"Did you know there are dogs that are autistic?" She looked at Blondie as she came through the kitchen to return to her chair.

"I don't think Blondie is. I think she was in a shelter too long when she was a puppy and then her heart broke when she was adopted and returned."

"Like I said, she is a very lucky dog." I offered Dinah an assortment of leftovers. It was like the United Nations of food in my refrigerator. "There's pad Thai, falafel and salad with pita bread, tikka chicken, and a platter of French cheeses." I looked around at the other food. "And there's plenty of deli stuff."

"It all sounds great, but what I'd really like is some of your scrambled eggs."

"I can certainly do that. It would be nice to cook something, even if it's just eggs." I went to gather up the butter and eggs and take out my favorite frying pan while Dinah asked me more about the conversation with Gabby's mother.

"She seemed fixated on Taylor's house. I half expected her to volunteer to take Marlowe to the mommy group the next time they meet there."

Dinah started typing something into the computer as the butter melted in the frying pan and sent out an appealing scent. Making the eggs made me think of Barry and all the times he just showed up and I'd made them for him. I was pretty sure that Carol wasn't swirling butter in a pan when she got off a shift at the ER. I started wondering if she felt like cooking after all the blood and guts she must have to deal with in her job. But then Barry had to deal with a lot of the same. It was hard for me to imagine how either of them dealt with their jobs and then just returned to normal life. Since they were on the same page, maybe they could be there for each other in a way that outsiders could not understand. I was so lost in thought, the butter started to sizzle before I thought to pour in the eggs. The actual cooking of the eggs took barely any time and I slid some for each of us on plates.

"Sherlock would be impressed," Dinah said from across the room.

"What did you find?" I asked, coming to join her at the table. I glanced out at the yard. The floodlights illuminated the row of orange trees. The white blossoms were just beginning to open. I realized I should have grabbed a couple of the oranges and sliced them for garnish.

"A lot," Dinah said. "That house is famous. I glossed over the stuff when it was the Beltron estate, though it is interesting that they considered it their second home and beach estate. Andrew Palmer and his first wife, Margo, kept up with the Beltron tradition of lavish parties. There are lots of photos." Dinah turned the laptop around so I could see.

I looked over Dinah's shoulder as she scrolled through some photos. I recognized some of the rooms, but the furnishings were different, though you could barely see them for all the people in the pictures.

Dinah moved to photos from a holiday party. The living room had a huge Christmas tree decorated to the hilt. I looked closely at the faces of the people around it. It was a candid shot and the people were holding cups of eggnog and were socializing. The first Mrs. Palmer was in the center of it. She was wearing a red cocktail-length dress and high heels to match. Her blond hair framed her face in the style of the day. "That's Andrew Palmer, a much younger Andrew Palmer," I said, pointing to the tall man whose hair was still dark. I tried to make out the faces of the people around them and noted some A-list stars.

"That's her," I said, excited as I pointed to a woman in tailored evening wear. "That's Daisy Cochran." Dinah leaned in closer to get a better view.

"Okay, now we make Sherlock proud and see what we can deduce from that," Dinah said.

"It's clearly from the time when Daisy was at the height of her power from the column. It looks to me like Daisy is in the middle of things."

Dinah looked at the pair again. "Look at the way Mrs. Palmer has her hand on Daisy's arm. It's a friendly gesture. Maybe they were actually friends." Dinah typed in something and more pictures of parties showed up, but the crowd was much sparser.

"No Andrew in these," Dinah said. "And by Margo's hairstyle, I'd say these were more recent."

"You don't have to do much deducing to figure that Andrew was the draw. Without him, she was just another ex-wife with a fancy house," I said.

We looked at more photos focusing on the house itself. "The house has eight thousand square feet." Dinah shook her head in disbelief. "Commander would have a field day turning off all the lights," my friend said with a laugh. "But seriously, that's a big place to live in alone. But then it seems the house was her claim to fame."

"And now it's Taylor's place," I said, thinking of how she had seemed so enamored with having the place. "Let's see what we can find out about Taylor." Dinah was in charge of the keyboard and typed in her name. A torrent of things came up and we skimmed through them before deciding which one to click on. We went for the stories connected to her wedding to Andrew Palmer. We stopped on a photo of them cutting the wedding cake. It was from six years prior and I was surprised at how different Taylor looked. She was model-thin now with cheekbones that looked almost sunken, but in the wedding her face was full and her bust seemed to be overflowing the white lace dress.

"I bet Sherlock would say she was pregnant," Dinah said, and I nodded before telling her what I'd heard about how Taylor had snared her husband. "It must have been a revolving door from his divorce to his wedding." Andrew was standing next to her. "If I didn't know better, I'd think he was the father of the bride walking her down the aisle," Dinah said. I had to agree.

We read more about her history prior to her marriage to Andrew. She had been a production assistant working on a film of his and apparently had managed to cozy up to him. "Enough so she got pregnant," Dinah said with a laugh.

"It's hard to believe that old ploy still works." I shook my head with disbelief. "It's surprising that such a powerful guy like him went for it."

"Back to what Sherlock would say," Dinah said, showing me yet another article. "Andrew seems to think of his children as his legacy. And men are so hooked on having a son. Once he heard she was having a boy, it probably locked the deal and he divorced the wife who he'd been married to for twenty years."

We had been neglecting our eggs and finally began to eat them as she told me about the latest hijinks her students were up to and mentioned again how there was one who made it all worthwhile.

Chapter Twenty-one

"I know what I said, but it's been long enough," Peter said in an irritated tone. "If there was anything to find, you should have found it by now. I'm running out of excuses why I can't give him an answer." Peter stopped and glanced out the front window at the street, where a couple was taking a Sunday morning stroll with a pair of large white dogs. "I have everything on hold until I lock in the money." He let out his breath and seemed conflicted. "But at the same time, I can't afford to have something come up about him once he's connected to me." We were sitting in my living room watching Marlowe roll around in the playpen. The dogs were spread around the room with Princess cuddled next to Peter. He was trying to appear indifferent, but I saw how tenderly he stroked the poodle mix.

"There's something I need to tell you," I said. I had not told Peter about Lily Langford hiring Adele for the kids' party, but finally broke the news to him. "I'm sorry." He sputtered like a shaken-up bottle of soda. Words came out in a jumble and his eyes closed.

"I thought you were going to make sure she didn't hire Adele," he said.

"What can I say? She liked the ridiculous idea I came up with and she's got a time problem."

I looked at my son as he considered what I had said. I could only imagine how much worse his reaction would be if he knew that not only had I talked to Barry, but he had confirmed that I was a person of interest in what happened to Daisy Cochran. Ignorance was definitely bliss in this circumstance.

"You have to go with her and make sure nothing goes wrong," Peter said, like it was a command. "Maybe I should just reject his investment now and see about finding someone else."

"You'd be in the same bind," I said, and Peter let out his breath as he realized I was right. "You don't have to worry, Adele has made me part of her party business and I will be there for Alexander's party."

"Alexander?" Peter said with a puzzled look, and I explained he was Lily and Miles's son. "Going back to Miles," I said. "Do you have a feeling in your gut that there's something hiding in his past?" I asked.

Peter let out a sigh. "He seems like another rich guy who wants to say he's in show business, but I don't know—that's why I got you into it. I thought the mommy group got you a perfect entry."

"You're right. They all gossip about each other, but so far the worst I've heard about Miles is that he's thin-skinned."

"It would help if you got an example of what they meant," Peter said.

"Did you know that Gabby and Taylor go back to the days they were both production assistants?" I said, changing the subject. Peter nodded like it was old news. "Do you know how she ended up married to Andrew Palmer?"

My son gave me a hopeless look. "I am not going to gossip with my mother," he said with a decisive shake of his head.

Everything got dropped then because more of the family joined us, ready to go. Peter had invited the whole crew to Sunday brunch as a thank-you for all the help with Marlowe. In the old days before his business exploded, it would have been to some fancy place where it would be good for him to be seen. The kind of place that Daisy had spent a lot of time at when her column was hot. But due to how many of us there were and his reduced circumstances, we were going to a café on Ventura Boulevard where you ordered at a counter and they brought you the food.

It took two cars to get us all there. Marlowe in her car seat and the whatnot bag of essentials we had to take along just in case took up the whole backseat of Peter's car. I didn't think much about the location until Peter was looking for a parking spot on a side street and I realized we were a block from Mason's house. The wood-paneled restaurant was busy and we took up the whole community table. My father got a high chair for Marlowe while Peter took over ordering for everybody.

The plan was he'd order a bunch of different dishes and we'd all share.

When I say he invited the whole crew, I meant everybody. My mother and her two She La Las backup singers, my father, Samuel and Beth, the babysitter who filled in when the rest of us weren't there. Though actually she seemed to stay on when my mother and the "girls" were practicing and my father would have been fine looking after Marlowe. It felt like Beth was adopting the family and I suspected that she and Samuel had a connection. I just hoped she didn't have any pets to leave behind. I was already up to my ears in family and at the legal limit for dogs.

The food came and was placed in the center of the table and we all got plates and started to help ourselves.

There was a lot of passing plates around and serving food to each other. The place was noisy and it was hard to say much more than *will you pass me the lemon ricotta pancakes*. I was holding out Marlowe's sippy cup of juice when I saw someone come in. There was no mistaking Mason, and since it was near his house, it made perfect sense why he would be there. I watched him go to the counter and pick up a to-go order. He had a great house that I'd been too many times. It was not one of the cookie-cutter white farmhouses. The dark brown wood exterior looked mysterious, but inside it was warm and comfortable, like Mason. Or at least how he used to be. The clerk packed the order in a big shopping bag and it was clearly for more than one. I let out a sigh. What did I expect? That he would stay alone forever? He was a catch. Nice-looking, fun, a successful lawyer at a big Century City firm. He loved animals. Even now, his toy fox terrier Spike was tucked in his arms as he reached for the shopping bag.

It was then that Peter noticed Mason and went over to talk to him. I knew Peter still had some contact with him, and why not. Mason had been great about helping my son pick up the pieces when the last production deal fell apart. Peter had been devastated. Who could blame him? He had a commitment for shows, had hired a whole crew and was ready to go into production when the bottom fell out because of the sexual misconduct of the creator, chief writer and star.

I knew Mason would look our way as soon as Peter met up with him. I stared down at my plate as if the lettuce garnish was the most fascinating thing on the planet. I stole a glance up after a moment and saw that Mason was heading toward the table. He and my parents had become quite chummy, which was why my mother still had not gotten over me breaking up with him. It made sense that he'd come over to talk to them and to see Marlowe. And when he looked at me there would be the stone face again. I couldn't take it and slipped away to the bathroom.

When I came back, he was gone and the family was passing around the platter of desserts that Mason had sent over. On top of all my other regrets, I realized that Mason probably knew about the Palmer house, and since he specialized in naughty celebrities, probably knew a lot about Daisy Cochran, too.

• • •

Seeing Mason again was still on my mind the next day and I was anxious for the Hookers to get together to tell Dinah about it. I knew she would understand my ducking out since she saw his reaction when we ran into him at the pet store. There were a number of conversations going on when I sat down and it all came across as a jumble of chatter. Dinah hadn't arrived yet. CeeCee was helping Elise fix her granny square striped blanket, which involved unraveling, as Elise had forgotten that she needed to alternate the two basic rows. Rhoda was pointing out the difference in the rows from her own work. Eduardo was talking to Sheila, who was showing him a piece she was working on. The mixture of blue, green and lavender was stunning as always. When she lifted it, I realized it was one of Lily Langford's cocoons.

I was going to compliment Sheila on the cocoon jacket, but Adele slid in next to me and demanded my attention. "Pink, uh, I mean

Molly, we have a problem." She flipped open a file and scanned a clipboard that was in it and immediately started sputtering complaints. "This isn't the one I need," she said, reading it over. "It's the new list of story-time kids. The names these parents choose. What happened to Bob and Barbara? Now it's all Ezekiel, Rance, Aire, East, Bertha." Her eyes went skyward and she reached around in the tote bag hanging on the back of the chair and pulled out another file. "The only thing you can say about those names is that there is only one kid per name." She put the right clipboard on the table. The heading said *Langford Birthday*. "That woman keeps calling with another change. I knew it was too good to be true that she went for your idea so quickly."

I wasn't surprised that Adele was ready to dump everything on me and I had actually expected it. Now that I'd gotten past trying to get Lily not to hire Adele, I had the new chore of making sure it was a success, and I asked about the changes. It wasn't so bad. Lily had rethought the menu. She nixed using common hot dogs and a grocery store sheet cake. The hot dogs had to be organic with a vegan option. She preferred a cake created out of cupcakes so that there could be different kinds to suit everyone. She wanted some to be gluten-free, sugar-free, and all the ingredients to be organic. She had questioned pin the tail on the donkey since it might foster cruelty to animals and wanted it changed to pin the hat on Blippi, the host of a popular kids show. The cups of ice cream had to be custom-made on-site with something that would work for everyone no matter their dietary issue. Dinah came in at the end of Adele's diatribe and looked at me.

"You could just opt out. It is her business," my friend said, pulling me aside.

"No, I can't. I promised Peter I would help her with it. He's worried about her making a mess of the party and somehow it coming out that I'm his mother who he asked to investigate his potential investor." Dinah winced at the thought of me being uncovered and I was about to delve into recounting the brunch when Mrs. Shedd came up to the table. She had a light in her eyes and seemed excited about something. She greeted everyone first and admired their work before zeroing in on me.

"I just talked to Leslie Bittner, Daisy Cochran's assistant and podcast producer, and she had a wonderful idea. We could do the *Were They Murders* podcasts live from here. It would draw people to the bookstore and get interest in the podcast." She looked over the group. "Of course, I said yes." She turned to me. "Since it comes under events, I'll leave it to you to make all the arrangements." She started to go and then turned back. "Mr. Royal and I will be leaving for our dance lessons." She did a little demonstration of the cha-cha and gushed that it was so much fun.

I was letting it all sink in when Samuel came up and grabbed my shoulder. "I'm sorry to do this." He had Marlowe in his arms and handed her to me with her whatnot bag. "I have to drive to Rancho Cucamonga for a gig. It's an important one." It took a moment to register and then I asked about Beth, the babysitter. He said she went home not feeling well. My mother and the girls were performing at a charity luncheon and my father was acting as their roadie. "I'll just call Peter," I said, shifting Marlowe so I could get to my phone, but Samuel shook his head.

"I tried that," my younger son said. "He's in a meeting." Samuel's voice dropped before he continued. "With Mason." He gave Marlowe a snuggle and backed away. "Got to go."

I put her on my lap and was considering my options when CeeCee leaned in to me, ignoring that I was holding an eight-month-old. "I know I said I wouldn't host the podcast, but having it here and live makes it all different. Maybe I should do it. I'd look contemporary and have an audience. You have to talk to that woman and tell her I'll do it before she finds someone else."

I held back a laugh at her self-absorption. Rhoda came and took Marlowe from my arms and walked around playing peek-a-boo with her. But when Marlowe got squirmy, she handed her back to me.

Needless to say, I never got to tell Dinah about Mason, or spend any time crocheting. I took Marlowe to my cubicle and let her loose while I called Daisy's assistant and pitched her CeeCee's change of heart.

A meeting between them was set up for the next day.

• • •

Even if CeeCee hadn't demanded my presence, I would have wanted to go along since it involved the bookstore, despite it being my day off. We met at Daisy's condo, which had also been her office. It was located in Encino and surrounded by beautiful grounds with lots of trees. I glanced around the interior as we went in. The walls were lined with photos from Daisy's glory days. She was in all of them with an assortment of famous people, movie sets and award ceremonies. The furniture was off-white and the only color came from some red-toned oriental rugs.

Leslie did not seem concerned that I'd come with CeeCee. "I'm using this place while I straighten everything out with Daisy's affairs." She took us into the dining room and invited us to sit at the table. "I've turned this into my office," Leslie said. "By the way, I don't want to be referred to as Daisy's assistant anymore. My title is podcast producer. I was thinking I'd do the podcast from here before I came up with doing it live from the bookstore." She looked at CeeCee. "So, you changed your mind. I already have several other people who are interested. You're going to have to convince me why I should choose you."

I didn't want to listen to her making CeeCee squirm. I knew that I would end up jumping in and try to smooth it all over. It was really up to the two of them. I walked back into the living room and checked the view out the front window at the trees and grass. It looked so bucolic; it was hard to imagine that Ventura Boulevard was on the other side of all the greenery. Peter had been pushing me to move to a condo before it had become convenient for him that I had the big house. I had never thought about it seriously, but if I had, I would have considered a place like this.

I was curious about the kitchen and went to have a look. It was better than I expected and open to the den area with a breakfast bar separating the two spaces. There were a few dishes sitting in the sink along with a long, serrated knife just like one I had. It was great for cutting bread and watermelons. They were not supposed to be left soaking that way. I'd probably never get a thank-you for it, but I pulled it from the sink and was wiping the blade off with a paper towel when I was startled by something brushing against my ankle and the knife slipped out of my hand and fell on the counter.

When I looked down, a tan and white long-haired cat was working its way around my legs. Its fur felt silky as I gave its back a stroke, and when I stopped the petting, it rubbed against my leg again and began to meow. I gave it a few more strokes, thinking that's what the meows were about, but then the cat started to walk down the hall, meowing as it went. I knew enough about animals to recognize that the cat was telling me it wanted something. I followed it down the hall and into a bedroom that Daisy must have used as her office and apparently a cat feeding station as well. The bowl had a few crumbs of dry food and the water bowl was empty.

"You poor kitty," I said. "You must have belonged to Daisy and now she's gone." The water bowl was easy to take care of in the bathroom, and then I looked around the room for a bag of dry food. The cat food was in a drawer of the desk, and as I pulled out the bag I saw a folder marked *Podcasts*. I tucked it under my arm as I filled the bowl with the dry morsels. The cat immediately started noisily chewing after lapping up a lot of water.

Now that I'd seen the podcast folder, I couldn't ignore it. Since I was getting dragged into it, it seemed like it would be okay to have a look. As I thumbed through the pages inside the folder, I realized these were the infamous notes that Leslie had been looking for on the computer. How funny that it hadn't occurred to her to look for written ones. The first page had a heading that said *Case 1. The House.*

The cat jumped on the desk wanting attention and I knew that at any moment Leslie might come looking for me. I used my phone to capture images of the pages, and as a concession to her left the folder on the desk where she would be likely to find it. Then I slipped back into the living room just in time as I could tell that their conversation was winding down. The cat had followed me and was at my side when the two women walked in from the dining room.

"I'll let you know," Leslie said, clearly enjoying having the upper hand with the well-known actress.

I could see that CeeCee was perturbed but knew how to hold it in. I was going to get an earful when we got in the car. As we started to leave, the cat walked with us.

"You better keep an eye on him or her," I said, "or it will try to go out with us."

Leslie shrugged indifferently. "So what. I'm going to take it to the pound anyway."

I looked at her, horrified. "You can't," I said. "That poor cat will wonder what happened and why it's in a concrete enclosure."

She shrugged again and I got it. She didn't care. "I'm not an animal person," she said finally.

"Then you don't mind if I take the cat," I said. I admit to not thinking it through, but it was an emergency and what difference would one more cat make?

"Be my guest."

"I certainly will." I asked if there was a carrier and Leslie went off to find it.

She came back with the carrier and the bowls and bag of food. "If you want the litter box, it's on you to get it," she said.

I assured her I already had one and packed up the cat, only asking what its name was.

"It's a she and her name is Buttercup," she said, barely giving the cat a glance.

Chapter Twenty-two

Dinah and I decided to end my day off with a girls' night out and met for a late dinner at an Israeli restaurant that stayed open late. I had left her hanging at the Hookers meeting the previous day and she wanted to hear all. We sat outside on the patio area next to a heater for comfort. Being outside made us feel freer to talk without regard for being overheard.

There was so much to talk about that telling her about Mason's appearance seemed like old news and something to be left for later.

"I'm going to tell you some observations," I began. "And then we can play the Sherlock game and see what we think it means."

Dinah sat upright in her chair, eager to hear what I was going to say. I went back to the Hooker meeting and Mrs. Shedd's arrival with the news about the live podcast.

"That was sure dumped on you," Dinah said.

"It's an event and that's my job, so not really dumped. But there's so much more," I said, and Dinah gave me back the floor. "You know that when CeeCee heard there was going to be a live audience, she changed her mind and wants to host the podcast." Dinah looked to say something, and I rushed and said that CeeCee's change of mind wasn't the point and brought up the meeting I had arranged for them and which I'd gone to.

"The meeting was at Daisy's condo in Encino. I think Leslie worked out of the condo when Daisy was alive, but now it feels like she's living there, too. Her demeanor has definitely changed. She made it clear she didn't want to be known as Daisy's assistant anymore, now that she has anointed herself as the producer of the podcast. She seemed on a real power trip. It made me uncomfortable the way she was making CeeCee squirm." Dinah was listening with rapt attention as the server brought the plate of silky hummus and the freshly baked chewy flat bread. We took a pause in the conversation and both pulled off some of the bread and dipped it in the hummus. It was amazing how they'd turned lowly chickpeas into such a fabulous dish.

I explained that it was uncomfortable for me to listen to my fellow crocheter be treated like a bug on a pin and I was afraid I'd say something, so had left the room. I mentioned the hungry cat and how she had led me to Daisy's office.

"I saw the notes Daisy had left." I mentioned how they were handwritten rather than on the computer, where Leslie seemed to be looking.

"Handwritten notes, that is old-school," Dinah said.

"I just really saw the first page. The title was the House or something like that. I stopped to pull off another strip of the bread and had some more of the appetizer.

"What about the cat?" Dinah said. "Tell me you didn't leave it there."

"How could I? It was the pound or die from dehydration. Buttercup has her own part of my house when I'm not home until she acclimates. Sherlock would probably say that I'm a crazy cat lady," I said with a laugh. Then I corrected myself. "Sherlock would say crazy pet lady since there are actually more dogs than cats."

"I think Sherlock would say you were softhearted and couldn't abandon that cat to a horrible fate." Dinah took another bite of the bread as she seemed to be thinking over what I'd said. "I would deduce that Leslie was glad to have Daisy out of the way, and seeing that she was there when Daisy died, could have made it happen."

"And she could have been the one who put the note on my car," I said. Dinah looked perplexed and I realized there was even more that I had not told her. I detailed what the note said. "I thought it might have been from Garth since he'd been at the bookstore earlier, but now I think it came from Leslie. Rick Carlson has implied the smoothie was tampered with. Would anyone have noticed if Daisy's assistant hovered over the drink?" I said. "I know that it had a lid and a straw in it when I left it, but was without the lid and straw when Daisy drank it. Leslie has been around the bookstore enough to have overheard something about me poking around in what happened to Daisy," I said with a shrug. It was impossible to tell her about finding the note without mentioning Barry acting like a stalker and we got sidetracked again as I told her about Carol. "They seem perfect for each other."

Dinah smiled at me. "You sound like you really mean it."

"I guess I do." Then I told her about Mason and the brunch.

• • •

Garth was only partially off the hook about the note. I hoped I might find out for sure either way during the next mommy group meetup at his house. He'd prepared me for it not to be as opulent as Taylor's mansion or as trendy as Lily's fake farmhouse and I was curious what his place would look like.

Gabby had sent me a text asking how her daughter was. Even without a request from her, I had been sending her updates and pictures of Marlowe, but had been too busy dealing with everything, including Marlowe, to remember to text her recently. I sent her a photo and a text back that Marlowe was enjoying the mommy group.

Garth was right about his house being different from the other two I had seen. It was in Woodland Hills in a section that still felt a little rural. The lots were big and full of wild foliage rather than lawns, or even the planned drought-resistant replacements for the lawns. Bushes along the wrought iron fence hid his yard until I walked in the gate. I had the feeling that I had walked into a magical sort of space. There were patches of grass with some flowers and a pond with lily pads and fish swimming around. Several wooden Adirondack chairs were arranged near a firepit. A number of tall old trees shaded the whole area. A brick walkway led to the house. The house was a wood-frame ranch house shaped like an L and was surrounded by bushes, which gave it a hint of mystery. The door was open and I wheeled Marlowe in, calling out hello. A voice directed me to come to the den. Garth greeted me and pointed to the backyard, which seemed like a children's delight. An elaborate playground set was next to a sandbox and water table. He explained his sister was doing the honors with the kids. I handed over Marlowe and went back inside. I was the first arrival and Garth invited me to get something to drink while we waited for the others. The eat-in kitchen was big and rambling with wood-paneled walls and a built-in table. The window that looked out on the yard had stained glass accents. Another window looked out on a side yard that had a kitchen garden. The place looked lived in and as if a lot of good times had been had there. He had coffee, water and juice set up, along with grocery store bagels and plain cream cheese.

The two nannies showed up together and offered their employers' apologies, saying as they had before that next time the parents would come with the kids. Once they'd walked their charges outside, they took a seat in the corner of the den and pulled out their phones.

Lily came in and did a model-style swirl to show off yet another model of her cocoon wrap. She described the mixture of fibers. Without missing a beat, she started to talk to me. "Your Hooker friend is amazing. I love the cocoons we have been making, but the ones that I've commissioned her to make are a higher level. They're one-of-a-kind and handmade. Our Malibu customers will snatch them up as fast as she can turn them out."

Taylor came in, filling the area with the scent of her floral perfume. She looked around the smaller house in a dismissive manner and then became effusive about the unique cocoon wraps and how she had to have one. Lily was acting as the middle man and I stayed out of it.

Kath was the last arrival. She seemed a little disorganized and took Plum out to join the other kids. Garth offered the drinks and she half-heartedly took a glass of juice and looked at it as if she wished it was something else. "Channel 3 is doing a story on the Belle Visage clinics. It's their consumer reporter and he's interviewing some unhappy clients." She let out a sigh. "Luckily, no one famous or we'd really be in trouble." She turned to Garth. "We're having our lawyers go over the script you wrote for our infomercial." She looked at the rest of us. "You have to be so careful what you say or it will come back to bite you."

Garth assured her that he'd be happy to make any changes necessary. "Writing is rewriting until the client is happy."

"Speaking of writing," Taylor said. "I talked to Andrew about you. He's setting up a meeting about a book they optioned for a streaming series."

Garth folded his hands prayer-style and bowed his head. "A most grateful thank you." So Garth was right when he said to me that the group was about networking for him.

It had been more of an accident than a plan, but I had done my own networking helping Adele get the birthday party. The only ones who seemed to be missing out on working the group were the two nannies.

A cat walked in the room and stopped in the middle, looking at all of us. It had the same tan and white markings as Buttercup, but its fur was short. Garth snatched the cat up and apologized. "She's supposed to stay in my writing room when we have company."

When he returned, I mentioned the new cat at my house with the story how she'd ended up there. "Daisy's assistant seems to have one-upped what Daisy had planned. It's lucky that Leslie isn't here to hear me call her that," I said with a groan. "She wants to be referred to as the podcast producer now. She's taking it to a whole new level and is going to do it live from the bookstore now." Since they only seemed vaguely interested, I didn't go into the matter that Leslie was still struggling with the content of *Were They Murders.*

"Is it too early for wine?" Kath asked, changing the subject.

I left Garth's not any closer to knowing if he'd been the one to leave the note, or getting an example of Miles's thin skin. But on a plus point, it gave me hope that having them come to a special story-time with some treats from the café would be acceptable. I didn't know why I cared since I was a stand-in, but I was representing Marlowe. I had gotten Adele to agree to it, convincing her it was a chance to pitch her party business, but now that she had been hired for the one party, she was less enthused and I was worried she would try to back out.

As soon as I got back to the bookstore, I snagged a red-eye from the café and went to the children's department to talk to Adele about the planned mommy group story-time. The dark blue carpeting with the cows jumping over the moon always made me smile.

Adele was standing at the entrance with her clipboard, dressed in her favorite version of the queen costume. The silver crown was crocheted out of a thread and then starched to death to keep its stiff shape. The decoration around the low-cut bodice was all done in fun fur that tended to shed. Adele said it was like leaving a trail of fairy dust. She didn't seem concerned it was a pain to clean up. She gave me a roll of her eyes as I approached. "Whatever it is will have to wait," she said in her queenly voice. "I have to check in the story-time arrivals."

When I looked back across the bookstore there was a straggly line of adults with kids in tow headed our way. "It'll just take a moment," I said, not letting her dismiss me.

A woman in yoga pants with two kids in tow stopped in front of us. "This is Phyliss and Ryder." Adele checked her clipboard to make sure they were members of her story-time crew. As soon as Adele gave the woman a nod and looked at the kids, the little girl curtseyed and the little boy bowed before they ran inside and the mother headed off.

Adele had them bowing to her now, I thought, choking back a laugh. It was clear my coworker wasn't going to talk to me, but I couldn't tear myself away and had to watch as more kids arrived.

Adele glowered when one little boy started to run in without a bow in greeting first. "What are you supposed to do first, Rance?" Adele said. The little boy froze and stuck out his tongue at Adele and ran into the area carpeted with the cows and moons without looking back.

The mother apologized to Adele as she turned to go. "It's been a tough time for us and he's acting out."

I might have wanted to watch, but Adele wanted me gone and finally asked what I wanted while giving her version of a queenly glance to a pair of customers who passed by on their way to the romance section.

I brought up the story-time plan and she reacted as I feared. "Now that we have our first party set up, why should I do that?" she said.

"Because you still need my help to pull off the party," I said. She acted as if she hadn't heard me as a little girl wearing a princess costume stopped in front of Adele and curtseyed.

I shook my head in disbelief as I walked away. Adele continued to outdo herself.

Mrs. Shedd and Mr. Royal had gone off for an early lunch at a Brazilian restaurant with a fabulous lunch buffet, and I made the rounds to make sure everything was okay before I took my now lukewarm coffee to the yarn department. I needed a little crochet time to release my hunched-up shoulders. I definitely understood now why my fellow Hooker Sheila carried her emergency crochet kit everywhere. *Kit* was a stretch as it was just a hook and a small ball of string. I thought about doing what Sheila did to release tension and started to make a long row of chain stitches, not caring if they were wobbly since they would only be temporary. I started back over them, making single crochets as I felt the tension release. I chuckled to myself as I unraveled the whole thing, glad that Elise wasn't there or she would want to create kits and sell them at the bookstore. Though I had to admit that it wasn't a bad idea.

I moved on to working on the granny square stripes. I let out a happy sigh as my shoulders relaxed even more. If only it had lasted.

"There you are," CeeCee said in an upset tone. Ever the actress used to being in the public eye, she didn't look the way she sounded. Her blondish hair was nicely done in her ageless style and her burgundy velour tracksuit was casual yet made her look together.

I had just finished a row and the last of my cold coffee, and was about to go back to my cubicle. I invited CeeCee to sit and she slid into her usual chair at the head of the table. Since she sounded like there was a problem, I skipped over the small talk and asked her what was wrong.

"That woman was so disagreeable," she said. "She should have been thrilled that someone of my stature would be interested in doing that podcast. And then not to get back to me when she said she would." CeeCee looked at me directly. "You seem to be in touch with her. Did she go with someone else?"

It was clear she was talking about Leslie Bittner, and after our last visit with her I definitely went along with the description of her being disagreeable or worse. Her horrible mistreatment of Daisy's cat was enough reason. The poor cat was so traumatized that she had attached herself to me since I had brought her to my house.

"I don't know," I said. "Do you want me to call her?" There was no reason for me to feel responsible for the situation, but I did. CeeCee trailed me as I went to my cubicle to get her contact information. She was hanging over me as I put in the number.

I expected it to go to voice mail since nobody seemed to answer their phone anymore and was surprised when it was answered after only a few rings, and more surprised by the male voice.

"I'd like to speak to Leslie," I said in my business voice.

"Who's calling?" the man said. I gave my name, which didn't seem to satisfy him, and he asked more questions about my connection to her and what the call was regarding. I'd had enough of his grilling and simply said that she knew me and asked to speak with her again.

"That won't be possible," the man said. "I'm afraid she's dead."

Chapter Twenty-three

I had hoped to get some details from the man on the phone, but once he'd said that Leslie was dead, he hung up. His voice had been loud enough that CeeCee heard it all. Her eyes were wide with upset when she looked at me. "Oh, no, dear, now I regret the unkind things I said about her."

"My thoughts were worse," I said and brought up the cat. "At least now you have closure about the podcast. She didn't go with someone else. I guess after this, the whole thing will really be dead for good now." I cringed at my word choice and thought about breaking the news to Mrs. Shedd.

"Yes, dear, I think that is a safe estimation." CeeCee put her purse on her shoulder and exited the cubicle and went to the door.

I needed another red-eye after that. I was in the café when Dinah came in. "I was looking for you. I hoped we could get coffee," she said brightly. "I guess we can." She looked at the mug that Bob had pushed toward me. She glanced up at my face and when she saw my expression, knew there was something wrong. "What happened?"

Bob asked if she wanted her regular café au lait and said he'd bring it to her. The two of us took the table in the corner that we favored. I waited until we sat to drop the news about Leslie.

"The way she was acting and how she'd taken over the podcast and the fact that she was there when Daisy died," I said, shaking my head. "I was hoping to find a way to get the heat off of me by putting it on her."

"How did Leslie die?" Dinah asked and I shrugged. "You do know who would know, though."

I let out my breath. She was right. I did know who would know, and since it was hardly personal, it didn't break any rules of our forever breakup that I had set up in my mind. It seemed even more okay if I made the call with Dinah across the table.

I had never taken his number out of my phone and clicked on it.

Unlike most people these days, Barry did answer his phone most of the time. "Greenberg," he said in his cop voice. For a moment, I considered hanging up, but it was pointless because if he checked his phone, my number would be at the top of the list of calls.

"This isn't a personal call," I said finally.

"Okay," he said in a slightly less formal voice and waited for me to continue. I explained my call to Leslie Bittner and what had been dropped on me.

"A man said she was dead with no details." This time I left it open for him to say something.

"So you're calling me for information," he said in an amused tone. I heard him let out his breath. "I suppose I could still do that." He stopped for a moment. "About the other night. I wasn't stalking you. I would have done the same thing for a stranger if I thought they were in danger."

"Okay, fine," I said. "You were about to tell me about Leslie Bittner."

"She was stabbed and the place was tossed. Could be an interrupted burglary. You probably talked to a cop," he said.

"Any suspects?" I asked, and he laughed.

"That goes beyond my rules of our after-the-breakup relationship. Got to go." There was no sound on cell phones when someone hung up, but I knew he had.

Dinah was pouring coffee and steamed milk in her cup. "That wasn't so bad," she said.

"I guess not," I said with a shrug. "At least I found out what happened."

• • •

I was back in the yarn department getting ready for the Hookers afternoon get-together when Mrs. Shedd came into the area at the back of the store accompanied by a man walking a step behind her. She seemed a little uncomfortable as she pointed me out. I already had a sinking feeling about it, and her announcing his identity was unnecessary.

"This detective said he wants to talk to you." She made a hasty exit and left me with him.

"I just wanted to ask you a few questions about something that came up," Rick Carlson said. "You want to grab a cup of coffee? I don't know about you, but I get a four o'clock slump." An outsider would have thought it was a friendly offer, but I wasn't falling for it and stayed on guard. He suggested we go to the café and the truth was even with all the red-eyes, I did have a four o'clock slump and needed some more caffeine.

He led the way and invited me to sit while he ordered. He was not being bland and cop-like, but had an expression on his face. He came to the table with coffee and several of Bob's most popular item, the chocolate chip cookie bars.

"I'm tasked with this job a lot," he said, pouring some cream in his coffee. "There's never a good way to say it." He looked at me. "I don't know how well you knew Daisy Cochran's assistant Leslie Bittner, but she's deceased."

"How terrible. What happened?" I said, pretending to be surprised.

"But then you already knew that," he said. "An officer noted that you called."

I fumbled around trying to cover myself. "It was just such a shock that I'm still in disbelief."

I couldn't tell if what I said pacified him, but he continued on. "Of course, we're still investigating Daisy Cochran's death. You know that once someone has killed one person and crossed that threshold, it's easier a second time around." He glanced up at me and looked me in the eye. "There's some debate about what exactly happened to Leslie Bittner. It could have been a burglary gone wrong. The condo belonged to Daisy Cochran and it wouldn't be the first time a deceased person's place was ransacked, but it also wouldn't be the first time a murder was made to look like a burglary. I was just wondering if you had any thoughts," he said.

"I barely knew Daisy Cochran and her assistant even less."

"Really?" he said, peering at me. "One of the neighbors remembered seeing two women leaving the residence carrying a box. They recognized one of the people as CeeCee Collins, who was there the night that Daisy Cochran died, and the other one sounded a lot like you." He peered at me.

"Was it you?" he asked. I saw where he was going and I didn't like it. The whole spiel about a second killing being easier once you had done the first one. And me leaving with a box of something. I wanted to tell him what was actually in the box, but then he'd probably twist it and think I'd killed Leslie so I could steal her cat. I felt a pressure to answer his question and I was stuck as to what to do, but then I remembered something I'd done before.

"Did they say which day they saw the two women?" I said finally. I had learned it was a cop trick to answer a question with a question. He did not look pleased. Barry had told me that cops liked to be the ones to ask the questions. It was information in for them, not out.

"What difference does that make?" he asked with a flash of annoyance. So much for his friendly approach, and so much for me being cooperative. I decided to exercise my other option.

"I really don't think I can help you," I said, and got up and left. I hoped I sounded more confident than I felt. It seemed the same as taking the fifth or asking for an attorney—moves that made you look guilty. I did not look back as I walked away, and I knew he would be back.

The first thing I did was call CeeCee and let her know what Detective Carlson had said. She squealed, upset. "I can't be a murder suspect. I want to be known as an Academy Award–nominated actor who leads a crochet group, not prisoner number 249. It doesn't matter if you're famous anymore, they'll ship you off to jail anyway. I'm calling an attorney before that detective shows up at my door." She didn't say who the attorney was, but I knew exactly. She was going to call Mason Fields.

I certainly couldn't call him. With the way he had looked at me, I was sure he hoped they would cart me off to jail. My only option was to find out who killed Leslie, who I bet also killed Daisy. All while taking care of everything else, including breaking the news about the podcast to Mrs. Shedd.

Chapter Twenty-Four

It was two days later and I was back in the yarn department cleaning up the mess made by a bunch of try-before-you-buyers, and worse still they were knitters. I had told Mrs. Shedd about Leslie's demise and with it the podcast. She had taken it better than expected and I was feeling relieved until she said that just because that podcast hadn't worked out, there was no reason to give up on the whole thing and floated the idea of the bookstore doing their own. She thought it was an event and therefore something for me to handle.

This group of knitters had really taken trying the different yarns to the hilt. There were skeins all over the table with strands that had been pulled out and knitted in swatches. I wanted to get all the stitches pulled out and the skeins rewound before the Hookers got there.

I was focused on what I was doing until a noise startled me. "Psst." I looked out into the bookstore to see where the hissing sound meant to get my attention was coming from, but saw no one and went back to what I was doing. I heard another *psst*. This time it sounder even louder and more insistent. I stared out into the area of bookshelves with a sprinkling of easy chairs and display tables. This time I saw an arm sticking out from behind the bookcase devoted to cookbooks. The hand waved me over. I hesitated for a moment, wondering if it was such a wise idea to follow the beckoning of a disembodied hand, considering how things were going.

But curiosity won out and I walked out of the yarn department to the cookbook shelves. When I was close enough the hand grabbed my arm and pulled me into the dark space between the bookcases devoted to cookbooks and the one behind it filled with diet books. It wasn't my idea to arrange them that way, but whoever did either had a sense of humor or figured they all had to do with food.

An overhead light must have burned out because the opening between the one-sided bookcases was fairly dark and the space felt narrow. It took a few moments for my eyes to adjust and then I felt a little claustrophobic.

"CeeCee?" I said, surprised to see who the hand belonged to. She was dressed in a dark velour tracksuit and almost blended in with the darkness. "What's with all the cloak-and-dagger?"

"You have to ask?" She sounded indignant. "Any minute that detective is going to show up and want to grill me," she said, shaking her head with concern. "I rue the day I let myself get involved with that unpleasant woman. I wanted to host a crime podcast, not be the subject of one."

"I'm sorry I let you get involved," I said, giving her a hug. "We know we didn't do it, and what evidence could they have to say we did?"

"You're right. You said she was stabbed." The actress let out a squeal. "How up-close and personal. It's certainly not how I'd kill somebody," CeeCee said. "I'd use poison." She froze. "What am I saying. Isn't that what happened to Daisy?" She looked around in a panic, worried that someone might have heard her.

I was going to try to calm her, but then I had a sinking feeling as I remembered something. I had gotten so distracted with taking care of the cat, I had forgotten all about rescuing the knife from the sink. I had wiped the blade with a paper towel, but my fingerprints had to be all over the handle. I tried to calm myself by thinking there was nothing to say that it was the murder weapon anyway. Wouldn't the killer have come equipped with their own?

"Why are you being so quiet?" CeeCee said. "Is there something I don't know?"

"No. I just thought about something with the cat." The knife didn't involve her anyway. The fingerprints would be all mine.

"Right after I talked to you, I called Mason Fields," she said. I felt my stomach clench at the mention of his name. I could only imagine what he had to say about me. "He told me that as long as the police weren't trying to question me, there was nothing for him to do. He was very reassuring and told me not to worry. As soon as he heard you were involved, he said that you'd figure a way to get us out of trouble."

"He said that?" Here I was expecting him to trash me and he'd expressed confidence in my abilities. I'm not a crier, but I felt my eyes well up in remorse, regret and . . . I couldn't think of something else that started with an *R* that would have completed the thought.

I finally got her to come out of hiding and join me in the yarn department. She was glad to help me clean up the balls of yarn, and by the time the group got there, the table was clear.

She showed off what a good actress she was during the time the group met. She seemed her normal self and spent the time making normal conversation. I told Sheila that Lily seemed thrilled with the idea of hand-knitted cocoons. Adele looked up at the word *knitted* and it seemed like her nostrils flared. If anyone brought up knitting it was like waving a red cape in front of a bull. I was glad that CeeCee stepped in and got Adele onto something else.

"How is your party business coming, dear?" CeeCee said in a friendly voice.

It might not have been the best choice as Adele still had a stormy expression, which seemed at odds with the black sweater decorated with crocheted sunflowers. If there was such a thing as a happy flower, it was the sunflower. Even the crocheted version made me smile.

"I shouldn't have gone with your idea—" There was a pause before she added, "Molly." She still seemed to be having a hard time saying my first name, but it was becoming a little more natural and she was slipping up less. "That woman keeps changing everything, except what she'll pay. She's got the successful business selling those cocoons for ridiculous prices and her husband is rolling in cash from his family's business and she's trying to stick to the price I gave her based on our original proposal. Everything she's demanding costs more. But she doesn't want to pay more." Adele seemed to deflate. "She knows it's the first party I'm doing and that I can use doing her party as a reference."

"It's not the price that attracted her to Adele's business," I said. "It was the idea that she would be doing something original, be a leader instead of a follower, and the time factor. That couple is so concerned with what people think of them. But then so is Taylor Palmer. She goes on every time about that house."

"It is a historic house with lots of stories connected to it," Dinah said.

"I'd love to get a listing for a place like that," Elise said. "I think I'll do a little research." Looks were deceiving when it came to Elise. Her bird-like voice and wisp of brownish hair made her seem like her mind was somewhere else, when really she was always on point.

"When I hear about a house like that, all I can think about is that I'm glad I don't have to clean it," Rhoda said. Eduardo was silent for most of the time, only asking the group what they thought of making fondue a theme for the restaurant he had in the works.

The group broke up and CeeCee hung back. As soon as it was just the two of us, she reverted to a look of worry and I had to reassure her that she wasn't going to end up being prisoner 249.

Dinah and I had already arranged to get together. Beth was trying to make up for her early exit the other night and offered to take care of Marlowe, free of charge. I think it had something to do with Samuel being there as well. He had said she was someone who worked at the coffee place when he pitched her as a babysitter, but I had sensed all along there was something more.

I made a pit stop at home to make sure everything was going as planned. Samuel and Beth were in the living room with plates of food. Peter was in the kitchen making himself a plate and Marlowe was cruising around the living room in the seat she propelled with her feet.

Everything seemed peaceful and I was relieved that neither of my sons had any idea I was a person of interest in another murder.

I picked up a pizza from Paoli's on the way to Dinah's. She lifted the lid of the box and took a deep inhale of the pizza scent. "Good. You got the half alfredo and half traditional cheese," she said, shutting the box and taking it from me. She led the way to her she-cave. I was surprised to see Commander sitting in one of the chairs. He looked up when I walked in and smiled. "I hope you don't mind if I join you."

Dinah gave me a helpless shrug, as if she wasn't sure how she felt about his being there. She appreciated the effort he was making to stay up, but not so sure about him being included in our girl time. "It's fine with me. There's plenty of pizza," I said.

He went off to get some plates and Dinah pulled me aside. "I love that he's trying to stay up, but this is our time and you said you have a lot to tell me." Her voice dropped and she seemed to be having an inner conversation with herself. "But how can I not let him stay when he's trying so hard?"

I got it. Despite him being a day person and her being a night owl, she didn't regret marrying him. She focused on what made him dear to her. As in the way he used his Mail It center as more than a place to have a post office box or to deal with shipping a package. In addition to realizing that a lot of his customers worked from their homes and arranging events to get them together, he also volunteered at a retirement place and arranged fun night activities. As long as everything ended by eight, he was good.

He was holding back a yawn as he came back with the plates. I wasn't about to start talking about Daisy and Leslie's deaths and Detective Carlson's treating me like a person of a lot of interest, but it seemed okay to talk about the job Peter had given me. I explained the situation to Commander, adding that Peter was getting pressure from Miles Langford to make a decision about accepting his investment in the project Peter was putting together. "If Peter accepts the money, Miles will get an executive producer credit." I explained the situation with Miles and his brothers and how he was trying to make his own way and gather producer credits, and that I hadn't had much to pass on to Peter about Miles other than he and his wife appeared to have paid big bucks for an imitation farmhouse that had clones all over Encino and Tarzana.

"Maybe he is what he appears," Commander said. "There are people who don't have dark secrets hidden away. I can understand Peter's concern, though. I have to be sure who I rent post office boxes to. I don't want to be connected to someone using a post office box to run an illegal business." Commander asked what else Miles had worked on and Dinah told him about the western.

"A western, huh, I haven't seen one of those in a long time," Commander said. He had picked up the remote and asked for the exact name of it. A moment later, the opening scene appeared on the screen. Dinah and I traded glances and shrugged as he looked at the screen with interest. As the movie continued, we both kept stealing glances at him, expecting that the carbs in the pizza and the lull of the TV would send him off to dreamland, but he was alert until the end and insisted on keeping it on until the final closing credit. Then he stopped it and got up, yawning and stretching.

"I did it," he said triumphantly. "It's ten o'clock and I'm still awake." He collected the pizza plates. "But I reached my limit. If you'll excuse me, my pillow awaits." He leaned down and kissed Dinah and left the room.

She watched him go. "What a sweetheart." Then she turned to me. "Now spill."

It felt like I'd popped a cork on a champagne bottle as I told her everything about the detective's visit and the neighbor who had seen me and CeeCee leaving Daisy's condo carrying a box. "And what's worse, I realized that my fingerprints are on a knife." I told her that I'd been trying to save the knife from getting ruined by sitting in water and taken it out of the sink and wiped it off.

"Did the detective say anything about the knife?" my friend asked.

"No. He just asked questions and threw out that we had been seen leaving the place. The only reason I knew she had been stabbed was that Barry told me." I took a moment to think back to Carlson's visit. "He did imply that there was a connection between Daisy's death and Leslie's and done by the same person that just might be me."

"We know it wasn't you. Any ideas of who it really was?" Dinah asked.

"I think it's connected to the podcast," I said. "Leslie had made it sound as if Daisy had left an outline for some of the shows. Though all I saw were some notes that seemed pretty vague."

"What was in them?" Dinah asked.

"I was distracted with the cat and concerned about getting caught. All I remember was a heading for the first case. I think it said something like house or home." I strained to remember the rest and came up blank. "Barry said the place was ransacked. You can bet those notes are gone now. If it's all about information that was going to be divulged in the podcast, whoever did it feels safe now."

Dinah nodded and offered me a cup of tea. "I had to tell CeeCee about what the cop said. He pointed out that she had been there when Daisy died and was seen leaving Leslie's place. Poor CeeCee came unglued. She was going on about celebrities going to jail. She rushed and called a lawyer."

"A lawyer? Who?" Dinah said, pouring herself a cup of tea.

"Who else? She called Mason." I felt myself blushing when I remembered the rest of it. "You won't believe what he said."

Dinah put down the cup and gave me her full attention. "He said something nice about me. He told her something like I would take care of getting her out of trouble."

"Wow," Dinah said.

"But you were there at the pet store. You saw how he looked at me. He still probably hates my guts personally. Though it's nice that he recognizes my skill. Or maybe he was just trying to make CeeCee feel better." I drank the rest of the tea and set down the empty cup. "Time to call it a night."

I wanted to help her clean up, but she said she would take care of it.

The menagerie was waiting for me when I got home. I let the dogs out, and after greeting me Mr. Kitty and Cat Woman, as we'd come to call the two cats, went off into another room. Buttercup stuck close to me as I went into the living room. Samuel and Beth were watching TV in the den and Marlowe was asleep nearby in the portable crib. I transferred the baby to the crib in my room and got ready for sleep myself.

I was just settling in when the phone rang. It was Dinah with some startling news.

Chapter Twenty-five

"I'm sorry I didn't think of this before," Dinah said. I was in her office in the English Department of Beasley Community College waiting for her star student. Dinah explained to me that after I had left her the night before, she'd decided to watch the late news. The TV was still paused on the very last credits of the western, which turned out to be an *in memoriam* for someone named Billy Erickson. She had tried to turn it off and had hit the wrong button on the remote, and the credits started going backward. While she was trying to stop it, she recognized the name of her star student and recalled that she had written her extra-credit paper on working as a production assistant on a movie.

"I didn't pay attention at the time since I didn't recognize the name of the film. What a surprise when I realized she worked on the movie Peter's money guy was one of the executive producers for," Dinah said.

"It's perfect timing. She was coming in to meet me anyway," my friend added. "She wants to get into a special class and needs my recommendation." She looked at the door to make sure it was still closed. "I'll introduce you and then I'll pretend to get a phone call I have to take and leave the room."

I got it. I'd have a few minutes to see what her student knew about Miles Langford.

Just then the door opened and a young woman walked in. Dinah greeted her and introduced her to me. "This is Roberta Tockle." When I heard her last name I understood how Dinah had recognized it. How many Tockles were there in the world? Dinah gave it a moment before looking down at the phone in her hand, as if it was vibrating. "I have to take this," she said in an apologetic voice and gave me a nod.

It was easy to start the conversation. All I had to do was tell her the nice things Dinah had said about her. "She said you work, too," I said, pretending to be vague about the details. "Something on a production?"

"I'm a production assistant, or was. I was hoping to get another gig, but I lost the guy who was my 'in.' The pay isn't great and the hours are crushing, but still there are tons of people who want the jobs. I'm hoping to get something over the summer. In the meantime, I thought I'd go to school."

I went on about how interesting it must be and asked what she'd worked on. She mentioned *Back Home on the Range* and seemed apologetic that it was a low-budget western. All I said was that it must have been interesting and she took off from there.

"Who would have guessed that the perfect location for a western would be so close. Base camp was on a flat area at the top of a hill at the north end of the Valley in Chatsworth." She stopped herself. "It was really more of a mountain. *Hill* implies something soft and rolling. This was covered with slabs of jagged rocks and steep cliffs. A lot of people hike around there, and I heard there have been a lot of rescues where a helicopter has to come because they got stuck somewhere. We had to be on the lookout for rattlesnakes, tarantulas, mountain lions, coyotes, and falls." Her expression dimmed. "Even with all the warnings, one of the PAs fell off of a cliff. Billy Erickson, rest in peace." With no segue she started on about food. "They really kept us fed well, though. There was a whole setup for cooking and eating, even though there was a nicer tent and faster service for the key people." She started going over the menus and I realized Dinah could only be gone for so long.

It was a little awkward, but I interrupted her as she was describing how even the production assistants had gotten grilled steak on the last day of shooting.

"I think I know someone who worked on that project," I said. "Miles Langford." She responded with a blank look at first, and after a moment nodded with recognition. "He was one of the executive producers. I heard he came on the set, but I'm not sure which one he was." She looked at the door and then at her watch. "I hope she comes back soon. I have to get to work. But it's nothing as exciting as being a

production assistant. I'm an assistant manager at a fast casual place."
She gave the name of a local eatery.

Dinah must have been listening and a moment later came back in
the room. I had to get to work myself and only stayed for a few
minutes after Roberta got her letter and left. "Did she say anything
helpful?" Dinah asked.

"Just more of a hint that there's nothing," I said with a shrug.

"How will you know when you're done checking him out?" my
friend asked.

I had been debating about that. I knew that Peter was anxious to
settle things with Miles and take the money for the production, but I
wanted it to look as if I had done a complete job. "I think it would look
better if I found something negative about Miles. Not enough to be a
problem, but something that made it seem I had really checked him
out." I mentioned the party Adele was putting on for the Langfords.
"I'm sure I'll turn up something. Lily has already changed everything
she initially agreed to, except what she wants to pay."

• • •

Adele grabbed me as soon as I walked into the bookstore. "You have
to help me," she said in a panicky voice. She was dressed in a new
outfit for story-time. This time as Snow White, if Snow White knew
how to crochet. The high collar that was part of the costume had been
created out of thread and starched to stiffness. The bodice was
crocheted as well. Adele was tall with an ample build that made her
seem imposing, and that made Snow White look a little menacing to
me. But apparently not to the kids, who somehow were drawn to her
anyway.

"What is it now?" I said, glad that at least she had not called me
Pink.

"I heard from another one of the people in your mommy group
who wants a proposal about a party. She heard about the one I'm doing

for the Langfords and she wants me to do one for her, but it has to be grander than what we're doing for them and different. I agreed to going there with a proposal." She looked at me. "You have to come up with something and go with me."

"I thought this was your business," I said. I had a reason to want to help with the Langfords but had thought that would be it.

"It is," she said defiantly, "but I thought you'd want to help with the people from that mommy group."

I started to protest, but realized she was right. If she messed things up with any of them, it would reflect on me, and maybe get Marlowe kicked out of the group. If Gabby came back to that, I would never hear the end of it. But I choked when Adele told me who it was and how soon she expected us to pitch her on an idea. "Taylor Palmer wants it this afternoon?" I said.

She saw the kids beginning to arrive for story-time and told me to get back to her with a plan. I followed her, trying to get any details of what Taylor had said and all I got was that it was for her older son, Andrew Junior. There was a clump of people waiting by the entrance to the children's department. The parents were anxious to drop off their kids, who were bored with waiting and were rolling on the floor and dancing around.

Adele grabbed her clipboard and started checking kids in with their bows and curtseys. A harried mother was trying to get her son away from pulling books off of one of the bookcases. I remembered having seen her before and felt like I should step in. All the time with Marlowe had reawakened what it was like to deal with children.

Seeing the wild kid stirred memories of how I had managed my boys when they were his age. "I wonder if you could help me," I said to him. He stopped what he was doing and looked at me. I told him how people would be coming in the store looking for books and if the books were all mixed up, they wouldn't be able to find anything. He looked at the pile of books. "Why don't you hand them to me one at a time and we'll put them where they belong." His mother's face relaxed and she gladly let me take over. As Adele continued her duty, the little boy and I cleaned up the mess he had made and he finally skipped in to join the others.

"Thank you," the mother said when it was just the two of us. "He's having a hard time dealing with his father's death. He can't understand that his dad went out for his usual bike ride and never came back." She seemed close to tears. "They just left him there, too." She swallowed back her feelings and pulled herself together. "If we didn't have this story-time I don't know what I would do. Queen Adele has a way with the kids. She makes the stories come alive." She peeked into the area closed off by bookcases. I looked over her shoulder and she was right. Adele had the kids mesmerized and I had an idea for the party we had to plan.

• • •

Mrs. Shedd and Mr. Royal had taken a day off from their midday outings and had lunch brought in, and there was no problem when Adele and I took our lunch break at the same time.

Adele insisted on driving, and like everything else she did, it was over the top. She was busy looking out the window at the rugged terrain along Malibu Canyon Road. The winding roadway hugged the mountain on one side, with a steep drop on the other. Malibu Creek ran through greenery at the bottom of the cliff and Adele kept taking her eyes off the road, attempting to see the water. Beyond the creek, there were rock-covered mountainsides with houses perched on the top.

It made me think of my conversation with Roberta Tockle. I bet there were lots of rattlesnakes, tarantulas and more in the area we were passing. I let out a sigh of relief when the expanse of blue water showed up and I knew we had made it through the canyon.

I had discussed the idea I came up with for the party on the ride, when I was not holding my breath at Adele's driving. She liked the idea, but wanted me to pitch it to Taylor. "You can go on about how great I am and it will sound much better than if I say it." Adele was still wearing the Snow White costume, insisting that it was a plus.

It was a lot quieter without the mommy group and I had a chance to really look at the house as Adele parked in the motor court. The grounds around it included a perfectly manicured lawn with some bushes for interest. Now that I had a chance to look at it again, I noted how grand the massive exterior appeared with the creamy-colored walls and terra-cotta tiled roof. I knew from my past visit that the large arched window with mullioned panes looked in on the living room. The entranceway was lined with huge terra-cotta pots of flowers.

The door was opened by a woman in a white uniform who I recognized as Elena, the person who had entertained the kids while the parents hung out. She recognized me and smiled, but when she saw Adele in the Snow White costume, a look of "what is this about?" crossed her face, but only for a split second and then she invited us in.

"Mrs. Palmer is occupied at the moment. She asked me to take you to the guesthouse." She gestured for us to follow her and we went outside through a side door. The backyard had a pool with a cabana, a tennis court and a grassy area. Two umbrella tables sat near an outdoor kitchen. Beyond all that there was a step up and the guesthouse with a whole other yard that seemed like a kid's dream. Along with the swings and slide, there was a playhouse and a picnic table. Some old trees added some shade and I could see that they were outfitted with tiny lights.

Elena led the way inside the guesthouse, which was bigger than a lot of people's primary houses. Elena said the guesthouse would be home base for the party and offered to let me look around. There was a full kitchen with an eating area that flowed into a comfortable space with couches and chairs. I wandered on to a hall that led to the back. I started opening doors. The first one led to a large bedroom with a connecting bath. As I moved on to the next door the handle didn't turn. "There's nothing to see in there," the housekeeper said. "Just some boxes of stuff that belonged to the former Mrs. Palmer." She crossed herself. "May she rest in peace."

"Did you know her?" I asked and Elena nodded.

"I worked for her. And now I work for Taylor Palmer. You could say I came with the house," she said with a touch of humor. She pointed out the window at another structure I hadn't noticed. The garage had three separate garage doors and a second story. "It's the only way I'd get to live in a place like this. Everybody who lives here wants to stay forever."

Elena was close to me in age and she seemed to sense that in the scheme of things I was more a working person rather than a friend of Taylor Palmer's. I have no idea what she thought of Adele, other than she seemed to be keeping her eye on my companion.

"It must have been different working for Margo Palmer," I said. Elena raised her eyes skyward.

"The money she spent on shoes—I wish I had it for a retirement fund. There were brand-new ones she never wore." She glanced toward the main house. "She wears them now." The way she shook her head showed that she didn't approve. "All that money and she barely wore them anymore. Only when there was someone other than me to see them. Then she wore those stilettos no matter how uncomfortable."

"It's too bad what happened to her," I said.

Elena's expression froze. "I'm sorry now that I wasn't here, but it was my day off. When I left, she was stretched out on a chaise lounge watching a game show and painting her toenails. She didn't like anyone touching her feet. I left her a salad for lunch and a plate of cold cuts for dinner and then I left. I went into Santa Monica to meet my daughter." She said it as if she'd said it many times before, probably to the police.

Adele was getting fidgety and grumbling that she, the head of the party business, was being kept waiting.

Elena and I traded glances and probably had the same thought. Adele needed to know her place. We were just the little people.

Taylor swept in and glanced over the group of us. After what the housekeeper had said about Taylor wearing Margo's shoes, I looked at her feet. She was wearing sling-back beige heels and I could just see a bit of the trademark red soles of Christian Louboutin. She dismissed Elena, looked back and forth at Adele and me. "I don't have a lot of time, so tell me what you've got."

I tried to give Adele the floor, but she pointed at me. "She's better at explaining it than I am." I chuckled to myself. Adele had stopped calling me Pink, but still had a hard time calling me Molly, so now I was just "she."

"You haven't been to one of our story-times or you would understand that Adele doesn't just read stories to the kids. She entertains, takes them on an adventure. That is what she can do for a deluxe party. I'm sure you know that children now like interactive entertainment. No more watching something—they want to be part of the action. That's exactly what Adele will do. She will take them on an adventure that has an obstacle course and is a treasure hunt. There will be a celebration at the end of the journey with a confetti cannon, prizes, balloons and a themed lunch."

Taylor interrupted. "How is this different from the party you're putting on for the Langfords?" She looked from Adele to me. And Adele gave me the floor. "Adele is putting on a nostalgic party with a contemporary touch. Simple games, like pin the tail on the donkey, but with no notes of animal cruelty, vegan hot dogs, cupcakes for every diet and the same for the ice cream. No themed setup or the high adventure your party will have."

"That sounds good, but way too vague. I need something more detailed. What's the theme and how is it carried throughout the party? And the cost, and we'll go from there." She glanced around the guesthouse. "You can use this and the yard. I'll need something for the adults in the house." She took another look at Adele. "Never mind on that. I'll use my usual caterer." With that, she turned to leave. "Elena will show you out."

• • •

Adele spent the whole ride back trying to convince me that I had to do the proposal. "I'm the talent, not the one who deals with the nitty-gritty stuff," she said just as we got to the part of Malibu Canyon Road where it flattened out and changed names.

She was still going on about it and still dressed as Snow White when we joined the rest of the Hookers in the yarn department.

"But it's your business," I countered, taking a sip of yet another red-eye. I was beginning to think I was immune to caffeine, or maybe it was just that with everything like Marlowe waking up in the middle of the night, I wasn't getting enough sleep.

"The idea was yours, so you know the details more than I do," Adele said. I gritted my teeth with frustration. And tried to think of something to say.

"Maybe we can help," Dinah said. "What's the problem?" Adele insisted on speaking first and told them about her party business to make money so she and Eric could live independently of Mother Humphries. Of course, Adele didn't notice when everyone at the table let out a groan at what she called Eric's mother.

"The business is really taking off. I have one definite commitment and this one in the works." Adele stopped for a breath and I took the opportunity to tell the rest of the story, but Adele interrupted and complained how Taylor Palmer had left us waiting with the housekeeper. "Instead of taking care of business, Molly was talking to the housekeeper about expensive shoes."

Rhoda's head shot up from her crochet work. "What kind of shoes?"

I recounted the whole story of the housekeeper working for the former Mrs. Palmer and her employer's love of expensive shoes. "Heels," I said, looking at Rhoda, who rocked her head with disapproval. "But she said something you would probably agree with," I said to the heel-hating Hooker. "She said that Margo only wore the heels when there was someone to see them."

"That makes a lot more sense," Dinah said. My friend looked down at her blanket in progress. She was at the end of a row with black yarn and looked at the array of small balls of leftover yarn she was using for it. "What color should I do next?" They voted on a golden yellow and she joined it on the last stitch of the black and began the next row. She was working her way across, when her head shot up and she gestured for me to go away from the table with her.

"No fair, secrets," Adele said, watching us go. The rest of them joined in and we sat back down.

"Okay," Dinah said, feeling like a naughty schoolgirl. "I was going to tell Molly a thought I had. I didn't think the rest of you cared, so I was just going to tell her." She looked around the table. "You all know about the Sherlock Holmes game Molly and I play—well, see what you deduce from this. Margo Palmer fell down the stairs, it was thought, because the heel of her shoe caught on the carpet. She died because she was home alone and there was no one to call for help. But Molly just heard that she didn't wear heels unless there was someone to see them."

"I get it," Rhoda said excitedly. "If she was wearing heels then someone was there."

"Unless she was going out," CeeCee said.

"If she was going out, she wouldn't have put the shoes on until she was ready to walk out the door. Or at least, I wouldn't have," Rhoda said.

"What about the housekeeper?" Sheila asked.

"She left on her day off and said when she left Margo Palmer was barefoot and spending the day alone," I said.

Eduardo seemed perplexed by the whole thing, and then his face lit up. "If I were playing your Sherlock Holmes game, I would deduce that something doesn't add up."

Chapter Twenty-six

I went home to find the nightly circus at my place. My mother and the girls were practicing. By now I'd realized that more than rehearsing for a show, they just liked singing and doing their routines. My father enjoyed watching them and they all loved spending time with Marlowe after not being able to see her while Gabby had held her prisoner. Samuel obviously liked Beth, so unless he had a gig, he hung around. Peter was settling into the idea that he was a father and it was one step forward and two steps back as he formed an attachment to Marlowe.

This time things were a little rocky because Marlowe was cranky and none of their usual tricks could pacify her. As soon as I walked in, my mother handed Marlowe off to me. I carried her with me as I took care of letting the dogs out for a run.

I had said I would never do it, but I started talking silly baby talk to her as I carried her to the kitchen and got something from the freezer. When I came back into the living room, I waved a frozen bagel at them and then put it in her mouth. "She's teething."

"Of course, I knew that," my mother said.

When things calmed down, Peter asked me for an update. I had the whole trip with Adele on my mind and started to tell him about the party plans. He gave me an impatient sigh. "I don't really care what's going on with the Palmer kid's party," he said. "All I care about right now is Miles Langdon." He paused for a moment. "If you're such a hotshot sleuth, you must have found out something."

"Right," I said, glad that I had stopped before bringing up the whole shoe discussion and the fact there was something off about Margo Palmer's death. I thought over what Roberta had told me and tried to find something I could pass on to Peter. "I talked to Roberta Tockle," I said, quickly going over our conversation to find some tidbit about Miles.

"Who's Roberta Tockle?" Peter said with a chuckle as he said her last name.

"She's a production assistant who worked on that western that Miles got the executive producer credit on." Peter seemed unimpressed as he waited for me to continue. "She told me that there's a whole hierarchy of what and where people get to eat. And there were problems with the location because of tarantulas, sharp drops and rattlesnakes." Peter rolled his eyes and gave me a hopeless shake of his head.

"It was a western, so they had to shoot in that kind of locale," Peter said. "And I doubt that Miles had anything to do with choosing the location." The frozen bagel slipped from my hold and Peter caught it before it hit the floor. He tried to hold it so that Marlowe could gnaw on it. He looked drained and I knew what he was going to say and said it for him.

"I know. You're going to say if that's all I've got maybe I'm not such a hotshot detective and you want to shut it down."

"Those aren't exactly my words, but the idea is the same." He repositioned the cold circular roll. "I got another call from him and he wants to know what the holdup is. He implied he could invest in something else." Peter groaned. "The money is the difference between me having a production company and not having one. But I don't like him putting the pressure on me." Peter sagged as he let down his defenses and reminded me of the little boy he'd been once instead of the ambitious producer he'd become.

I reminded him about the party at the Langfords' that Adele had hooked me into helping her with. We could make that an absolute deadline."

"Right," Peter said, brightening. "If nothing comes up by then, I accept his money and he's an executive producer."

"What? Did you say I was right?" I said, laughing, and then I gave him a hug with my free arm and for once he didn't resist.

• • •

I had made peace with the fact that I was stuck helping Adele with the parties for now. The next day, I took advantage of a lull at the bookstore and sat in my cubicle working on the proposal for Taylor Palmer. I had fun coming up with a story and how the kids would be part of it. It was like interactive theater. I had worked out a general plan with an idea of what we would have to provide beyond Adele. I made some phone calls to get an idea of costs and then set it all aside when it was time for me to take my afternoon coffee break. I was looking forward to the clearing of my brain that a red-eye would do and went to the café.

As soon as Bob saw me, he went into action making the espresso to pour into the cup of the coffee of the day. I was glad to see that he had brewed a medium roast, which had more caffeine than the darker ones.

I was considering whether I wanted to take the drink back to my cubicle or drink it in the café when I sensed someone behind me.

"You're suffering from the four o'clock slump again, too," a man said. I knew who it was before I turned and tried to keep my expression neutral. Although he was trying to make this sound like a chance encounter, I knew it was completely calculated.

"Detective Carlson," I said. "Glad to see you like our coffee." I picked up my cup and prepared to go back into the bookstore and then he made his move.

"Since I ran into you, I wonder if you could spare me a few minutes. I could use your help in going over the facts of the two homicides. I heard you were good at sorting out clues."

I almost laughed that he was trying that flattery again. Did he honestly think I didn't see through it? I could give him an excuse that I had to get back to work, but he'd just come back with something else. I figured I might as well play along and get it over with.

We took our drinks to the same table where I sat with him when he'd come with Barry. I focused on the coffee, waiting for him to speak. He was doing the friendly cop thing to the hilt and started off with small talk about the bookstore, asking what I did. He even feigned interest in the crochet group, but it was just a lead-in to talking about CeeCee.

"We're trying to put together the pieces of the two deaths and it seems that CeeCee Collins has a connection to both. You seem to know her well. It would help if I knew her relationship with the two women."

Did he think I'd help him trap CeeCee to get the heat off of me? I was glad that CeeCee wasn't here to hear him. She would have freaked out. "I'm not exactly sure," I said. It was my plan to answer him with no information.

"I thought it might have something to do with the information that Daisy Cochran had for the true crime podcasts that she was going to do and that Leslie Bittner took over," he said. "Maybe there's something in CeeCee Collins's past." He left it open-ended.

I wanted to tell him that if he was looking for a motive in Daisy's death, he'd just presented one. Leslie Bittner had been very quick to step into Daisy's shoes, moving into her place and going ahead with the plans for the podcast. I was startled at what I'd just thought. Someone stepping into someone else's shoes. Hadn't Taylor done that. According to the housekeeper, Taylor was wearing Margo's uber-expensive shoes, along with taking over the house. I thought about mentioning it to the cop. I would have if it had been Barry since whatever exchanges had gone on between us were more teasing and less him thinking I was guilty of something other than putting my nose where it didn't belong. I had noticed the handcuffs hanging off of Rick Carlson's belt and I was sure he was anxious to use them. No matter that he was asking about CeeCee, I knew he was trying to corner me.

"You know, we found fingerprints on the knife used to kill Leslie Bittner," he said. I almost let out an *aha, I knew it* as he turned the conversation off of CeeCee. I also knew that my fingerprints were on file because of past involvements I'd had and that he knew they matched.

He was looking for my reaction and I forced myself to appear nonplussed. When I didn't say anything, he kept pushing. "You know they were your fingerprints," he said, peering at me. "Do you want to explain?"

It was a trick question. I could not really say no. What was that saying about the truth will set you free? Okay, that's what he was going to get and then some. "I was curious about the kitchen. One of my sons has been on me about downsizing and that was the kind of place he had in mind. Most of these places have ridiculous kitchens designed by people who don't cook. I do cook," I said. "Actually, I'm a very good cook. The kitchen wasn't too bad, but I would really want more counter space than that and the trouble with condos is that you can't really remodel the kitchens that easily." I knew he was itching to tell me to get to the point, but I had decided not to leave out the slightest detail. "And then the cat walked in. I have a lot of pets and I can recognize when they need something, and the way that cat was meowing, I knew there was something wrong."

He was maintaining his benign cop expression, but his body language said he was getting impatient. I had switched around the way things had happened, but it hardly mattered. "That poor cat had an empty bowl and no water. You know cats need their water."

Finally, he couldn't take it anymore. "You were going to tell me about the knife."

"Knife?" I said, feigning a blank look to give the impression I was a little ditzy. "Oh, yes, the knife with my fingerprints. I don't know if you know this, but I'm an experienced cook and I know how to treat my utensils. You never leave a good knife soaking in the sink. It's my nature to take care of things, like getting that cat food and water. And taking it home with me since Leslie Bittner planned to take it to the pound. You do know what would happen to Buttercup if that was where she ended up. That's her name, Buttercup. Do you have any pets?"

He closed his eyes in frustration and nodded. "I have a dog." His voice was terse, but it opened the door for me to ask him for details.

"What kind?" I asked. I had cut through his copness and touched on his humanness.

"A German shepherd mix," he said. He pulled out his wallet and showed me a picture.

"Mine are all mutts. They're the best. One of them used to be Barry's dog." He nodded with interest and then remembered why he was there.

"The knife?" he prompted me.

"So sorry," I said. "You never leave a good knife soaking in the sink, so I took it out and wiped off the blade and left it on the counter." I glanced toward the entrance of the bookstore. "I have to get back to work. I hope I was able to give you the help you needed."

I was smiling to myself as I walked away. I snuck a look back and he was shaking his head and muttering, "I should have listened to Greenberg. He warned me she was trouble."

I went back to my cubicle and took a few minutes to recover from my coffee date. I felt like I'd won that round, but knew there was more to come. The proposal for Taylor's party seemed rather trivial after that and I gave it a quick going-over and emailed it off to Adele.

A woman came up to the cubicle and asked for some help finding a book. I had barely finished sending her off to the location of what she was looking for when Adele showed up. She seemed as if she'd lost some of her usual presence. "I tried to email the proposal to that woman, but she wants us to go over it in person so we can work it out," Adele said with annoyance. "I said she could come to the bookstore and we could talk here."

"How'd she respond?" I said, already knowing how well that must have gone over.

Adele appeared indignant. "She said I had to bring it there." She stopped talking and seemed to be having an inner conversation. Finally, she looked up at me. "I can't do it without you. Will you come with me?" She added a *please* under her breath. I was astonished at her manner. She had lost all her bravado and seemed vulnerable.

I actually had no problem agreeing to go along. After my revelation that Taylor had literally and figuratively stepped into Margo Palmer's shoes and thinking about what the Hookers had figured out—that Margo was wearing the heels for a reason before she fell down the stairs—I was curious to talk to the housekeeper again. I was shocked when Adele thanked me after I agreed to go with her. She gave me a quick hug and muttered something about me being her best friend in the world.

Chapter Twenty-seven

I drove this time and Adele was free to look out the window all she wanted without making me feel like we were going to go over the cliff. She had returned to her usual self and was giving me orders to let her do the talking. I had no problem with that.

Elena answered the door and sent us back to the guesthouse without accompanying us. When I tried to make conversation, she seemed uneasy. "I have to take care of something in here," she said. Then she dropped her voice. "I'm not supposed to talk to anyone here to see Mrs. Palmer." She pointed us to the side gate.

Adele was out of costume, but that didn't mean that her outfit was bland. She had worn the black sweater with the crocheted sunflowers on it. It was over the top, but of all her crazy outfits, it was my favorite. I loved sunflowers in any form. We walked into the guesthouse expecting to find Taylor there, but the place was empty. Adele started rocking her head around and making annoyed sounds that we were being kept waiting. I tried to ignore her fussing, but finally decided to give her some friendly advice.

"If you want to succeed at this party business, you have to understand your place," I said. "You can't make a fuss if you have to wait. They have the upper hand. Maybe someday when you are considered the primo kids' party arranger, you can act like a prima donna, but you have to get there first by doing whatever to please your clients."

She grumbled at what I said and reluctantly agreed. She pulled out her phone and started scrolling through something, and I took the opportunity to look around the guesthouse and zeroed in on the room Elena had said held what was left of Margo's things. No surprise, the door was locked.

Remembering my conversation with Detective Carlson, I went to have another look at the kitchen in the place. It was small but had all high-end appliances and the window had a view of the ocean. Taylor was really taking her time and I went to poke around some more. I opened a door off the kitchen and found a bathroom. It seemed like a weird setup until I saw the door on the other side of it and opened it to see where it led. As soon as I walked inside the adjoining room, I figured out it was the one that held Margo Palmer's leftover belongings and been locked from the other side. The curtains were drawn over the windows and it was dimly lit. I didn't want to turn on a lamp or even use the flashlight on my phone for fear Taylor might see it when she finally came to meet us.

I knew I had to be quick because she had already made us wait to prove who was in charge and would come back there soon. I opened the closet and saw a stack of shoe boxes with designer names on them. I opened the top one and saw a pair of black pumps with stiletto heels. When I checked the sole of one of them, it was scuffed and clearly had been worn. I assumed it was true of the shoes in the boxes below. Back in the room, I noticed a pile of stuff on a desk. When I checked through it there were framed photos of Margo and some kids, who I assumed were her daughters, who were now grown. There was an appointment book, and more photos that appeared to be of parties. I flipped through the appointment book, amazed that anyone still used a paper one. I flipped to the last week of her life to see what appointments she'd had. She seemed to have written everything in shorthand and small letters and seemed involved with the minute details of running the house. It mostly had reminders, like having *d cl* picked up and needing *oj*. All that was listed on the day she died was *el off* and *tp*. There were more photos, which were much more interesting than the ones with her kids. There was a picture of Margo and Andrew flanked by Elizabeth Taylor and Brad Pitt standing in front of a floor-to-ceiling Christmas tree. There was a face behind them I couldn't quite make out. I looked closer and realized it was Daisy Cochran. She must have been a fixture at their parties.

I froze when I heard Adele talking to someone. I set down the photo in my hand carefully and then left the way I had come. I walked out of the bathroom holding one of the guest paper towels as if I had just washed my hands.

Taylor greeted me and seemed to treat me with more regard than Adele because even though I was a stand-in for Gabby, I was still part of the mommy group. I let Adele handle giving her the written proposal and a price. I'd learned from dealing with the Langfords to offer a price for the entertainment and separate the food and supply costs with a *TBA*.

I thought the whole thing was going to explode when Taylor tried to negotiate the price down by diminishing Adele, saying that she was just starting out and the only reason she was considering her was because of my recommendation. She also pointed out how doing a party for her would open the door to lots of business for her. Adele started to fume, but I gave her the evil eye and she pulled herself together, and I took over mediating the negotiations. By the time Adele and I left, we were one step closer to a deal. Taylor criticized what we'd brought, saying there were still not enough details of the theme and how it would play out through the party.

"What are we going to do?" Adele said as we were on our way back to the Valley. "I wouldn't know where to begin." I was surprised by how toned down and vulnerable she sounded and I immediately melted for it and assured her we would work it out.

We had taken our lunch break time to see Taylor. It took longer than expected and I was hungry when we got back to the bookstore. I made a short detour to the café and Bob hooked me up with some leftover Eggy Squares and a red-eye and packed it up for me so I could slip it into my cubicle unnoticed.

I set aside working on the proposal for Taylor's party and went back to my real job at the bookstore. I had been spending so much time on Adele's party business, I had forgotten about the newsletter I had been working on.

I was trying to eat, drink and look at some photos for the newsletter. Mrs. Shedd had taken them at the event with Daisy,

CeeCee and Elise. Considering how it turned out, showing photos of the speakers seemed like a bad idea, but I needed to find a way to use some of the photos my boss had taken. I was caught with a mouthful of food when I looked up as someone approached my cubicle. I swallowed so quickly I almost choked on a strand of spinach, and I set aside what I was doing to help them locate a number of books. I had just gone back to eating, drinking and working on the newsletter when another figure approached and I rushed to swallow again.

"Take your time," Barry said. "I don't want to show off my skills and do a Heimlich maneuver on you." When I looked surprised at his comment, he continued. "I saw you almost choke when you went to deal with your last customer."

"Are you doing the stalker thing again?" I said. I looked at the dark suit, white shirt and tie. "But if you're looking to blend in, that outfit won't work." I glanced around at the customers who were dressed in jeans and joggers.

"No. I was being considerate and waiting until you finished with the customer."

"Are you looking for a book?" I asked.

He shook his head. "I came to give you some friendly advice. It was different when you played around with me answering my questions with a question, but it won't work with Rick Carlson. He wasn't happy with the convoluted story or that you got him to show you the picture of his dog. He's seriously looking at you and CeeCee as suspects."

"Can't you say something to him?" I put my hands up in a helpless gesture. "Really? CeeCee and me knocking off two women?"

"I guess you know that your prints are on the knife that stabbed Leslie Bittner and the two of you were seen leaving the place."

"But was it even the day she was killed?"

"You didn't hear this from me, but the neighbor was confused about exactly what day and time she saw CeeCee and her companion," Barry said. "And before you ask me, he has motive. The same neighbor who saw you leaving the place overheard the two of you complaining about the victim and that you'd said you'd taken care of it."

"I was talking about the cat," I said. "She had neglected the cat and then was going to take it to the pound. So I took it with me."

"Cat?" Barry said. "You don't have enough animals without adding another one?"

"It wasn't a choice. I couldn't leave it there," I said. "I told your detective buddy about the cat."

"It seems like you told him a whole lot of stuff," Barry said, shaking his head.

• • •

I was ready for the crochet group and looking forward to some time to let go and get lost in the yarn and my hook. I didn't have to worry about talking because Adele had center stage, going on about what a success her party business was and how she was sure there would be more to follow. All her bravado had returned.

CeeCee slipped in unnoticed, and when I caught her eye, she gestured for us to talk away from the table. After what Barry had said, I already had a feeling I knew what she was going to say.

"That detective showed up at my house and said he needed to speak to me. He was all steely-eyed and intimidating and wanted me to go with him so we could talk at the station. I was all flummoxed, imagining being locked in a room with bright lights. Then I thought to pretend I was you and I got all huffy and said I wouldn't talk without my lawyer. Mason Fields is supposed to meet me here. He already worked it out that we'd talk in the café instead of the station." She looked around, as if expecting him to appear.

I told her what Barry had said about Rick Carlson. "He thinks we're real suspects," I said.

"That's what I was afraid of," she said, appearing upset, "even though when he came to my house, he claimed he was looking for information about you. You better tell Mason whatever you know," the actress said.

"You can tell him," I said.

"Oh, no, I can't. I'll get it all mixed up. He's coming before the detective is supposed to meet us. You have to tell him what you know. Put on your big girl pants and suck it up," CeeCee said in a sharp tone. Then she apologized. "Sorry, that was from a bit part I had as a guard in a woman's prison."

I thought about just leaving but I was at my place of employment and the Hooker meetup was really part of my workday since it was an event and I was supervising. And then I saw him come in the door. It brought back a wave of memories. He had a solid build and a broad face. He was dressed in his work clothes of a finely tailored taupe-colored suit. His dress shirt had a sheen from the high thread count. His hair had a few more strands of silver and was cut in a conservative style. Somehow a lock of his hair always fell loose and hung over his forehead. Our eyes met and his face warmed with a smile, for a moment, then it seemed to register how he felt about me now and his expression turned distant.

He greeted CeeCee and put his hand on her shoulder in a reassuring manner. "You don't have to do a thing. I'll do all the talking," he said.

CeeCee tugged at my sweater. "Tell him what you know," she demanded. Mason kept the distant expression, which was now tempered with interest.

"I'm listening. Shoot," he said, giving me the floor to speak.

"Interesting choice of words," I muttered. I took a deep breath and told him about the neighbor and the question of when they had seen us. I mentioned how my fingerprints had ended up on the murder weapon along with my explanation of rescuing the cat.

"The story of the cat notwithstanding, that does all seem to point to you," he said, looking at me before he quickly turned back to CeeCee.

"He might see you as an accessory, but that's it." He waited a beat and turned back to me. "You should think of getting a lawyer."

I shook my head. "I'm good for now."

"You should really think it over. I can recommend someone, if you like."

I was stunned that he didn't even want to be involved with me professionally. I shook my head again and thanked him.

"If you change your mind, you know how to reach me," he said. Then he and CeeCee walked to the café and I went to rejoin the group. Everyone but Adele had their eyes glued to me.

"What was that about?" Rhoda asked. There was no choice but to tell them the whole story. They all reacted in their own way. Sheila got so tense, she had to pull out her emergency crochet. Rhoda said I shouldn't have been so quick to turn down Mason's help in getting a lawyer.

Elise said she was sorry now that she had taken part in the event with Daisy. "They'll be coming after me next."

"If you need a place to hide out," Eduardo said, "the windows are all papered over at the restaurant. There's nobody there now. I'm waiting for the inspector to come." I wasn't sure if he was joking or not and I answered with a thank-you and an uncertain shrug.

Dinah grabbed my arm to get my attention. "I'm not so sure that Mason's as mad at you as you think," she said. "He did give you some advice."

"It's probably some lawyer code that if you see someone in legal jeopardy, you have to offer help."

"I think that's doctors or first responders," Dinah said.

"I'm fine," I said. "I'm sure that whoever really did it thinks they're scot-free and will get careless or I'll think of something that I missed. Remember, Mason told CeeCee I was good at getting out of trouble." I tried to sound light, but really, I was hoping that he was right.

Chapter Twenty-eight

Nobody showed up with a SWAT team to arrest me during the night. And life had to go on. I had said nothing to my family about Rick Carlson's repeated visits or that he seemed to think I was a killer. I got Marlowe up and changed into her day clothes and fed her some of my breakfast then she had a bottle and I had coffee. She was starting to say some sounds and by the way she reached out her arms toward me and said La La, I figured that was her name for me.

Gabby had begun to text me more often about Marlowe. I gathered that Peter had been short on details and mostly just said that Marlowe was alive and not sick. The communications had been fine until I started mentioning the mommy group, and asked questions about the other members, like did she think that Taylor was overly possessive of her house. Gabby had sent me a snippy text asking me to stay out of their business or I would ruin it for her to take Marlowe to the meetups when she came back.

"Don't worry, Marlowe. I won't ruin it for you and your mommy." We were headed to Kath's, as it was her turn playing host. She lived in a house overlooking Corbin Canyon. When I looked down into the wilderness in the space between two ridges all I could think of was that it was where the deer and coyote played and probably not with each other.

It was a single-level house that was deceptive from the street. It was only when I saw the C shape of the back that I realized how big it was. The living room and front of the house were all immaculate and toyless, and I remembered that little Plum had been a surprise and their other kids were beyond the toy stage. She took me back to a large room on one side of the C shape. It had been turned into an indoor playroom. There was a slide and a little car that ran on foot power, both of which were beyond Marlowe. She did a fast crawl toward a tube that led to an enclosure filled with balls to roll around in. Kath was dressed in expensive casual and introduced me to her au pair from

Switzerland, who would be in charge of the kids.

She directed me to a whole other den for the adults just as Lily came in. She was checking Alexander's face with a worried look. "He's been getting the nosebleeds again. Maybe I should leave this with your au pair."

"You didn't have to bring your own ice cubes. We have plenty if he needs them," Kath said as Lily took a small case from an insulated bag. "If you're in the plastic surgery business, you always have lots of ice. Michael advises his patients to use ice for swelling or whatever. There's a refrigerator with ice in the children's room and my au pair is trained in CPR and first aid." Lily put the case back in the bag and we both followed Kath to the other den. Garth was looking through a stack of pages. Taylor was on her phone and the two nannies were off to the side talking. Kath pointed out the platter of fruit and cheese, along with an assortment of drinks and wine. She invited everyone to help themselves. Lily poured herself a glass of white wine and sat next to Taylor.

"Do you have something for me?" Kath said, looking at Garth.

He looked down at the pages he had been going through with a moment of hesitation and then gathered them up. "Let me know what you think of this version of the script for the infomercial."

She thanked him and gave it a cursory glance. "I'll read it over and pass it on to the lawyers to check it out." She let out a discontented sigh. "We have to make sure we're covered. Stuff happens during procedures, even deaths, and we have to slip in that there are risks in all the procedures. We play cheerful music over the voice-over with the risks, and have shots on the screen of a woman in a bikini wowing her boyfriend with her fabulous shape. I'm a lot less worried now that something that was going to bite us has been successfully buried."

She grabbed a glass of wine, found a seat, and began reading through the pages.

Garth got a plate of fruit and cheese and took the seat next to me. He seemed nervous as he watched Kath read through the script. I had felt a kindship with him since the first meetup when he'd been friendly and filled me in on the group. "I understood what she meant about covering gloomy warnings with happy music and shots of people having fun, but what was that last thing she said about?" I asked.

"I'm not sure, but I'm guessing that they've had complaints or suits from unhappy patients. Maybe someone in the public eye."

I had a sudden thought. "Did she know Daisy Cochran?"

He shrugged. "Probably. It was Daisy's business to know everybody and Michael had some celebrity clients. No names were ever given—doctor-patient privacy." He put down his glass of juice. "Why do you want to know?"

"No reason other than curiosity," I said with a shrug.

• • •

When the meetup was done, I loaded Marlowe back in her car seat. The kids seemed to have had a good time. She was asleep before I pulled out from the curb. It was a whole process of taking care of Marlowe's needs when we got home before Samuel took over until Beth got there. I tried to leave things as easy for everybody as possible, so I made sure she had a fresh diaper, was fed and was in her baby walker. I watched for a few minutes to make sure all was well. Samuel was on one of the couches as she rolled around the living room. He was strumming his guitar, working on a song. After a few chords and some lyric about lost love, he morphed into a song about rainbows that had been in a Muppet movie. Kermit sang it in the movie and Samuel did his impression of the frog. Marlowe stopped rolling and watched him.

All seemed good and I left, turning my thoughts back to the bookstore. My mindset instantly changed from baby stuff to business and by the time I walked into Shedd & Royal I was ready to finish up the newsletter.

I had written most of it with information about upcoming special events and a calendar with story-times listed and meetings of Hookers and some other groups we hosted. All I needed was to add some photos from the ones Mrs. Shedd had left me. I had been in a quandary what to use when I'd worked on the newsletter before and I couldn't put it off any longer. I discounted all the pictures of Daisy and realized my only option was to put in some pictures of the crowd and keep the caption general. As I was trying to pick one, I looked over the faces and then I saw one that made me stop. I even enlarged it on the screen. I had been right all along.

"Pink," Adele said, interrupting my thoughts. She caught herself. "I mean Molly, how's it coming with the plans for the Langford party? I should have really charged them extra for it being so last-minute and all. And I heard from Taylor Palmer. She's all hot and bothered and wants to know when we can bring her the more detailed proposal. She implied that if it was too much for me to handle, she would go with someone else. I told her it was almost ready and we'd bring it to her." Adele took a breath. "I can't believe we have to go there again." Taylor seemed to be playing the grand lady a little too much, but I also knew that if Adele wanted to make a go of the business, she was going to have to deal with people like that.

Adele handed me a stack of books. "I thought these might help figure out a theme." I was shocked at her offer of help instead of the usual complaining that she was the talent. I knew it was business as usual with her when she started fussing about a kid who was ruining story-time and needed to be removed. "You should be the one to tell his mother. I saw you talking to her."

I knew who she was talking about. "There has to be another way," I said. "He really needs story-time."

"Maybe, but he keeps interrupting me and causing trouble. I can't tarnish my reputation by telling his mother he can't come anymore. You are the assistant manager, which makes you customer service. Work it out."

The worst part was that I knew Adele was right.

Chapter Twenty-nine

It didn't seem fair to deal with Adele's problems during my work time, except the part about removing the kid from story-time. I knew I would deal with it better than Adele. Still, it was not something I looked forward to taking care of, and I gladly put it off. I wished I could put off the party planning too, but time was of the essence.

That afternoon when the Hookers met, I took Dinah aside and told her all about it. True-blue friend that she was, she offered to help.

The crew was taking care of Marlowe, which left me free. "Let's talk about it over dinner," I suggested. Dinah was ready for another girls' night and agreed. She even had a restaurant in mind.

• • •

"Roberta keeps talking about this place," Dinah said as we approached the glass doors of City Dishes. It was at the high end of what was referred to now as fast casual. The dining area was appealing, with wood tables and nice décor. We went to the counter to order and Dinah waved at her student, who walked behind the order taker and was carrying a tray of food. I smiled at her, too.

We perused the menu on a big board hanging over the cashier's area. I chose the salmon with asparagus and mashed potatoes and Dinah ordered the Chinese chicken salad. We were given a number and found a table near a window. As soon as we sat down, we started to talk about how I'd gotten mired in the mess with Adele and her party business. "I'm going to see it through with these two parties, but then Adele is going to have to step up and be more than the prima donna talent." I had made some notes on what I needed and put them on the table. I was glancing through them when Roberta showed up with our food.

"I'm one of the assistant managers, but I do everything," she said as she set down the plates. She saw the notes on the table. "Is this a business meeting?"

"If you call putting together a kid's birthday party business, I guess it is," I said. I didn't mean to, but I segued into the situation of one being a last-minute affair and one being complicated.

"Maybe I can help," she said. "Being a production assistant has given me a lot of experience dealing with all sorts of things beyond just looking out for rattlesnakes. I had to arrange for all kinds of stuff, like getting one the producer's Saint Bernard groomed and snagging last-minute reservations for a director at a trendy place that was booked out for a month. That's just the tip of the iceberg."

I mentioned dealing with Adele, and Roberta laughed. "She sounds like everybody I dealt with. They all have fragile egos. It can cost a production assistant their job if they don't treat the top people right."

"You probably dealt with the food service since you seem experienced in it," Dinah said.

"Even there egos clash," she said. "If someone gets in the wrong food line, it's a mess all the way round. It's not a good place to make a mistake." She looked at the notes again. "What do you need?"

"More than I can tell you in a few seconds," I said

She said she was due for a break and would come back. "Ms. Lyons-Blaine is the best and I'd be happy to help."

"Ms. Lyons-Blaine?" I said when Roberta left. The last I had heard was that Dinah was going to keep to Lyons as her last name when she married Commander.

"I know it's a mouthful, but it seemed to be really important to him that I add on his last name. I recently did it. It seemed like a small request. It's so confusing to get married again when you're in your fifties and have a life and identity."

Roberta returned with plates of cake and said they were complimentary. And then she listened while I explained the situation. "The games and decorations aren't a problem for the first one," I said. "I can do all that with a stop at a party store, but the food is another story." I showed her Lily's demands for vegan hot dogs and an organic sheet cake.

"No problem. I can arrange that for you," she said. She glanced back at the food area. "We can do it here."

"You're hired," I said and gave her the kids' menu. "I don't think the other party is going to be that easy," I said before describing the adventure I'd sold Taylor on. Roberta asked some questions about the child the party was for and the location. As soon as I mentioned it was for Andrew Palmer Junior, her face lit up.

"You don't need to consult the books. It should be a treasure hunt with an Indiana Jones–style adventure. Give them all hats and set up an obstacle course toned down for a five-year-old's style. This Adele person can lead the way with the kids being her helpers. I would be happy to help with it. Making a good impression on the Palmers would help me get my next PA job," she said. She had ideas for the decorations and knew where to get everything. She said she would call me with costs and even offered to come with us when Adele and I delivered the detailed proposal and again for the actual party.

"Thank you," I said. "You're fantastic. I don't suppose you know a way to tell a mother that her son can't come to story-time anymore."

She smiled apologetically. "I'm afraid that's on you." One of the other workers came to the table and told her there was a problem in the kitchen and she left.

"That was easy," I said, letting out a big sigh of relief. "Problem solved."

Unfortunately, it was not the only one.

• • •

I had hoped that CeeCee getting Mason Fields involved would keep Rick Carlson off of me, but he was sitting in his Crown Vic when I came into work the next day. I knew without looking behind me that he had followed me into the store. There was no use trying to avoid him, so I turned abruptly and faced him.

"Did you want something?"

He let out a little grunt of displeasure, as it appeared that I had taken charge. "I was hoping to ask you a few questions," he said. He made it sound like I had a choice, but I knew I didn't. The Columbo act had gotten tired. I was even thinking of asking Mason for that lawyer referral.

I took him to the yarn department, which was empty at the moment. It gave a semblance of privacy and I invited him to sit at the table.

"What do you want to know?" I asked. There was another grunt of displeasure as I had taken charge again.

"What do you know about the podcast that Daisy Cochran was putting together?"

"Only that it was supposed to be one of those true crime things and she was going to use information she had to shed new light on some old incidents. She was calling it *Were They Murders.*"

"What were the crimes she was going to cover?" he asked. "Maybe something from your past?"

I couldn't help myself and laughed. "I'm sorry but I don't think there's anything I've done that would be that interesting."

He didn't seem happy with my answer and asked how developed the audio shows were.

I gathered that CeeCee, through Mason, must have explained that she was there to be considered as the host of the podcast, which would imply there was a plan for the shows, and I remembered the notes I'd seen. All that I recalled was that the beginning of the notes had a heading of *House* or maybe it was *The House*. I thought it was better to say nothing, and I simply told him I didn't know.

He wasn't pleased with my answer and kept hammering at me about who the subjects of the podcast were supposed to be. After the fifth *I don't know*, he finally gave up and left.

He was becoming less like Columbo and more like a terrier. Only I was the pants leg he had latched on to. I really needed to find a way to get him to let go.

When he finally left, I knew I needed something to perk me up before I had to deal with Adele. We were going back to Taylor's with the more detailed proposal during our lunch break. I still had to tell Adele about Roberta, which I knew would be a problem. Bob saw me and pulled out a paper cup. "Make it a black-eye," I said.

"You're really getting into the hard stuff," he joked as he worked on getting two shots of espresso to add to the cup of coffee. It only took a few sips for the drink to start to work its magic and I felt ready for anything, except for Adele. She balked when she heard the theme was settled without me consulting her, even though she was happy about what it was.

"I guess you don't remember that you put it on me," I said. Roberta had come through as she had promised and I wrote it all up.

"Even if I did, you should have cleared it with me before you wrote it all up." She was being extra ridiculous. She had toned down her attire and there was no costume or explosion of crocheted flowers on a sweater. She had loose-fitting lavender slacks on with a long tunic top in the same color. And then she wrapped a shawl around her and tied it, leaving the knot over one shoulder. It was made of granny squares in all different colors. No one could accuse her of being dull.

I wasn't compelled to explain any more, but I did. "I was lucky enough to get some help," I said. "Her name is Roberta and she's coming with us to explain the setup."

"What do you mean someone is coming with us?" Adele said in a petulant tone. "You should have talked to me first. Remember, it's my party business."

How convenient of my coworker to start acting all possessive when there was nothing for her to do.

"She's not charging us anything. All she wants is an introduction to the Palmers," I said, and Adele agreed.

I shouldn't have worried. Roberta was used to dealing with difficult people and won Adele over before we even pulled out of the bookstore parking lot by complimenting her on her shawl and asking if she'd made it. She was enthused about seeing the Palmers' house and went on about the history of it from the time it was the summer house of the Beltrons to Margo Palmer's fall. "All that glamour and then she died there all alone," Roberta said in a wistful voice.

Elena answered the door as before and sent us back to the guesthouse to wait for Taylor. I wondered if she was really that busy or if it was just to let us know who was more important. Roberta wanted to see what we would be working with and looked over the guesthouse and went outside to check out the grounds. I knew she really wanted to see the inside of the main house but was taking what she could get.

"Wait for me," Adele said, rushing out after her. "I'm the principal in the party business and should be involved in every decision." Now that I was alone in the place, I wanted to have another look at Margo's things. I did a repeat trip to the bathroom hoping to use the unlocked door to get in. But this time the door leading from the bathroom was locked. I remembered the headline on Daisy's notes for the podcast had been something about a house. I had seen her in two photographs of parties held there. I knew now that Taylor had been at Daisy's event. Could the house Daisy was referring to be this one? If there was any chance to find something to throw at Rick Carlson to get him off my back, I wanted to get in that room. Normally, I would not have done it, but I felt like I had to do what I had to do. I pulled out a credit card and used it to push the locking mechanism out of the way.

I went right to the desk and looked for the appointment book, and at first I thought it had been moved, but it had blended in with the other things on the desk. I opened it to the day of Margo's accident and read over the notes with a fresh eye. And then I realized it was all right there in front of me all along, coupled with some information Elise had given me. I just hadn't recognized it.

I got my phone out and was going to photograph the pages when the door whipped open and Taylor walked in. "What do you think you're doing?" she demanded.

"Checking for evidence that Margo wasn't alone when she fell. I was right when I said you were at the author event. You almost had me believing that I was mistaken, but then I saw you in the photo of the crowd. Daisy knew you were here when Margo *fell*, if that's what really happened. It was all about getting this house, wasn't it? With Margo out of the way, you could finally live in the legendary house."

"That's ridiculous," she sputtered. "The police, coroner, and Andrew all agreed that Margo was home alone when it happened. It was her own fault. She should have left when they got the divorce. Andrew was softhearted and wouldn't evict her."

Elise had told me about the research she had done on the house. I had not paid much attention at the time because she had gone off on the lack of romance in marriages of the powerful and wealthy. Her point was that the house belonged to Andrew Palmer and it was spelled out in the prenuptial agreements with both of his wives. Now it made sense.

"Was she really here alone?" I said. "Margo only wore high heels when she had company." The color drained from Taylor's face and she gave me a cold look.

"There's no way to prove that it was me," she said in a panicked voice.

"It's right here," I said, holding up the appointment book. "I thought it was a reminder that she needed toilet paper, but the *tp* was for Taylor Palmer and that you were coming to see her. You were here when she fell, or was she pushed? And somehow Daisy knew." I watched the change in her demeanor. She seemed to be falling in on herself. "Daisy knew you were there with Margo and when you heard about the podcast, you had to get rid of her. And then when you heard that Leslie Bittner was going ahead with the podcast, she was next." Taylor was rocking her head from side to side and closing her eyes. Was she trying to make it all go away?

She opened her eyes and stared directly at me. "Why couldn't you have paid attention to the note I left on your car? No one can know that I was there the day that Margo fell. I thought that I could talk her into leaving the house since Andrew wouldn't do it. He could have, you know. It belongs solely to him, but he didn't want to go through the embarrassment of evicting her. All she did was go on about how she was staying there and that she was the real Mrs. Palmer and that I had just tricked Andrew into divorcing her because I was giving him the sons he'd always wanted. And then to make it even more insulting she got a phone call from Daisy Cochran and went upstairs to talk. By then I realized it was hopeless and I left. I was so upset by the whole thing I had to get myself some self-care to calm myself."

Taylor's mouth tightened with annoyance. "When I heard you talking about the podcast she was doing, I realized that Daisy must have known I was there when she called Margo, but never said anything. With her column over, Daisy needed money and was doing whatever she had to. I heard she was even doing PR work under another name. I was going to offer her money to keep me out of her podcast. I had bought a copy of her book and was going to approach her to get it autographed. I had an envelope of cash."

It seemed as if her throat had gone dry and she stopped to swallow. "When I saw Daisy get sick, I left." She gave me a hard look. "No one knew I was there and I wanted to keep it that way." I glanced out the window and saw Adele and Roberta wandering around the yard. "And without you, there's no proof that I was."

I wondered if she was telling the truth or just buying time while she figured out what to do with me. It wouldn't have been the first time someone tried to get rid of me because I confronted them with what they'd done. I tensed, waiting to see if she was going to make a move. Did she have a tiny gun in her pocket or was she planning to grab one of the kitchen knives?

I made a move toward the door and she came up behind me. "No one can know that I was there the day Margo went down the stairs," she said in a low voice. I prepared to jab her with my elbows if she stuck a weapon in my back, but she didn't do anything.

Adele and Roberta came in and Adele instantly took center stage and began to give the exact details of the party. Adele described the Indiana Jones–like adventure with a description of the hats the kids would get, the pit of plastic snakes they would have to climb over, and the treasure chest they'd find at the end. Adele was lost in her own performance and never noticed that Taylor and I were both lost in our own thoughts. Taylor gave her approval at the end and didn't even try to negotiate the updated costs. She left with barely a goodbye, assuming we would find our way out.

I was so rattled by the confrontation with Taylor, I had a hard time taking part in the conversation on the ride back. Roberta was all charged up and wanted to help with the mother whose son was causing trouble at story-time. She sparked when she heard his name and knew the details of what had happened to the boy's father. We both agreed it was a shame to remove him from story-time and convinced Adele to let us figure out something else.

• • •

"You know the appointment book will disappear after this and even if Elena tells the shoe story, it's no proof that Margo's company was Taylor. Daisy is the only one who knew Taylor was there and she and her notes are both gone," I said to Dinah. "That just leaves me." My shoulders sagged as I tried to make sense of it all. She had met me at the bookstore as soon as Adele and I returned and Roberta had rushed off to work. We'd forgone coffee and were in the yarn department with our hooks out which for the moment were idle.

"If she knocked off Margo, Daisy and Leslie, why not me too?" I said. "Not that I'm upset with her decision." I punctuated it with a mirthless laugh. Dinah was just letting me talk and I continued. "Maybe it was just because Adele and Roberta were there." I scanned the area nervously. "And she has something else planned. And I still have nothing to get Detective Terrier off my back."

"Or, she was telling the truth," my friend said.

Whatever it was, I dealt with it the only way I could. I shoved it to the back of my mind and got on with the rest of what was on my plate.

"The Langford party is this weekend. It's the official end to my investigation. I barely got Peter to wait until then to make the deal with him. I don't think he has any confidence in my ability and regrets getting me involved." I sighed. "Peter will get his money, Miles will get another executive producer credit and 1 will go back to being just Peter's mother. I'll probably be stripped of my grandmother role when Gabby comes back and finds out that I accused one of the people in her mommy group of being a serial killer and investigated another one. She didn't like me before and it can only go downhill from that."

Dinah gave me a sympathetic pat on my arm. "The only bright spot is Roberta Tockle. She's great," I said.

"We're sitting in the yarn department. It feels like we should crochet," Dinah said. We both took out the granny square striped blankets. I was doing two rows of colors to one row of black yarn. Dinah was doing all the rows in color.

I didn't mean to, but I couldn't help myself and went back to the encounter with Taylor. "Is it possible I was wrong?"

Chapter Thirty

Weekends did not mean off to me since the bookstore was open seven days. I had always worked a lot of Saturdays and Sundays, but even more so now that my social life was a zero. I felt a tug of loneliness when I came home Saturday evening with no plans. There were no rehearsals going on and my parents had gone to dinner and a movie. Samuel had a gig and Peter had told me he had plans. He didn't discuss his social life beyond mentioning seeing a "friend." Beth was the only one there and she was anxious to leave. She didn't say anything, but I was pretty sure she wanted to be in the audience for Samuel's time onstage.

Samuel had taken care of the animals before he left, and other than letting the dogs out for a run in the backyard, they didn't need any care. There had been so many people around giving them so much attention, so after giving them all some pets and treats, they were happy to settle into their favorite spots and sack out.

Everything was ready for the Langford party the next day. Both Adele and I had arranged for the afternoon off. Adele had left it to me to bring everything, and the party favors, decorations and games were in boxes in my car. Roberta had arranged for the food from the place she worked. She had offered to stay for the whole party and help. I didn't wait for an okay from Adele and had accepted her offer with relief.

"It's just you and me," I said to Marlowe as I carried her into the kitchen. Her teething pain seemed to have stopped and she gave me a sleepy smile. "Well, maybe it's just going to be me." Beth had already bathed her and put her into her sleepwear. The baby didn't complain when I laid her in the portable crib in the den.

The United Nations of food was gone and I was actually going to have to cook something for my dinner. I wanted comfort food, and to me that meant spaghetti. I had a basic recipe for sauce using ingredients I always had on hand. I poured the can of tomatoes in the pan, quartered an onion, added some butter and assorted seasonings and some balsamic vinegar and set it on to cook. I started a pan of water for the noodles and sat at my kitchen table looking out at the yard. The sauce had begun to simmer and fill the air with a delicious scent and I regretted having no one to share it with.

I considered calling Dinah, but I remembered that she and Commander were volunteering at the senior center. Once a month they helped put on a social evening with dinner and dancing.

I talked myself out of the blues and began to relish the peace, particularly since I knew it was only temporary. After eating too much spaghetti, I took the granny square striped blanket I was working on and went into the living room. The rhythmic repetition of the movement of my hook put me in a meditative state and I began to think over everything. I had said that I'd shelved the whole episode with Taylor, but it kept popping up in my mind anyway. I kept thinking if I could find some evidence that would make it clear whether Taylor was involved in any or all of the deaths, it would help. I didn't even know any details of the police investigation of Margo's death. I considered calling Barry. There was the chance that he would think I was calling to try to start things up with him, but I decided to take it since he was the only shot I had.

"Greenberg," he said in his cop voice tinged with tiredness. After I greeted him, I rushed to tell him this wasn't a personal call and launched into what I wanted. "Any details about Margo Palmer's death would help."

"Why do you want to know?" he asked. He didn't wait for me to speak. "That's okay, I probably wouldn't like your answer anyway." He was quiet for a moment. "You want me to deliver the info in person?"

"No," I said almost too quickly. "I'm sure Carol is expecting you."

"Actually, she's working, too."

"A phone call is fine," I said and he agreed to call me back.

My phone rang again shortly after I had hung up, but this time it was Roberta calling to tell me that she was confirming the food and went through the list for the party the next day. "I probably should have called Adele, but, well . . ."

"I know," I said and got ready to end the call, but she went into prattle mode about how excited she was to be working on the party and brought up her connection to Miles Langford. "I don't really *know him* know him, if you know what I mean, and he probably won't remember me," she said. She started on how production assistants were mostly interchangeable and then told me she was glad she wasn't the production assistant who handled the food line. She went into the details of a mix-up because Miles had been an extra. I debated whether it was something I could mention to Peter.

My phone began to beep that there was another call. I knew it was Barry and wanted to end the call with her. She was still rambling about the food line and seemed surprised about something that she'd remembered and said a name. I finally had to just interrupt her and tell her I had another call.

"Do you want the gory details or the nice version?" Barry said. He'd dropped the cop tone and sounded friendly.

"I just had a plate of spaghetti," I said. "All that red sauce and squiggly noodles—I'll go for the nice version."

"Was it that homemade sauce?" Barry said.

"Yes," I said.

"That's the best." He was quiet after that and I knew he was probably hungry and looking for an invitation, but that wasn't happening.

"I can text you the recipe and you can give it to Carol or make it yourself." I stood and stretched. "You were going to give me the nice version."

"She was found at the foot of the stairs by the housekeeper. She was wearing high heels and the stairs were carpeted with some loopy stuff. The conclusion was that she had caught her heel in the carpet and fallen, hitting her head. They determined the time of her fall by her watch. The crystal was smashed and the watch had stopped at four thirty-three. And that's it."

It didn't seem like it would help, but I thanked him. "Is there anything you need?" he said.

"No," I said and hung up before he could say anything else.

Chapter Thirty-one

I went into work on Sunday morning and took care of things at the bookstore until it was time for Adele and me to go to the Langfords'. Miles and Lily were off having brunch and the housekeeper let us in and then went off to take care of Alexander. I was so glad that Roberta had offered to help when I saw how above it all Adele was acting. She believed she was the talent and didn't have to do anything until the kids got there, and then it was only to lead the kids to the games and help blow out the birthday candles. She went out in the yard to do vocal exercises and prepare herself for the inaugural Queen Adele party, or so she said. I thought it had more to do with not wanting to help with the setup.

The plan was that the kids' party would be in the backyard. A canopy covering a table and chairs was already set up. Roberta had brought in all the boxes and was decorating. She oversaw the setting up of the food. The parents were going to hang out in the great room and socialize. As I was looking around the large room where the mommy group had met, it hit me for the first time that Taylor was going to be at the party with the rest of the group.

Should I be worried? If she wanted to get rid of me, the party was a perfect cover. Just like Daisy, I would collapse in front of the crowd. I simply would not eat or drink anything while I was there. Just what I needed, something else to worry about. Peter literally was just waiting for the party to end before he sealed the deal with Miles. What if I had missed something and it turned up after they had a deal? I would feel terrible that I had failed my son.

On top of it all was the concern about the party being a success. I gave myself a pep talk and reminded myself that I had survived swimming with electric eels.

Roberta had commandeered the person who had delivered the food to help her with the decorations, which left me free to wander around the first floor. Since Miles and Lily were off at brunch and the housekeeper was upstairs with Alexander, it seemed like a good time to have another look around so I could honestly say I'd done my best. I checked out the laundry room again, admiring how pleasant it was. A door at the end of the hall opened onto the garage. This time it struck me as strange that their SUV was parked in there since they seemed to park in the driveway. The area was dimly lit by the light coming in through a row of windows at the top of the garage door. It was enough to make out some bicycles and sports equipment against the wall. I understood why the SUV was parked in the garage when I saw the front of it.

I left the garage and went back to the great room to see how things were progressing. A whole game area was set up in the yard. Bunches of blue and yellow balloons were attached to the posts on the patio, along with streamers and a banner. Everything seemed in order and it was getting close to time for the party to start. Instead of bothering with the other doors in the hallway, I went directly to the office. Lily's desk was littered with pictures of different designs for the cocoons, and I recognized one that Sheila had made. Miles's desk was clear in comparison. I went for another look at the photographs on the wall with new interest after what Roberta had told me about the location and her experiences. Time was running out and I realized I better hurry. The best plan seemed to be to use my phone to get photos of the pictures instead of studying them on the wall. I was getting nervous by now and my fingers slipped as I was trying to open the camera. Other apps started opening, and as I tried to close them, other stuff kept showing up on my phone. All my efforts were intent on closing everything until something showed up in the photos app that made me stop trying to get rid of things and instead read what was in front of me. Somehow, I had ended up with the notes from Daisy's podcasts. It came back to me then that I had taken pictures of them when I'd been at Leslie Bittner's. All that I had noted then was the heading that said *House* and now I saw there was a whole lot more. I was stunned for a moment and then went into action. I had to call Peter right away and make sure he didn't rush into making a deal with Miles.

I had my phone on speaker and was relieved when Peter answered his. He'd barely gotten out a hello when I interrupted. "Don't take Miles's money," I said. "He's a serial killer. I don't have all the details exactly figured out, but it seems like there are four people dead."

Peter was sputtering something and I was trying to hear, when a hand reached over my shoulder and ended the call. When I glanced up, Miles was hovering over me.

"Are you crazy?" he said, his mouth twisted in horror. "I didn't kill anybody."

"What about the production assistant—Billy Erickson? The one who got the *in memoriam* credit because he died during the shoot. The one who made you go in the food line with the little people instead of the higher-level line where an executive producer was supposed to be. It was humiliating to be treated like that in front of everybody." I had used Daisy's notes and put them together with what Roberta had told me to figure it out.

"I didn't kill him," Miles said. "It was an accident. I went to talk to him and let him know that what he'd done was going to cost him his job. He kept going on that I had been an extra and there was no way he could have known that I was an executive producer. He was in my face and I pushed him away so I could leave." He stopped and let out his breath. "I didn't realize the bushes behind him were hiding the edge of a cliff. It was chalked up to an accident with no connection to me."

"But somebody knew you pushed him," I said. "You mentioned Rance Butler, who had been your escort while you were on the set."

"He didn't do a very good job or he would have been there when the production assistant was hassling me about the food line."

"But he saw you push the guy. What was it? Did he try to blackmail you?" I said. "And then he mysteriously died in a hit-and-run accident." There had been a news article in Daisy's notes and Roberta had told me the details about Rance's death when she'd been trying to help me deal with Rance Junior, the boy who was acting up in story-time. Miles had a blank look as I continued. "Daisy did PR for the movie and it was her job to keep anything negative under wraps. She probably knew about your run-in with Billy and the coincidence of his falling to his death afterward, but looked the other way and kept it quiet. She didn't put all the pieces together until she got the idea for the podcast. She must have figured out that Rance was a problem for you. And then she was a problem for you."

"I don't know what you're talking about," Miles said. "I didn't kill anybody. Billy's fall was his own fault."

Lily had come in behind him. "Stop talking," she said in an angry tone. My eye went over the office and my gaze stopped on her desk. "Who do you think you are?" she demanded of me. "Snooping around and making accusations."

"It wasn't Miles," I said, looking at her husband, who looked confused for good reason. I picked up the strip of paper and small black box off of Lily's desk. "It was you," I said, looking at Lily. It had just registered that the receipt on her desk wasn't from the time she'd come to the bookstore with Alexander, it was from the night of Daisy's event. And I knew how she'd done it, looking at the black box I'd seen her with at the mommy group meetups. "You dropped an ice cube laced with cyanide into her smoothie," I said. "Who would have noticed that?"

"That's ridiculous. You have no proof," she said. "No proof about any of it."

"There's the damaged SUV," I said and she grew pale.

"What's going on?" Miles said, looking at his wife.

"You are such a fool. You thought Rance would keep quiet," she said. "Do you know what would have happened if it came out that you pushed that production assistant?" she said.

"It was an accident," he argued.

"With Rance gone, I thought it was all taken care of," Lily said. "But then when I heard about Daisy's podcast, I knew it was going to come up again, only worse, because now it would seem there had been a cover-up. Her stupid assistant should have let the podcast go," Lily said, as if it was all their own faults that she'd had to get them out of the way.

"You did it?" Miles said in shock. "You're a serial killer?"

"I did it for you. To clean up the mess you made. Nobody would have believed it was an accident if they knew you pushed that production assistant. It spiraled from there." She looked at me. "We have to take care of her—permanently." I saw her look at the closet. "We can lock her in there until I figure something out."

She tied up my arms behind me with the cocoon off the back of the chair and pushed me toward the closet. *I don't think so.* I used an old trick I had learned and stamped on her instep. She was crumpling in pain as a crowd of people rushed in.

Rick Carlson had his gun drawn and was flanked by Peter and Mason Fields.

"Where did you come from?" I said, looking at the group.

Chapter Thirty-two

I didn't get my answer right away. First, Detective Carlson handcuffed Lily to a railing in the bathroom. He used a second pair of handcuffs on Miles, anchoring him to a bar in the closet. It was lame and I didn't say it to anyone, but it seemed like I had found the skeleton in the closet, or more accurately, he'd become it. The detective called for backup and only then gave me the evil eye before he untied my hands.

I tried to direct him to the garage, but he told me he had things under control. By now guests had started to arrive for the party, and since we were all in the office, the partygoers had no idea what had happened other than their hosts seemed to be missing. Roberta stepped up and brought the kids to Queen Adele, who was now ready to interact with them. The parents hung around in the great room helping themselves to snacks.

Alexander seemed to be enjoying his party with no hint that his parents were both being arrested. The only time the detective listened to me was when I suggested looking for one of Alexander's uncles to take over his care instead of calling social services. Julian Langford came into the office and shook his head when he saw his brother with his hands connected to the lower bar in the closet. He said Alexander could go home with him and that he would get a lawyer for his brother. It seemed it wasn't the first time the more successful sibling had had to bail out his brother, but I doubted it had been this serious. Lily heard the voices and demanded an attorney as well.

The backup arrived and Barry Greenberg was with them. Detective Carlson made sure it wasn't Barry who took a statement from me. When I was done talking to the uniform, Barry was gone.

The party continued on as the yellow tape was put across the garage entrances and the two arrestees were taken out a side door.

When it was just Detective Carlson, Peter, Mason and me, I finally found out how they had shown up. Detective Carlson had me under surveillance and had followed me to the Langfords'. He thought all the packages I took in seemed suspicious. Peter was so sure that I had come up with nothing, he had arranged to meet Miles at the party to make the deal. Mason was acting as an advisor. When Carlson saw the two men sitting in a car out front, he had run the plates, and when he saw that Peter and I were related, he thought they were up to something. He was talking to them when I called Peter.

Miles had ended my call, but it stayed on the screen, and when the phone got jostled it had made a pocket call, so that the three of them had heard everything that Miles, Lily and I had said.

Peter had a sheepish expression as he apologized. "I'm sorry that I doubted you." He turned to Mason. "You were right."

"Right about what?" I said.

Peter let out his breath. "Who do you think told me to hire you?"

• • •

When I finally caught up with Adele, she gave me an annoyed stare. "There you are," she said. "I thought you were supposed to assist me with the games."

"Don't even ask," I said, flopping on a chair. The party was winding down and the kids were picking up their party favor baskets. It seemed as if they'd all had a good time, despite what was going on behind the scenes.

Kath and Garth told me their kids had enjoyed the party and wondered where Lily and Miles were. I left it that they'd had an emergency and had to leave. Taylor sensed there was something wrong and hung back. I told her the truth about Lily and Miles, and the notes about the podcasts that I'd forgotten I had on my phone. When I mentioned that the first set of notes seemed to be about her house and Margo's fall, she seemed to collapse on herself.

"But the cops are going to figure out that I was there the day that she fell. No one will believe that I didn't push her or just leave her there." Her mouth clenched in annoyance. "If only you had stayed out of it. You can forget being part of the mommy group and cancel the plans for Andrew Junior's party."

I still didn't know if I believed her, but I thought of a way I could find out for sure. "I might be able to help," I said. She seemed surprised and then wary. I asked her a few questions, promising to get back to her.

• • •

"And then what happened?" Rhoda asked. The Hookers were all working on their granny square striped blankets listening to me tell them about the part of Adele's party that she had missed.

"The police got a copy of Daisy's podcast notes from my phone. It was important evidence since the actual notes had been destroyed. They were really bad news for Miles and Lily since Daisy had connected the dots from the production assistant's death to Rance Butler's death. But the notes under the *House* heading also had sent them to talk to Taylor Palmer." I looked around the table, letting the suspense build before I continued. "But thanks to me, she was ready for them and was able to prove she wasn't there when Margo fell." I explained Margo's smashed watch crystal, which showed when she'd hit her head. Taylor had mentioned that she was so upset about her interaction with Margo that she'd gone for some self-care, which involved a trip to a Malibu spa. All I had to do was contact the place and compare the times. "Taylor was already on a table, getting a massage when Margo fell."

"Just like I said. Those high heels are what killed her," Rhoda said, giving her Crocs a grateful look.

"Pink," Adele said, forgetting that she had started calling me Molly. "Why didn't you tell me about all this? You ruined my party business."

"More like she saved it," Dinah said, looking to me.

"The party is back on with a bonus for you, and Marlowe is reinstated in the mommy group," I said, remembering how grateful

Taylor was that I had settled the whole situation with Margo once and for all.

• • •

A few weeks had gone by and things had settled down. I finally took a couple of days off. Lily was charged with three counts of murder and Miles was charged with second-degree manslaughter. They were too caught up in their defenses to worry about being in the mommy group and dropped out before they could be asked to leave.

I got Adele to make Roberta a permanent part of the party team as she prepared for Taylor's son's party. Adele was surprisingly gracious about everything and was completely agreeable about doing a special story-time with the mommy group. When Adele understood why Rance Junior was acting up, she agreed to give him another chance and let him stay. She gave him special treatment and his behavior issues subsided.

Peter realized that saying that when one door closes another one opens was true. He lost the financing money from Miles, but when Taylor heard who I really was and what I'd been doing for Peter, she got him together with her husband and they made a deal that was far better for Peter and had a real future. It was better than anything with Miles would have been.

My son decided to give a party both to celebrate his daughter's birth, a little late, and that his production was getting off the ground at last. Of course, he did it at my house since his apartment was too small. Gabby had announced her return, which meant it was kind of a goodbye party for Marlowe. I had all kinds of mixed emotions. Even so, Peter said that going forward he wasn't going to let Gabby keep Marlowe a prisoner and he was going to insist on part custody—at my house. I pushed myself to get out of my bedroom, where the dogs and cats were spending the evening, and into the living room where I could help play host.

Instead of a stiff party meant to impress, Peter had gone with something warmer and more fun. My father had taken charge of the food and there were copious amounts of comfort dishes instead of tidbits served on a silver tray. The She La Las and Samuel were the entertainment and Marlowe was in the middle of things sailing around the room in her foot-powered chair.

People were just beginning to arrive, but everything came to a standstill when Gabby walked in with her mother. She gave us all a look of horror as she saw her daughter cruising around the crowd. "What is she wearing?" she shrieked, looking at the comfortable shirt and pants the baby wore. "Where are all her dresses and hair bows? She should be wearing those Mary Janes I got for her instead of being barefoot."

"Lighten up," her mother said to her as she smiled and waved to my parents. "These people know how to have fun. You could learn something." She went over and hung by the She La Las and did a little of their dance steps.

When I saw Mason come in, I froze. I knew that Peter had invited him, but I thought under the circumstances he might not come. I should have known that he would not be put off by confronting me. He was used to going to court and confronting people all the time. Dealing with me was probably just small change.

I really appreciated that he had not let our breakup interfere with his helping Peter. And I certainly wanted to thank him for suggesting that Peter use my sleuthing skills to check up on Miles Langford. If he gave me the death stare in response, so be it.

He saw that I was making my way toward him and met me halfway. I tried to say something, but with the music and crowd, it was impossible to hear and I suggested we go outside.

The yard seemed silent after all the commotion in the house. I rushed to say my piece and Mason seemed surprised.

"I like Peter and I'm glad to advise him. And suggesting to have you ferret out what you could about Miles Langford," he said with a smile. "Well, it turned out to be good advice." He glanced around the yard at the orange trees full of fragrant blossoms. "You did such a good job, I have a proposition. I have PIs working for me, but there are times when they just aren't right. I need someone who blends in and people share gossip with. Would you consider working for me?"

I was stunned by his offer. "Are you sure you want to do that after the way things turned out?" I said.

"I get it, you don't want any connection," he said. "I should have figured it when you said you were sorry you couldn't even handle talking to me when we met at the pet store, and the way you took off when I was coming over to your table at the food place by my house."

"What?" I said, perplexed by his comments. "You gave me the death stare at the pet store and when I said I was sorry, it was for what a mess I'd made of everything. If it's any consolation, it was a complete disaster and Barry is back with Carol. As for the restaurant, I took off to avoid another cold stare from you."

"Oh," he said, genuinely surprised. "I wasn't aware that I gave you a death stare." There was an awkward moment and it seemed like neither of us knew what to say.

His face softened. "It doesn't have to be personal, but I'd really like to have your help. I already have a case I'd like you to work on." He assured me I could keep my job at the bookstore and whatever else I had going on. We looked through the glass door as Marlowe came through the kitchen on her foot-powered chair and we could hear that the She La Las were starting up a new number.

"I better go inside," I said.

"Will you at least think about it," he said.

I nodded with a smile. "I already have. You know your offer is too good to refuse. How about you start by telling me about the case."

CeeCee's Granny Square Stripe Blanket

This uses the combination of clusters and spaces as in a traditional granny square, but creates a straight line of stitches instead of a square. Rather than give a specific pattern, these are basic instructions that can be used to make different-sized blankets. The stripes can go lengthwise or the width of the blanket.

It is a good project to use leftover yarn with. The rows can be alternated with black yarn or it can all be done in colors. Once the first two rows are done, it is a repetition of two rows that are slightly different from each other. One row has a single double crochet at the beginning and end of the row. The other has two double crochets at the beginning and end of the row. Change colors at the end of a row, when there are two loops on the hook for the last stitch, finish the stitch with the new color. You can fasten off the old color or carry it along. If you carry the yarn along, do an edging around the finished blanket to cover the carried along yarn. Adding picot stitches to the edging will give it a nice look. To do the picot edging, chain three and then single crochet into the bottom chain and attached to the next stitch.

There is no set hook size, though CeeCee likes using a J-10 (6mm) or K-10-1/2 (6.5mm).

Chain a multiple of 3, plus 1.

.

Row 1: Sc in second ch from hook, sc to the end. Turn.

Row 2: Ch 3 & dc in the same stitch (the ch3 counts as a dc), *skip 2 stitches, 3dc in the next stitch*, repeat from *to* until there are 3 stitches left, skip two stitches 2dc in the last stitch. Turn.

Row 3: Chain 3 (counts as dc), 3 dc cluster in the space, continue 3 dc clusters in spaces, dc in last stitch. Turn.

Row 4: Ch 3 (counts as dc) dc in same stitch, 3 dc cluster in space, continue 3dc cluster in spaces, making 2dc in last stitch. Turn.

Repeat Rows 3 & 4 until desired length or width.

Last Row: Sc across, fasten off. Weave in the ends.

Edging as desired.

To make different-sized blankets, make a swatch and figure out the gauge of how many stitches per inch, then multiply depending on the finished size desired.

Approximate sizes for blankets.

Toddler: 42" by 52"

Lapghan: 40" by 48"

Small Throw: 52" by 60"

Large Throw: 60" by 72"

Bob's Eggy Squares

1 pound frozen spinach, defrosted
1 cup shredded cheddar cheese
8 eggs
⅓ cup half-and-half
seasoning salt to taste
sour cream and sliced scallions for garnish

Preheat oven to 375 degrees. Line 8-inch-square pan with parchment paper.

Squeeze excess liquid out of spinach using a colander. Arrange the spinach in the prepared pan. Sprinkle the cheese evenly over the spinach.

Crack eggs one by one into a cup, making sure there are no shells, and then pour into a medium-sized bowl. Beat with a whisk. Add half-and-half and seasoning salt, mixing until blended. Pour egg mixture evenly over the spinach and cheese.

Bake for approximately 20 minutes, until the center is not jiggly.

Let sit for approximately 10 minutes, cut in squares. Add a generous dollop of sour cream and a sprinkling of scallion slices.

About the Author

Betty Hechtman is the national bestselling author of the Crochet Mysteries, the Yarn Retreat Mysteries, and the Writer for Hire Mysteries. Handicraft and writing are her passions and she is thrilled to be able to combine them in both of her series.

Betty grew up on the South Side of Chicago and has a degree in Fine Art. Since College, she has studied everything from improv comedy to magic. She has had an assortment of professions, including volunteer farm worker picking fruit on a kibbutz tucked between Lebanon and Syria, nanny at a summer resort, waitress at a coffee house, telephone operator, office worker at the Writer's Guild, public relations assistant at a firm with celebrity clients, and newsletter editor at a Waldorf school. She has written newspaper and magazine pieces, short stories, screenplays, and a middle-grade mystery, *Stolen Treasure*. She lives with her family and stash of yarn in Southern California.

See BettyHechtman.com for more information, excerpts from all her books, and photos of all the projects of the patterns included in her books. She blogs on Fridays at Killerhobbies.blogspot.com, and you can join her on Facebook at BettyHechtmanAuthor.

Printed in the USA
CPSIA information can be obtained
at www.ICGtesting.com
LVHW042331070424
776711LV00027B/728

9 781960 511300